The death threats were in the third drawer

Hands shaking, Meg withdrew the envelopes. They had been mailed about a week apart, the most recent being yesterday.

Each of the threats was pasted together from newspaper clippings, the words different sizes and different typefaces. Each carried the same message.

If you don't stop poking your nose into ancient history, you will die. You know this is not a joke.

Meg could understand why Aunt Tilly had not taken the pages to the police. There wasn't enough information. Ancient history could refer to events far in the past, or it could be someone's idea of yesterday. Still, someone had taken the trouble to paste the threats and mail them.

And now Aunt Tilly was dead.

ABOUT THE AUTHOR

Margaret St. George has been satisfying a creative need to write since she was sixteen years old. She has written more than fifteen novels, many of which have been historical romances. A full-time writer, Margaret enjoys gardening and traveling. She lives with her husband and family in the mountains of Colorado.

Books by Margaret St. George

HARLEQUIN INTRIGUE

133–JIGSAW

HARLEQUIN AMERICAN ROMANCE

142–WINTER MAGIC
159–CASTLES AND FAIRY TALES
203–THE HEART CLUB
231–WHERE THERE'S SMOKE...
272–HEART'S DESIRE
323–DEAR SANTA
345–AMERICAN PIE
421–HAPPY NEW YEAR, DARLING

Murder by the Book

Margaret St. George

Harlequin Books

TORONTO • NEW YORK • LONDON
AMSTERDAM • PARIS • SYDNEY • HAMBURG
STOCKHOLM • ATHENS • TOKYO • MILAN
MADRID • WARSAW • BUDAPEST • AUCKLAND

Harlequin Intrigue edition published October 1992

ISBN 0-373-22198-3

MURDER BY THE BOOK

Printed in U.S.A.

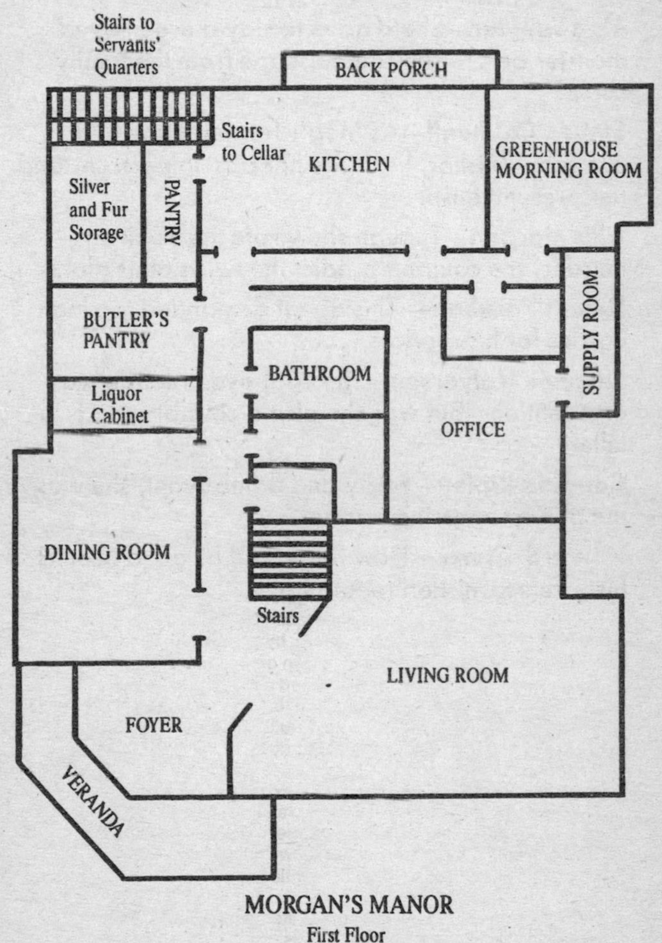

MORGAN'S MANOR
First Floor

CAST OF CHARACTERS

Meg Sandler—She'd have to slay a green-eyed monster before she could escape from the family curse.

Steven Caldwell—As Meg's former flame and current publisher, he made her past imperfect—and her present tense.

Tillis Morgan—Though she wrote the book on murder, she couldn't predict the twists of its plot.

Dennis Parnham—This agent demanded too high a price for his services.

Suzanne Halverson—The cool-eyed blonde was competition—but was she also a cold-blooded killer?

Candida Ripley—Feisty and flamboyant, she was the perfect sparring partner.

Howard Clancy—How far would he go to protect his wife's tarnished reputation?

Chapter One

"Each of you has a reason to want me dead." Tillis Morgan smiled at each of the diners seated at the long table, then raised her wineglass in a salute to her abruptly silent weekend guests.

Meg Sandler heard her aunt's statement, but the words didn't penetrate. From the moment Meg had come downstairs and discovered Steven Caldwell standing beside the cocktail cart, she hadn't been able to think of anything else. First came the shock of seeing Steven; a rush of adrenaline sent her heart pounding. And then joy, sheer joy that forgave everything. She had actually rushed toward him, her heart in her eyes, before she spotted Suzanne Halverson standing at Steven's side and realized she was about to make a colossal fool of herself. At the last moment Meg had stopped short, had given Steven a cool nod as she veered toward the fireplace.

Now Steven was seated across the dinner table from her where it was almost impossible to avoid meeting his eyes. Biting her lip and beginning to feel frantic, Meg wondered how she could get out of this weekend. She was a writer, surely she could invent an excuse for leaving that Aunt Tilly would accept.

Ignoring Steven, she looked at Aunt Tilly seated at the head of the table and resisted an urge to roll her eyes toward the shadows webbing the vaulted ceiling. Aunt Tilly was in fine form tonight, Meg noticed, from her needling comments to her flamboyant costume.

Tillis Morgan wore black, of course. It was her trademark. Meg assumed the funereal color was calculated to suggest mystery, or perhaps menace. Both befitted one of the world's premier mystery writers. Or perhaps Aunt Tilly always chose black to emphasize her creamy porcelain skin, still smooth and handsome at age fifty.

Whatever the reason, Tillis Morgan was famed for her unconventional attire. Tonight she wore a jet-black gown with a scattering of blood-red beads sewn onto the fabric. The beads formed a spider across her breast. With every movement, the spider expanded and glittered in the candlelight, appearing to reach for the black feather boa that alternately adorned Aunt Tilly's shoulders, arms or pale throat. Meg had no idea where Aunt Tilly purchased such singular gowns. She couldn't imagine there were hordes of women demanding feather boas, black crepe and beaded spiders.

"Really, Tillis," Candida Ripley said impatiently. Candida flicked her jeweled fingers in a gesture of annoyance. "Have you nodded off? We're all breathlessly awaiting the punch line."

Meg released a breath. It appeared she hadn't missed much by drifting into thoughts about Steven, not if the dinner company was waiting to hear a punch line. Because she sensed Steven watching her, she focused a determined smile on Candida.

Candida Ripley was no slouch herself when it came to flamboyant attire. Tonight she wore scarlet satin, which until moments ago had been covered by an iridescent feather cape that had to be seen to be believed. Ruby and amethyst flashed at her ears and throat; diamonds glittered on every finger. A feather plume swept up from the luxuriant mass of auburn hair gathered at her neck. Meg suspected Aunt Tilly was not pleased by the way the candlelight shimmered and glowed across her rival's scarlet satin bosom, drawing the eye to Candida and away from the head of the table.

"There is no punch line," Aunt Tilly said. With slow deliberation, she subjected each of her guests to an intense scrutiny as if she could read their minds if she applied herself diligently. "As I was arranging this board meeting it occurred to me that each of you would be pleased to see me in my coffin. Each of you will benefit when I die."

"What?" Meg jerked upright and a ripple of shock traveled down her spine. "You aren't joking," she realized aloud, forgetting Steven for the first time since she had discovered he was here. "Aunt Tilly, surely you can't think that I—"

"Well, dear, you are my principal heir. When I die you'll inherit all this." Tossing back the black feather boa, Tillis waved a hand to indicate Morgan's Manor and all its varied treasures. "Plus my research library, my notes and any works in progress. If something happened to me, you'd be a fool not to complete my current project, it's certain to be a bestseller."

Suzanne Halverson's blond head lifted and she narrowed her gaze on Meg. But everyone had turned to look at her. Meg was acutely conscious of Steven Caldwell's dark-eyed appraisal and felt a burst of heat color her cheeks. She would never have come to Colorado for the weekend if she had known Aunt Tilly had invited Steven and Suzanne.

"That isn't fair," she protested, leaning forward to see Aunt Tilly past the silver candelabra. "I didn't know I was your heir until this minute." The faces studying her registered polite disbelief. Not for the first time Meg cursed Aunt Tilly's eccentricities. It was just like Tillis Morgan to invite Meg and Steven for the same weekend. And trust Aunt Tilly to announce the contents of her will in the most dramatic fashion.

"I doubt Tillis's revelation can be much of a surprise," Candida drawled. "Even in her youth Tillis was too frigid and juiceless to have children of her own. She certainly isn't going to start producing them now. You're her only niece, Meg, therefore...plus you're a mystery writer, primed to follow in your aunt's faint footsteps." The candlelight falling from an old-fashioned chandelier gleamed on Candida's satin shrug.

Aunt Tilly's eyes narrowed. The mascaraed spikes of her lashes quivered like tiny black daggers. "How very like you to deduce the obvious, Candida. Perhaps this newfound facility with logic will improve your writing. I understand your latest book is such a bomb the distributors can't even give it away."

"That is a lie! You wish that were true because you're so jealous of me that you can't stand it!"

Dennis Parnham, seated on Meg's left, cleared his voice with a self-righteous sound. "*I* have no reason to wish you dead, Tillis." Dennis leaned closer to Meg so James, Aunt Tilly's manservant, could remove his soup bowl, then he shot his cuffs with a satisfied gesture.

"You smarmy slug," Candida hissed. The plume curving over her auburn hair trembled with intensity. Her eyes narrowed and blazed on Dennis Parnham. "You shouldn't even be here. Worms like you shouldn't be allowed membership in MAIMS."

"Need I remind you that MAIMS stands for Mystery Authors and Interested Mystery Supporters? I'm certainly interested in supporting the genre as my literary agency handles the top names in the field. I have as much right to a seat on the board as you do." He gave Candida a reproving look across the saltcellar and silver butter dish. "MAIMS isn't the problem, my dear. But let's resolve our little spat in private, shall we?''

"There's nothing to resolve. The instant I return to New York I intend to shop for a new agent!''

Although the exchange was embarrassing to everyone present, Meg listened with interest. She was also disgusted with Parnham and his practices and she, too, wanted a new literary agent. Eight months ago she would have solicited Steven's opinion, but now... how in the world was she going to endure this weekend?

"I'm sorry, darling. Your agency agreement is ironclad.'' Smug was the right word for Dennis's smile. Everything about him projected an air of self-satisfaction, from his perfectly coifed silver hair to his exquisitely tailored Bond Street attire. "Take your agency contract to your attorney if you don't believe me. You won't be free to shop for agents, as you so charmingly put it, for another four years.''

Meg's heart sank. If Candida was stuck, then she thought it probable that she was, too. The prospect depressed her.

"For once you and I agree, Candida.'' Aunt Tilly aimed her salad fork at Dennis Parnham. "As for wishing me dead, Dennis...have you forgotten how you tricked me into signing an agreement that assigns you the copyright ownership of my first four books in the event of my death?'' Frowning, Aunt Tilly gestured to James to remove the salad plates.

"That's common practice, dear girl. Many agents—''

"That explanation worked years ago when I was young and green, but I'm years beyond such swindles now. Everyone at this table knows reputable agents do not steal their client's work. I deeply regret that I didn't stop Meg before she signed with you.''

Meg also regretted that she hadn't sought Aunt Tilly's advice. She was tied to Dennis Parnham for another five years, paying a twenty-percent commission instead of the usual fifteen, and discovering just how miserable an agent could make a writer's life. She hadn't sought Aunt Tilly's advice because she didn't know her famous aunt all that well, didn't know if Aunt Tilly would welcome another mystery writer in the family and, stubbornly, she hadn't wanted to trade on her aunt's name or advice.

She should have swallowed her pride and telephoned Aunt Tilly the moment Parnham approached her. It would have spared her a great many problems and much frustration.

"Let's see now, where were we?" Having grasped the possibilities for character assignation, Candida cheerfully returned to the topic at hand. The feather arching over her head dipped toward Meg. "We know about you—with Tillis dead, you inherit everything. And with one of the contenders removed, you'd be a step closer to winning the mystery series assignment."

Once again Meg was the center of attention, agonizingly aware of Steven and Suzanne watching her. Suzanne was unmistakably enjoying the sight of Steven's former lover being embarrassed in front of the dinner company, but Meg thought she glimpsed a look of sympathy in Steven's gaze.

The last thing she wanted was pity from Steven Caldwell. Her chin lifted. "This is an idiotic discussion! I came here to attend a board meeting, not to..."

Then she noticed Aunt Tilly. Aunt Tilly was enjoying the conversation enormously, leaning forward, beaming and smiling. It was Tillis who had set the pot to boil, stirring people up, playing one of her famous pranks. It was no accident that Aunt Tilly had assembled such a volatile group for the weekend. Tillis Morgan loved drama, adored potentially explosive situations.

Meg drew a breath, feeling outmatched. "You're also competing for the Macabre Series, Candida. You, too, would benefit if the list of contenders became shorter." She felt Aunt Tilly's amused approval as strongly as she felt Steven's steady gaze.

All evening it seemed that Steven had been trying to catch her attention. Meg exhaled slowly and wished she had stayed home in New York City. Aside from Aunt Tilly, she didn't care about any of these people. Seeing Steven again upset her. The bad weather made her nervous. And she didn't like the forbidding atmosphere of Morgan's Manor. Discovering she would one day inherit the house caused her more dismay than pleasure.

"I'd like to win the series assignment," Candida agreed pleasantly. "But we aren't talking about me. Everyone knows I loathe Tillis. We're discussing why all of *you* want to kill her."

Meg started. "No one said anything about wanting to kill—"

Candida tilted her wineglass toward Dennis Parnham. "You really are a slug, Dennis. Did I understand correctly? When Tillis goes to the big publishing house in the sky, you'll own her first four books? You stand to make a bloody fortune, don't you?"

Dennis Parnham smoothed back a wave of silver hair and cocked an eyebrow. "If anyone here wants to dance on dear Tillis's grave—" he nodded a faint apology toward Tillis who rewarded him with a thin smile "—it's you, Candida. You've always been jealous of Tillis. Plus, your sales *have* fallen off. Meg and Tillis aren't the only writers desperate to win the Macabre Series. You're counting on the series to revive your career."

"You're fired, you toad! Do you hear me? Fired! I don't care what the attorneys say, I'll find a way!"

"Now, now," Tillis interjected when it appeared Candida might fling herself across the table at Dennis. "We all know manners aren't your strong suit, darling, but I really must insist that you don't throw yourself, your food or your utensils while dining at my table." To the others, she purred, "Lovers' spats can get so ugly, can't they?"

No one looked at Candida's husband, Howard Clancy. Everyone present was aware of the romantic attachment between Candida and Dennis, but it seemed churlish of Tillis to refer to it in front of Howard. An uncomfortable silence as thick as the deepening shadows spread through the room.

"You miserable no-talent bitch, Tillis." Candida's bosom heaved. "You can't stand to have an uneventful board meeting. You always manage to turn it into a dramatic fiasco because you don't know the meaning of the word professional. I didn't come here to be insulted. In fact, I can't imagine why I came at all!"

"You came because you lust after my position on the board and you hope to bludgeon the board into placing you on the new slate. You hate it that I'm president and you're not. You always want what I have." Enjoying Candida's outrage, Tillis waved her fingertips at James. "Please serve the prime rib."

Howard Clancy, the man who had been married to both Tillis and Candida, raised his glass. He had refused the dinner wine and continued drinking undiluted Scotch. "I must take exception to Candida's statement that Tillis is a no-talent bitch. We all know Tillis is talented." Dennis Parnham was the only person who laughed at Howard's failed attempt to lighten the mood.

Meg thought the contrast between Howard Clancy and Dennis Parnham was striking. Dennis was suavely handsome; Howard, who was balding and overweight, was a pleasant man but only mildly attractive. Age and alcohol had blurred the good looks that had once captivated two of publishing's most beautiful and flamboyant mystery writers.

When Steven spoke, Meg lowered her head and pretended to examine her prime rib. Steven wasn't a member of the MAIMS board. She didn't know why Aunt Tilly had invited him.

"I think this conversation has gone far enough," he said quietly.

"Really?" Candida leaned forward to glare at him. "At the risk of offending my publisher who, by the way, has done nothing whatsoever to promote my new book, I'd like to learn why *you* want Tillis dead. Does it have anything to do with Caldwell Publishing's recent slump? Gossip has it that sales are down."

"That's nonsense," Steven said. He glanced at Meg, then back at Tillis. "I have no reason to wish you anything but a long life, Tillis."

Tillis lifted an eyebrow. "Aren't you forgetting a certain half-million-dollar life-insurance policy naming Caldwell Publishing as beneficiary?"

Dennis Parnham stared at Steven, then at Tillis. "Whatever possessed you to take out a policy payable to your publisher?"

"I apologize," Steven said stiffly. "I did forget."

Candida's penciled brow soared toward the feather over her hair. "You *forgot* a half-million-dollar life-insurance policy?"

"Fifteen years ago," Tillis explained to Dennis, "when Steven's father was president of the company, Caldwell Publishing was experiencing financial difficulties. I wanted to help out." She shrugged. "Brice Caldwell sold me five percent of the company's stock with the proviso that I would sell my shares back to the company at a later date for the same price I paid for them. Any dividends earned in the interim were, of course, mine. In the event that I died before the company recovered financially, I agreed to a life-insurance policy payable to Caldwell Publishing so the company would have the funds to redeem the shares."

"We should have bought back those shares years ago," Steven said, frowning.

"Your father tried, but I wouldn't sell them." Tillis smiled. "It's been a good investment."

"So," Dennis said, staring at Steven. "If Tillis dies, Steven gets half a million dollars to buy back shares now worth three times that much. Very nice."

Steven's expression of contempt eased when he looked at Tillis. "Why did you invite me, Tillis? I thought I was coming to Colorado to discuss the new book and the explosive revelation you promised. Now I'm not sure that's the entire reason."

For a fleeting instant his expression froze as if he had committed a blunder. A glance of dismay passed between Steven and Aunt Tilly, gone before Meg could be certain what she had seen.

"It appears this weekend was originally scheduled as a MAIMS board meeting," Steven continued smoothly. He nodded at Howard Clancy, then at Suzanne Halverson who had not spoken. "But since you've included guests who aren't members of the MAIMS board, perhaps you have something different in mind."

"Isn't it obvious?" Tillis asked.

While everyone pondered what was supposed to be obvious, Meg studied the snow melting down the long gothic windows that lined the back wall of the dining room. Observing the worsening weather was preferable to looking at Steven, who seemed to be watching her whenever she risked a glance in his direction.

Damn him. The romance between herself and Steven Caldwell was as dead as a corpse. It shouldn't hurt this much to see him again. But it did.

Maybe she was just fooling herself. If it was really over, if Steven was out of her life and out of her heart, then why was the handsome sexy detective in her latest novel a dead ringer for Steven Caldwell? If Steven wasn't on her mind, then why had she created a detective who was tall, broad shouldered and athletic, with dark curly hair and chocolate eyes? Why had her heart flip-flopped when she walked down the staircase and saw him standing in Aunt Tilly's living room? Why did his deep baritone voice still send seductive shivers down her spine? Damn him.

She stared at the thickening snow and remembered things about Steven Caldwell that were better left forgotten. Like the thrilling pressure of his lips exploring hers. Like the night of passionate lovemaking when they celebrated her second book making the bestseller list. Like . . .

"I get it." Howard Clancy interrupted her reverie. "This weekend is a re-creation of the pivotal scene in *Murder at Eight*."

"Good boy." Tillis beamed.

"I wouldn't know." Candida tossed her head, sending the feather plume into spasms. "I don't read Tillis's trash. I prefer mysteries where you can't deduce who did it on page ten."

Even Tillis smiled at so patent a falsehood.

"Have you forgotten the complete set of Tillis Morgan's work in our library?" Howard reminded her.

Candida shot him a look that dripped venom. "Those books belong to you, not me! A sentimental reminder of your ex-wife to hold over my head when you're mad at me."

"*Murder at Eight* is the book where the main character assembles all his enemies on a Caribbean Island," Suzanne Halverson supplied. It was the first time she had spoken since they entered the dining room. She fixed a thoughtful look on Tillis. "One by one the host murders his guests."

"That's correct," Aunt Tilly said, not looking at Suzanne.

"Good God." Howard Clancy's eyes widened. He tried to focus on the snowstorm building outside, considered aloud the excellent possibilities for being marooned in the storm. "Is that why you invited me, Tillis? To have your final revenge?"

"I'd say it's you who have cause to seek revenge," Tillis replied softly. "I made your life hell while we were married, then dragged your name through the tabloids during the divorce."

"Let's not rehash old history, shall we? *Murder at Eight* is shot full of clichés." Candida sniffed and flicked a jeweled hand toward Meg. "If you haven't already, my dear, you will eventually write a novel where the suspects are marooned at an isolated site and corpses start dropping like flies. Agatha Christie did it, Tillis did it, even I did it. Of course *I* added a fresh twist."

Tillis smiled. "Indeed. In your book the corpses fall like hippos, and the reader knows the murderer's identity on page two. But Suzanne has the right idea," she informed the table.

Meg frowned, her thoughts jumping to the plot of her work in progress. The book was set in an isolated station in the Australian outback. Perhaps she should rethink the story line. When she glanced away from the snow beginning to pile against the windowpanes, she noticed Steven's dark eyes twinkled with amusement as if he had guessed what she was thinking. Her chin rose and she swiveled toward Dennis Parnham.

"Oh?" Dennis asked lightly. "Then you intend to murder us all, Tillis? Did you poison the mousse?" He spoke with determined amusement, but he pushed his strawberry mousse to one side. Ignoring Tillis's disapproval, he twisted a cigarette into an ivory holder, lit it, then blew smoke toward the chandelier.

"Don't be silly," Howard Clancy said, digging his spoon into the mousse. "Poisoning would require Tillis to enter the kitchen." He winked and blew Tillis a kiss, pretending not to see Candida's murderous scowl. "Take it from a man who was once married to her—Tilly wouldn't recognize a kitchen if someone tied her to a stove."

"I'm flattered that at some point during our marriage you were sober enough to notice where I went or what I did," Tillis said.

"And with whom." The smile on Howard Clancy's lips turned sad. "Let's not forget that, Tilly. With whom."

"It's you who flaunted your infidelity, Howard. You and Candida popped in and out of bed practically under my nose."

"If it's any comfort to you, events have traveled full circle. Now it's my turn to play the jealous fool." Howard glanced at Dennis and Candida. A flush spread across Candida's high cheekbones, and Dennis developed a sudden interest in the ash growing on the end of his cigarette.

Meg cast a desperate glance toward the snow flying past the windows, wondering if Steven and the others felt as uncomfortable as she did. If this evening was any indication, the weekend was going to feel like a year.

Sneaking a peek at her watch, Meg wondered if she could concoct a decent excuse and escape immediately after the brandy. She'd need five minutes to pack her luggage, twenty minutes to drive down the mountain, an hour and a half for the drive to Denver. That would put her at Stapleton Airport in time to catch the red-eye flight to New York City.

She had to decide soon since the storm appeared to be gathering force. Wind hummed in the chimney, rattled the panes. Snow piled against the windows. If she didn't leave almost immediately, the eight-mile stretch of road from

Morgan's Manor to Breckenridge would drift over and she'd be stuck.

Slowly, and skipping past Steven, her gaze moved around the table as she contemplated spending the weekend with these people.

She knew Candida Ripley from reading Candida's books and from having run into her in Dennis Parnham's office. They were both on the MAIMS board of directors. And they had both been invited to compete for the Macabre Series, a plum assignment that could revive Candida's career or boost Meg toward wider recognition and readership. Candida had wasted no time letting her know that Meg was an upstart of limited talent who should never have been a contender for the series in the first place.

Then there was Dennis Parnham, famed in mystery circles as an agent who routinely obtained lush advances for the writers he represented. Maybe he did so for established writers such as Candida, but he hadn't done much for Meg except make promises, request endless rewrites and offer lame explanations why he hadn't read her latest submission or sent her royalty checks yet. When she expressed frustration, Dennis offered a practiced smile, patted her shoulder in a condescending manner and reminded Meg that she was in her growth years. She needed to be patient.

Everyone in the industry knew Dennis and Candida were having an affair. A rather stormy affair if gossip could be believed. That's why Howard Clancy's presence at Morgan's Manor was such an awkward surprise. Aside from the relationship between Candida and Dennis—which appeared to be in one of the stormy periods—there was also the tension of ancient history. Meg felt the undertow of hostility flowing between Aunt Tilly, Candida and Howard. It was clear the others felt it, too.

Years ago, Candida had stolen Howard away from Aunt Tilly, whereupon Aunt Tilly had stolen him back again. But in the end, Candida won the prize: Howard. Afterward, murderesses appeared in each writer's books bearing remarkable resemblances to each other and a flurry of lawsuits had followed accompanied by lavish tabloid coverage. The tabloids pondered in gleeful headlines why the queens of mystery, both beautiful women, battled for the affection of a mild-mannered insurance salesman.

Howard became a figure of ridicule from coast to coast. In the end he lost his job, his pension and possibly his self-respect because of the publicity. Meg considered him with a degree of sympathy, wondering what on earth had induced Howard Clancy to return to Morgan's Manor.

Next, she straightened her backbone and studied Suzanne Halverson. If Meg had to describe Suzanne in a novel, she would have depicted her as the type of remote blond beauty who invariably attracted tragedy. Men often found such women irresistible. Perhaps it was their vulnerability, an image of being buffeted by unkind fate, the implied need for a safe haven and a protector. However one labeled the force, men seemed helpless before it; they felt compelled to rush to the rescue.

A year ago Suzanne's husband, Whitney Halverson, had been murdered. Whitney Halverson was found shot to death, slumped over the wheel of his Mercedes. Less than a week later, Suzanne's maid had committed suicide.

Naturally the double shocks had devastated Suzanne. And naturally Suzanne had turned to Whitney's friend, Steven Caldwell, for comfort. In the beginning, Meg had even encouraged Steven to spend time with Suzanne.

She lowered her head and looked away from Suzanne's blond perfection. And felt the scorch of jealousy.

When she glanced up Steven was watching her, wearing that same judgmental expression she knew so well. Anger flared in her eyes. How dare he judge her? Whatever they had together was over.

And yet . . . She gazed into his dark eyes and her body tightened and her breath quickened. The chemistry was still there even if the affection was not. Her gaze touched his firm wide lips and strong jawline, paused at his tie to imagine the hard muscled chest beneath his striped shirt.

She didn't need this. Biting her lip, Meg wrenched her gaze toward the head of the table and willed her thoughts to cool.

As soon as it was decently possible, she would leave. The other MAIMS board members could propose a slate of officers without her.

Howard Clancy finished his mousse and surrendered his empty dish to James. "Tillis, you really can be an annoying woman. Just what is so damned obvious?"

"You've let this silence go on so long that I've forgotten the question. If it was a question," Dennis Parnham complained.

"Tillis is about to solve the great mystery of why we're all here." Candida rolled her eyes. "Obviously we don't need Mrs. Halverson, Howard or Steven for a board meeting."

Tillis drew out the moment, enjoying the drama she had created. The beaded spider swelled across her breast. "I've received three death threats." She paused. "I have reason to believe one of you sent them."

They stared at her in silence.

The darkness in the room had deepened to the extent that when Tillis stood it was as if a disembodied head floated up from her chair. Pinpoints of candlelight shone in her bright eyes when she smiled.

"Shall we take our coffee and brandy in the living room?"

Chapter Two

"Meg, I need to talk to you."

Meg sensed Steven's presence behind her before she heard his voice and had been praying that any conversation between them would be banal and strictly superficial.

"There's nothing to discuss," she said in a low voice. If she looked at him she was afraid she would humiliate herself by bursting into emotional tears. Suddenly it was all there again, the confusion, the pain. She was glad when the table lamps scattered about the cavernous living room flickered, sputtered a moment, then blinked back on and steadied into a dim glow. The momentary distraction allowed her to move away from him.

"Oh, for God's sake, Tillis. Isn't this pile of rock spooky enough without you playing pranks with the lights?" Making a face, Candida threw herself on a Victorian sofa and arranged a fan of scarlet satin over the stiff cushions. She glared at Dennis Parnham when he moved toward the seat beside her. Instead, he chose a wingbacked chair beside the fireplace and pushed a cigarette into his ivory cigarette holder.

"This place is an antique," Meg murmured, moving farther from Steven. Morgan's Manor had been built in the twenties by Aunt Tilly's father, Meg's grandfather. He had purchased the stones in Germany, had them shipped to the

United States and then to Breckenridge, Colorado. Out-of-work miners had hauled the stones up the mountain to a craggy overlook where they were reassembled into something that looked like Dracula's castle.

Crenellated balconies jutted here and there. Narrow-paned leaded glass overlooked steep valleys and soaring peaks. Inside, the house was a rabbit warren of twisting corridors and odd rooms that made little sense to a logical mind. Some rooms, like the living and dining room, were massive. High ceilinged, chill and shadowed even on bright days. Other rooms were undersized, lending themselves to no discernible purpose. It was as if Theodore Morgán had designed the manor for a household of giants and dwarfs, attempting to accommodate each.

"Don't act like more of a fool than you already are, Candida." Aunt Tilly accepted a snifter of brandy from the tray James offered, then seated herself on a gilt-backed thronelike chair the rest of them had avoided. "How do you suggest I manipulated the lighting? I dashed to the basement, toggled the switch, then dashed back upstairs? In seconds? Without anyone noticing?"

Meg experienced difficulty following the conversation. All she could think about was Steven Caldwell. After her curt reply, he had moved into the room and reluctantly seated himself in an ornate armchair. Suzanne perched on the arm of his chair, her fingertips moving over his shoulder.

"One of your prankster stooges could be in the basement," Candida complained. "A hundred people could be creeping around this place and none of us would know it!"

"The lights are effected by the storm, madam." James inclined his head toward the windows. Frost spread fern-like patterns across the panes. Snow collected on the sills. "The electricity has been flickering for the past hour. It's very nasty outside. Hilda heard on the radio that most of the major roads are closed—drifted over with snow.''

''You see what I mean?'' Candida threw out her hands. ''Who the hell is Hilda? This is the first I've heard of any Hilda.''

''She's my cook,'' Tillis said. ''James's wife. You didn't think I cooked the prime rib, did you?''

Meg accepted a snifter from the tray. ''James, are you saying we're snowed in?'' Thoughts of catching the red-eye to New York evaporated when James nodded. She was stuck here for the duration. There would be no escaping Steven and Suzanne.

''I'm afraid so, miss. If the major roads are closed, it's certain our road is impassable.''

The moody silence that followed suggested others besides Meg had considered departing immediately instead of remaining for the weekend. As a single body, they turned to consider the frosted windows and the snow flying out of the blackness.

''If I didn't know it was impossible, I'd think you personally arranged this storm, Tillis, so we'd be trapped here.'' Candida sighed, then tasted her brandy. She offered a grudging nod of approval. ''Your taste in liquor is infinitely superior to your taste in fashion. I must say that spider is grotesque.''

Rather than watch Suzanne's fingers curling idly through Steven's hair, Meg gripped her brandy snifter and turned to the fire popping in the grate. How could she still feel jealous after all this time? What was wrong with her?

Aunt Tilly cleared her throat. ''There's something I wish to confess,'' she said.

''There's poison in the brandy?'' No one smiled at Dennis Parnham's lame attempt at humor.

Tillis ignored him. ''As I was planning this weekend, I realized I was eager to see each of you again.''

"Even though you believe one of us sent you death threats?" Howard asked. Lamplight gleamed on his balding head.

"In your own way, each of you has added spice and zest to my life. It occurs to me that I've enjoyed loathing my enemies more than I've enjoyed caring about my friends. You've been more exhilarating and infinitely more irritating and interesting."

"Good God." Howard stared at her. "How much have you had to drink, Tilly? Are you taking those threats seriously?"

"I just wanted you to know that I've—appreciated you over the years. That isn't the right word, but it's close."

Candida crossed long shapely legs, then turned her hands in front of her, watching the firelight sparkle across her rings. "If I were the person threatening your life—and I only wish I had thought of it first—I would not be deterred by that sentimental little bit of sop, Tillis. You would have to do much, much better to make me reconsider wringing your scrawny neck."

Tillis laughed, the sound as charming and girlish as it had been in her youth. She smiled at Candida with an expression almost of affection.

"You're unique, Candida. Nasty, ambitious, greedy. Jealous, vain and reckless. A cat in heat possesses a greater sense of loyalty than you do. You have made an exemplary enemy and a challenging adversary. And you prove the old adage about beauty being only skin-deep."

Candida's smile melded glistening teeth and cold eyes. "A skunk smells its own tail first, Tillis dear. Every slanderous word you uttered applies to yourself before it applies to me."

When Steven spoke, Meg looked up from the fire, the reflex one she instantly regretted. In the dim light his brown hair looked almost black; his hard jaw was shadowed. He was breathtakingly handsome. As Meg tried to squelch such unwanted thoughts, Steven moved away from Suzanne to stand beside the suit of armor guarding the archway.

"Tillis, you still haven't explained why I was invited for the weekend. Or why Suzanne and Howard are here."

Meg's eyebrow arched and she frowned. His phrasing made it sound as if he and Suzanne had not arrived as a couple.

"There's no mystery." Aunt Tilly wandered to the card table set up by the fireplace near Meg. "I've assembled the people who might wish to see me dead."

"You're being overly dramatic," Steven protested. He sounded annoyed. "No one here wants to see you dead."

"You couldn't be more wrong. But we'll leave that point for a moment. I asked you to come because I wished to review my notes for the new book with you."

Everyone present knew Tilly's new book was to be a nonfiction account of Whitney Halverson's murder.

Meg should have remembered Aunt Tilly was gathering facts and background information regarding the murder. Though it was tactless, her gaze involuntarily darted to Suzanne. Suzanne's aristocratic profile was turned toward the windows, away from the group gathered before the fireplace. She wore an expensive silk blouse with heavily padded shoulders, and a slim cashmere skirt. Her blond hair fell in soft waves toward the pearls glowing against her throat.

Meg admitted Suzanne looked tragic and fragile. What woman could hope to compete with a beautiful and wealthy young widow? Even one with curiously cold eyes. Suzanne turned those cool eyes from the window and followed the conversation between Steven and Aunt Tilly.

"Do I sense reluctance in your voice, Tillis?" Steven asked. "Have you changed your mind about discussing the Halverson book?"

"I've changed my mind about writing the book. The timing doesn't seem as fortuitous as I originally believed." For the first time Tillis looked directly at Suzanne. "As you know, there isn't an ending. The murderer was never apprehended." Aunt Tilly ran her fingertips across the card table. "Without an ending, the project isn't worth pursuing." Again she met Suzanne Halverson's steady gaze. "I've destroyed my notes. Everything is gone."

"Oh, no, you haven't," Candida said briskly. "You're lying. Less than an hour ago you referred to your notes and advised Meg to use them to finish the book if you croaked."

Tillis shot Candida a poisonous look that would have felled a lesser woman. A hint of alarm flickered behind Tillis's lashes.

"I know what you're doing, Tillis—you're playing coy." Candida rolled her eyes toward Steven. "Don't you get it? First she dangles the bait until you're salivating to get your hands on the new project, then she bats her false eyelashes and says, oh never mind. You're supposed to up the ante, dear Steven. The next move is yours and it's going to cost you plenty."

"Shut up, Candida," Tillis muttered.

Steven's expression turned thoughtful. "Has something happened that I should know about?"

"Only that I've decided not to do the book." An odd urgency charged Aunt Tilly's voice. "Steven, please. This isn't the proper moment to discuss business."

"Of course." He hesitated. "I understand."

"I'm sure you do," Candida said. "It's going to cost a fortune to change Tillis's small mind and put her back to work again." She waved at the smoke drifting her way from Dennis's cigarette. "If we're not going to be entertained by sitting in on the negotiations for Tillis's on-again off-again book, and I use the term loosely, then what is the plan for this evening? Shall we conduct the MAIMS board meeting and get it over with?''

Aunt Tilly shook her head. "There'll be time for MAIMS later. Tonight we'll relax and enjoy ourselves. Perhaps cards, conversation..." She touched Meg's shoulder. "I wonder if I might have a word with you in my office?''

"Of course." Anything to escape Steven.

Dennis eyed the card table and sighed. "Oh, very well. If we're forced to enjoy ourselves...anyone for bridge? Suzanne? Howard?" He grimaced. "For heaven's sake, Howard. We're civilized people. Surely we can share the same bridge table."

"Like we share everything else?"

Dennis stiffened. "Honestly Howard, can't you give that tiresome subject a rest?"

Eager to escape, Meg followed Aunt Tilly down a long shadowy corridor, wishing she had a flashlight. The wall sconces were placed at infrequent intervals and the corridor was dark and smelled faintly of dust and age.

Aunt Tilly laughed when Meg muttered that she felt as if she were wandering about in a late-night mystery rerun. Entering her library-office, Tillis moved around the room turning on low table lamps. The bulbs flickered, then steadied.

"When your grandfather built Morgan's Manor, electricity was still new in these parts. I have an idea he believed the supply was limited, that one was allotted a finite amount. So he spaced the outlets rather far and few between. This house really is a monstrosity, isn't it?" She smiled at the room with affection.

Floor-to-ceiling bookshelves covered three walls, ran up and around a small fireplace, threatened to enclose the windows. Behind Aunt Tilly's massive old-fashioned desk was a door that led into a room too large to be a closet, too small to be anything else. Aunt Tilly used it to store office supplies. A full skeleton hung from a hanger on the coatrack. A plaster of paris skull served as the base for a table lamp. Another skull had been sculpted to serve as a pencil cup. Several bottles labeled Poison were scattered here and there.

"A bit outré, I admit, but amusing." Tillis laughed when she noticed Meg examining the skulls and bottles. "The poison bottles contain bath salts, I believe."

Meg seated herself in a comfy worn leather chair and placed her brandy snifter on the table next to her. "Aunt Tilly, I don't want you to think I'm unappreciative regarding Morgan's Manor—"

"But you really don't care for the old place." Tillis took the seat behind the desk and folded her hands on the blotter with a smile. "Morgan's Manor grows on one. It's a perfect site for a mystery writer. Inaccessible, filled with secrets and possessing a certain brooding charm." When she spread her hands the beaded spider flattened across her breast. "Your inheritance doesn't come with strings attached, Meg. If you don't want Morgan's Manor, give it to someone who does, sell it or tear it down if you like. But when the time comes, give the old place a chance. Live here awhile. Maybe you'll find you enjoy having a home away from the city—even a Gothic monster like this—some place to run away to when flight seems the best solution."

Meg smoothed her hands over her wool skirt. There had been times when she had longed for a hideaway, when she had yearned to escape the heat and pressures of New York City. Aunt Tilly had guessed correctly. But Morgan's Manor?

"I regret that you and I have never really had a chance to know each other," Aunt Tilly said suddenly. "I have a feeling we would be good friends if time and proximity allowed."

"I'd like to know you better, too. I've admired you for years. From the time I read my first Tillis Morgan novel, I wanted to be like you. I wanted to write wonderful mysteries." A blush heated Meg's cheeks, deepened at the suggestion of moisture glistening in Aunt Tilly's eyes. It surprised her to discover Aunt Tilly possessed a streak of sentimentality.

"Oh, my, will you look at me," Aunt Tilly said, managing a smile. "I'm getting weepy in my old age. What would Candida say?"

The dining room had been illuminated by flattering candlelight. Here, with the desk lamp shining full on her face, Aunt Tilly looked tired, thinner than the last time Meg had seen her. She looked achingly vulnerable, a state Meg usually did not associate with Tillis Morgan.

"Aunt Tilly, are you feeling well?"

"Thank you, Meg, for the sentiments you just expressed. I'm very proud of you, you know. If I'd had a daughter, I would have wanted her to be as lovely and bright and gifted as you." Aunt Tilly drew a deep breath. "That's why I'm so distraught that I may have placed you in danger."

"I beg your pardon?" Meg stared and her eyebrows rose.

"I committed an unforgivable blunder. I made that impulsive statement at dinner and I shouldn't have." Shaking her head, Tillis pressed her hands together until the knuckles whitened. "Lately my brain seems to be running three sentences behind my mouth. I can't think properly."

"I didn't notice any blunder. What did you say?"

"I announced that you're my heir, that you'll inherit everything, including my papers. It was stupid to blurt it out like that just to score a dramatic point."

Meg frowned. "I'm afraid I still don't understand. How is that dangerous to me?"

"I can't say for a fact that it is—and I tried to repair the damage. But it *might* be. It might be very dangerous." She gazed at Meg, but it was clear her mind had jumped to another topic. "I've solved it, of course. The proof is in the photos. I should have telephoned someone immediately, I see that now. But the storm blew up, and it seemed too dangerous to risk being snowbound if..." Her voice trailed and her brows came together. She examined a point in space, working something out in her mind.

Confusion wrinkled Meg's brow. "Aunt Tilly, I'm sorry, but I'm not following this conversation."

"You need to remember that Morgan's Manor has secrets." Tillis looked at Meg, as if recalling she was present. "Your mother is very good at ferreting out secrets. Did you know that? We used to spend our summers here when we were girls. It was Helen who discovered the manor's secrets."

"What secrets?" Meg felt baffled by the skips and jumps in the conversation.

"All in due time." Aunt Tilly's gaze softened. "You remind me of Helen. The curly dark hair, bright green eyes, slender figure. You're as beautiful as Helen was at your age. I could never fool your mother for long. She always saw right through me."

Meg would rather have discussed the secrets of Morgan's Manor, but Aunt Tilly seemed to have abandoned the subject. "Mother says you used to pull the worst pranks..."

Tillis laughed. "I do love a good prank. The problem is sometimes you can't be present to enjoy the denouement. It would spoil the whole thing. Your mother can sniff a prank almost from the outset. Can you?"

Meg was feeling more puzzled by the minute. She didn't understand the swift topic changes or where the conversation might be leading.

"I'm not sure. Frankly, I'm beginning to suspect this weekend is something of a prank," Meg said finally, feeling her way. "I don't think you intend to murder all of us," she said, smiling. But maybe one of the guests is primed to do a little playacting. Like those role-play mystery weekends she occasionally read about. "I suspect the reference to *Murder at Eight* was no accident—the isolated site and a gathering of enemies. Am I on the right track?"

"I won't deny it." Tillis Morgan smiled.

"So you're confirming there's a prank in the making and you've given us the setup. Therefore, I'd guess the death threats are part of the prank. You made them up and at some point one of us is supposed to find them."

"You're wrong on that point." Aunt Tilly's slim hand dropped to a desk drawer. "The threats are very real. It's also true that any one of my guests could have mailed them. All the postmarks are stamped New York."

Meg stared. Until now, she had assumed the threats were the product of her aunt's fertile imagination. The revelation that they were genuine shocked her. "Have you taken the threats to the police?"

Aunt Tilly shrugged. "The police would read the notes, mutter a bit and advise me to contact them at once if something concrete develops."

"You can't possibly suspect that I..."

"No, dear, of course not. I apologize if I embarrassed you tonight. Benefiting from someone's death and wishing it are quite different things. But the others..."

"Are you including Steven?" Meg asked in a low voice. She hated herself for asking, but couldn't help it.

"Tell me something—is there any danger that Steven is actually involved with Suzanne Halverson? I know their association began innocently enough, but..."

"I wouldn't know," Meg answered stiffly. The familiar and hated jealousy bit into her. "I no longer keep track of Steven's social affairs."

"He hurt you, didn't he?" Aunt Tilly asked softly.

For a moment Meg considered lying, then gave it up. She didn't have the complexion for lies. A fiery blush gave her away every time. "The breakup was my fault," she said finally. "I drove Steven away." Closing her eyes, she passed a hand over her forehead, finding the admission terribly difficult. "I don't know what's wrong with me. I smothered him. I never thought of myself as possessive before. But with Steven . . ." She spread her hands in a helpless gesture. "I was jealous of everyone he spent time with. I . . . I drove us both crazy."

A full minute passed before Aunt Tilly responded. "Jealousy is a lethal poison, my dear Meg."

"I know! I just . . . I couldn't help it."

"There are other names for jealousy. One is fear. Another is self-doubt. You know, of course, that jealous people bring about their own worst fears. You can't continue this, Meg. Jealousy burns up the person who feels it and the object of jealousy is driven away."

"I wish I could stop it, but I don't know how. Even now, when our relationship is over, I look at Steven with Suzanne and I feel terrible inside."

Sympathy filled Aunt Tilly's eyes. "So much heartache has been caused by jealousy." For a long moment she watched the snow pelting the windowpanes. Then she sighed. "I can't tell you how to believe in yourself or how to trust. You'll have to work that out for yourself. But I can tell you that it's the loose tie that binds, not the hangman's knot."

Smiling, Aunt Tilly rose behind her desk and slipped an arm around Meg's waist when Meg joined her at the door. "You can beat the jealousy if you really want to. The process will be painful, but you can win. If you try, and if you really want to."

Meg swallowed the lump in her throat and told herself she absolutely would not cry. "I'm afraid it's too late for Steven and me," she whispered.

"Maybe. But maybe not."

"That wasn't the only problem. Steven's a workaholic, we didn't communicate as well as we should have..."

Aunt Tilly laughed. "And you're not a workaholic? By now you surely know that most men put their work above everything else. Steven is a publisher first. He was the one who spotted the bestseller potential of the Halverson murder. He's been an enormous help."

"I imagine he has been, being so close to the widow." Meg bit her tongue and moaned. "You see?" she said to Aunt Tilly. "It's like a sickness."

"It is a sickness, dear." Aunt Tilly pressed Meg's hand, then kissed her cheek. "The cure begins with believing in yourself."

Meg embraced her aunt. "I know you're trying to help. Thank you."

"There's one more thing I want to say to you. Dangerous people do exist outside the pages of the books we write, Meg. And they can hurt you. Never overlook the obvious."

"You're talking in riddles again." But she was glad the conversation had shifted from more personal problems.

Tilly pressed her cheek against Meg's, leaving the scent of an expensive French perfume. "Just remember what we've talked about."

When they walked into the living room, both women stopped short. Howard Clancy looked up from the wing chair when Tillis asked, "What on earth happened here?"

Steven paced in front of the fireplace, pausing to cast a murderous glare at Dennis Parnham, who sat pressed into the corner of the sofa, smoking furiously. There was no sign of Suzanne Halverson or Candida Ripley. Someone had overturned the card table and cards and score tablets lay scattered over the carpet.

Howard pulled himself upright in the chair and passed a hand over his balding head. After looking around he wet his lips with the last drops in his glass. "Someone ought to shoot Dennis," he muttered, then focused on Tillis as she moved to stand over him. "First, he made a pass at Suzanne Halverson—"

"I did *not* make a pass at Suzanne Halverson," Dennis snapped.

"Then, cool as ice, Dennis announces he's taking his writers out of Caldwell Publishing." Howard squinted at Steven. "That's when we lost the happy family atmosphere, so to speak."

Dennis glared at Steven. "Caldwell Publishing is no longer a major player—"

"I'll sue you, Parnham," Steven said, his hands in fists. "Your writers have contracts. You can't break those contracts on a whim. And you can't deny Caldwell's authors a legitimate market for their work."

"Caldwell Publishing is in a slump. You can't expect my authors to follow you down on a sinking ship. As to a legitimate market, there's a dozen legitimate markets." Dennis waved his cigarette. "You haven't done one damned thing to promote Candida's book, and—"

"That's the heart of this threat, isn't it? You're trying to patch things up with Candida by promising her that if she'll stay with your agency, you'll get her a better deal with another house." Steven glanced at Howard. "Forgive me, Howard, I wish you didn't have to hear this. But, Dennis, you are not going to solve your romantic squabbles at my expense!"

"Is that a threat?" Dennis asked, standing.

"If it comes to that, yes." Steven's mouth settled in a grim line. "I'll take you to court if you try to pull your authors out of Caldwell Publishing. And I'll see that every shady trick you ever pulled is exposed."

Dennis's face flushed an unhealthy red. "Fine. File your suit. Spend a fortune. I'll make sure that any court case stretches into years. And in the meantime, I'll take my writers to Ghost House or Shadow Days. You'll be bankrupt before you ever take the stand."

Meg drew a breath and stepped between them, hoping to put a stop to the argument. "Where are Candida and Suzanne?"

Steven stared at her as if she had materialized in front of his eyes. "I don't know. I think they went to bed."

"Maybe all your authors don't see you as God, Dennis," Howard said. He appeared to have followed the exchange with greater acuity than Meg would have believed in view of how much he had drunk. "Maybe they won't want to break their contracts and go trucking off to Ghost House or that other place just because you say so."

Dennis flicked him a contemptuous glance. "If you're referring to Candida, Candida will do as I say."

Meg turned so she couldn't see Howard's face, embarrassed for him. He blustered and mumbled, then sank back into his chair. Tillis bent over him and spoke quietly in his ear.

"I won't do as you say, Dennis," Meg stated quietly. "I don't break contracts. I won't renege on my agreement with Caldwell Publishing." From the corner of her eye, she saw Steven's look of gratitude.

"We'll talk about it."

"No, Dennis. There's nothing to discuss." Although it was early, Meg decided to go to her room. An hour in the company of Aunt Tilly's houseguests felt like two days in a war zone. The hostilities exhausted her.

"Meg, wait." Steven touched her shoulder and a wave of electricity jolted through her body before she hastily stepped away from his hand. "I need to talk to you. Will you take a walk with me?"

The suggestion caught her unawares and was so outrageous that Meg laughed. "In case you haven't noticed, there's a blizzard raging outside. One of the worst storms in ten years according to James. Believe me, this is no night for a walk."

"We won't go far. We'll stay near the house."

It was exactly the kind of silly idea that usually appealed to Meg. Good sense, however, insisted she decline. She and Steven had nothing more to say to each other. There was no point opening old wounds.

"Good God, listen to him! The man's a lunatic." Dennis Parnham stared at them. "Meg, I won't allow you to go out in a damned blizzard with this idiot! It's too dangerous."

"You won't *allow* me?" Incredulous, Meg stared at him. "Dennis, you're my agent, not my father or my keeper. Ours is strictly a business relationship. You don't decide where I go or with whom." To emphasize her point, she turned to Steven. "Give me two minutes to change into a pair of jeans and find my boots."

Turning sharply, she headed toward the staircase, already berating herself for giving in to a knee-jerk reaction. She knew she was making a mistake.

"IT PAINS ME to admit this, but Dennis was right." Steven pushed his gloves into his pockets and ducked his head against the sting of flying snow. "Coming out here really was a stupid idea."

They huddled at the bottom of the veranda steps, their backs braced against the force of the storm. Meg could see only a few feet in front of her, and what she saw was dismaying. A sea of white rolled under the black night. Giant drifts, sculpted by the wind, floated across the grounds like foaming waves. The road had disappeared.

"We could be stuck here for days," she said, then sank her chin back into the folds of her scarf. She had overheard James discussing the worsening situation with Aunt Tilly. The county plows would clear the highways and major roads first. Then, because area economics depended upon the tourist trade, the plows would clear access to the ski areas. Then the town streets. Private roads figured last on the list of priorities. James had promised to try to locate someone willing to clear Aunt Tilly's road. He hadn't sounded optimistic.

"Maybe being stuck isn't such a bad thing," Steven said. "It's time you and I talked."

Meg watched the white flakes accumulating on Steven's dark brows and lashes, the dusting of white that covered his ski cap. And she remembered another place, another snowy evening. Only they had been laughing then, chasing and pelting each other with snowballs like breathless children.

"There's nothing to talk about."

"Now who's refusing to communicate?" He looked into her eyes. "You didn't return my calls."

She hadn't seen any point. Then after a few weeks the messages he left on her answer machine had stopped. And the silence stretched into months.

"Look, Meg. Suzanne needed a friend." He moved slightly to shield her from the force of the wind. "Her husband was murdered, her maid jumped off the balcony of the hotel's twentieth floor—"

"Suzanne went through a lot—she had a rough ordeal. I've never disputed that. I just . . . oh, Steven, let's not rehash this." Stepping away from him, she moved up one of the stone steps, wondering how long she had to remain outside to prove to Dennis that he didn't order her life. She drew a frosty breath and said the hardest words of her life.

"I wish you and Suzanne every happiness. Let's leave it at that, okay?"

"Will you listen to me? It's not like that." He followed her up the steps. "If you could get past this stupid jealousy, you'd see the truth."

"What do you want from me, Steven?" She had an awful suspicion that melting snow was causing her mascara to run and her hair to stick to her forehead. She was crazy to have agreed to this lunacy.

"I want you to be reasonable. It's not really so difficult."

"Oh, come on. It was obvious from the first that you and Suzanne were more than just friends." She had to shout to be heard over the wind whistling around the veranda posts. But that was all right. The anger she had been keeping inside suddenly overwhelmed her. Shouting felt good. And Steven's interest in Suzanne was not an example of stupid jealousy. The most reasonable woman in the world would have been jealous. "You brought Suzanne here. She can't keep her hands off of you. And I don't notice you resisting too strenuously. If you're trying to tell me you don't have a relationship with her, save your breath. I'm not blind!"

"I didn't bring Suzanne to Morgan's Manor. She was here when I arrived."

Meg halted with her boot on the next step. When she turned, she stood at Steven's eye level, close enough that the vapor from his breath bathed her lips and made her feel weak in the knees. His unexpected nearness sent her pulse racing, and she realized if she took one step forward she would be in his arms. Quickly she stepped backward. "I thought Suzanne came with you."

Now she remembered Aunt Tilly inquiring how involved Steven and Suzanne were. Would Aunt Tilly have asked that question if Steven and Suzanne had arrived together?

Steven observed the change in her expression. "Meg, you're wrong. You've been wrong about this from the beginning. I didn't know Suzanne would be here this weekend. But I did know you would be. One of the reasons I came is because I wanted to see you."

"Have you...are you sleeping with her?" Helplessly, Meg listened to the appalling words fall out of her mouth and she was powerless to halt them.

Hating herself, hating the poisonous jealousy that drove her, she clenched her teeth and looked at her feet, wishing miserably that she would blow away on the wind. She would have given anything to withdraw the question. And yet...

"I hoped things had changed," Steven said, closing his eyes. The wind lifted and fell, the howl swelling, then dropping to a whisper. Snow swirled around them. "I haven't slept with Suzanne," he said finally. "But you won't believe that, will you? You have to torture yourself by imagining the worst."

"I want to believe you," she whispered.

"What if I did sleep with her, Meg," he said angrily. "What if it really is a flaming affair? You and I are free to see whomever we please. You made that choice when you broke it off, when you refused to answer my calls and wouldn't take my messages. You made it damned clear that whatever you and I had together, it was finished."

"It is!"

He caught her glove. "Whitney Halverson was my friend. I couldn't turn my back on his widow." Stepping up beside her, he caught her shoulders between his hands. "You had no reason to be jealous."

As if jealousy needed a reason. But the words poured out of her traitorous mouth. "You continued to see her far beyond any duty to Whitney, Steven. Suzanne was using you. Coming on to you. At the end you were spending more time with her than with me." She sounded small and petty, pathetically insecure. "What's the point of fighting about this again?"

His hands tightened on the shoulders of her parka, preventing her from going inside. "Because there's so much you don't understand."

"Then tell me. You seem to think I can read your mind, but damn it, I can't!" She shouted against the wind. "If you and Suzanne aren't lovers, then tell me why she's all over you. Tell me why everyone here believes the two of you are a couple. Make me believe you're only playacting when you look at her or take her arm." Oh God, she couldn't stop the accusations from pouring out of her and she was making a fool of herself, unreeling her pain like an old movie. "Let go of me, Steven."

"You're always saying I won't communicate. Maybe the problem is you won't listen. Meg, I started seeing Suzanne because of Whitney and because I believed she needed comfort. But it quickly became something else."

"That's obvious." She tried to pull out of his arms, but he wouldn't let her.

"Damn it, Meg! You get one idea in your head and you won't allow the tiniest possibility that you may be wrong. The thing with Suzanne and me is not what you think."

Tears gathered in her eyes and she thanked heaven for the storm. With luck, Steven would believe the moisture on her cheeks was melting snow.

"If there's something you think I should know, then for heaven's sake just tell me."

Frustration darkened his eyes and she winced as his fingers dug into her shoulders. He said something, but the wind tossed his words away. ". . . wish I could, but I can't. Not yet. Please, Meg, trust me. This is almost finished. When it is, maybe you and I can start over."

"Trust me." Her laugh spun away in the wind and snow, sounding like a sob. How could she trust him when she didn't trust that he could choose her over someone like Suzanne? Meg Sandler was no one special. She wasn't blond and beautiful. She wasn't witty or profound. She was just . . . just Meg Sandler.

It had been a dreadful mistake to come outside with him. All the pain came rushing back. The hurt, the ache of losing him. An image of Steven's lean muscled body lying next to Suzanne rose in her mind, a torturous stupid image, and Meg winced. Why did she do this to herself? And she had been crazy to think she no longer loved him. Stupid, stupid. The pain, the sense of betrayal, was as raw now as it had been eight months ago.

"Let go of me, Steven, I mean it. I'm frozen, I'm upset and I want to go inside."

His hands dropped from her shoulders so abruptly that she stumbled and almost fell. Anger heated his eyes. "All right, Meg. Run away. Believe whatever the hell you want to believe."

For a moment she stared into his eyes, as angry as he was. Then she threw open the door and blew inside, pushed by the wind. James glanced outside, waited a moment, then closed the door against a whirl of flying snow. He took her wet cap, parka and gloves.

"Is Mr. Caldwell remaining outside, miss?"

"I don't know." And she didn't care. Wiping the snow from her cheeks and eyes, Meg ran up the stairs, almost colliding with Suzanne at the first landing.

Suzanne made a point of noticing the wet ends of Meg's hair, the smudges of mascara beneath her eyes. "Have you seen Steven?"

"He went for a walk," Meg muttered, examining the woman who had bewitched Steven. Light from the candle sconce gleamed in Suzanne's shining blond hair. A sapphire-colored Scottish wool bathrobe hugged her slim figure. Despite Suzanne's beauty, she reminded Meg of a baked

Alaska, pale and luscious on the outside, remote and cold inside.

Observing Suzanne's elegant perfection, Meg became depressingly conscious of her own ordinary "cute" nose, her unmanageable hair, the embarrassing suggestion of freckles scattered across her nose. She would never be tall and willowy; she would never possess a patrician nose or a cool detached attitude. She would always be ordinary Meg Sandler from a small town in Iowa. A down-to-earth unglamorous tomboy with an inquiring mind and a lack of confidence. She was not the type of woman men like Steven Caldwell fell in love with.

"Steven went for a walk?" One of Suzanne's perfectly arched eyebrows rose in disbelief.

"Yes." Meg brushed past her and hurried toward the heavy carved door of her room. Head down, she ran pell-mell into Aunt Tilly.

"I'm sorry." She pressed her hand over her eyes and peered through her fingers to see if Suzanne had witnessed her clumsy display.

Aunt Tilly frowned and watched as Suzanne descended the staircase. "That is a dangerous woman," she said softly.

"I know."

"Did Steven tell you...?" Aunt Tilly gave her a sharp look. "No, he wouldn't. It would only place you at greater risk."

"Communication is not Steven's best talent," Meg said irritably. "Aunt Tilly, I'm in no mood for mysteries. If you think I'm in some kind of danger, then stop beating around the bush and tell me what's going on. I'm entitled to an explanation."

"You're right, of course. But I want to speak to Steven first," Aunt Tilly said, still watching the staircase.

"Okay, have it your way. You and Steven decide what's best for me." Meg threw up her hands and reached for the door latch. "I give up. I'm going to take a hot bath and go to bed."

"Did you and Steven have an argument?"

"It's just not going to work out for us," Meg said in a low voice. "Even if Suzanne wasn't in the picture..." When she looked up Aunt Tilly was rubbing her temple. "Are you all right?"

"Just a headache. I've been having a lot of them recently." She brushed back a strand of Meg's damp hair and tucked it behind her ear. "You really are quite beautiful, you know."

A protest formed on Meg's lips, then she laughed. "It must be the dim light. Or you're losing your eyesight."

Whenever someone referred to her as beautiful, Meg shied away from them. She was pretty enough, she supposed, but nowhere near beautiful. Her hair was too curly, her mouth was too wide. Her features were too determined to be beautiful. And at five foot four, she was too short.

Tillis smiled. "I recognize a beautiful woman when I see one. But I have an idea you don't. Maybe that's part of your problem."

Meg leaned to kiss her aunt's cheek. "Good night, Aunt Tilly," she said fondly.

"Good night, my dear." Aunt Tilly placed her hand on Meg's cheek and looked at her for a long moment, then she moved down the dim corridor and rapped at Candida's bedroom door. Meg shook her head and smiled. Even Aunt Tilly's satin bathrobe was done in the trademark black.

Then Steven came up the staircase. He and Meg stared at each other, then Meg slammed into her bedroom.

Sometime near midnight someone knocked at her door. Meg glanced up from the book she was reading, but she didn't climb out of bed. She had nothing to say to Steven Caldwell.

Chapter Three

"Good morning, everyone." Stifling a yawn, Meg poured a cup of coffee from the silver service on the sideboard.

Everyone but Aunt Tilly had assembled in the dining room for the breakfast buffet James laid out. Meg wore jeans and a heavy lemon-colored sweater. She noticed Steven had chosen jeans, too. Candida still wore her pink satin bathrobe trimmed with dyed pink fur, though she'd made up her face before coming downstairs. The others wore casually elegant clothing *Town and Country* would have approved as suitable for a country weekend.

"Are you in a more reasonable mood this morning?" Steven asked, stepping beside her to refill his coffee cup.

"If that's supposed to be funny, it isn't." His after-shave teased Meg's senses. He looked fresh and handsome, his hair still damp from his morning shower. Meg looked at him and her heart sank. Already the weekend was a torment. She didn't know how she was going to get through the rest of it. "Did you knock on my door last night? About midnight?"

"Were you expecting someone else?" he asked, looking down at her.

"I wasn't expecting anyone."

"I've spoken to Tillis and she agrees it's time to tell you everything." Steven's gaze brushed her lips, then moved upward.

A helpless feeling sent Meg's spirits plummeting. He had such wonderful eyes. Warm dark brown flecked with tiny green specks. Thick long lashes that any woman would envy. "All right," she conceded with a sigh. "Tell me 'everything.'"

"Not here." He cast a pointed glance at the people in the dining room.

Meg lifted an eyebrow. "Not in front of Suzanne, you mean?"

"Meg, give it a rest. We need to talk privately."

Pink flooded her cheeks. But anger was easier to handle than regret or pain. "Anything you have to say to me you can say in front of everyone," she said sharply.

He frowned. "You couldn't be more wrong. And you're making a big problem worse. When I knock at your door tonight, let me in. I mean it, Meg. Don't fool around. There's a situation involving Suzanne and it's imperative you know about it."

"Involving Suzanne." She hid her face by bending over her coffee cup. "An announcement of some sort?"

"Do you have to personalize everything?" Anger flickered in his eyes. "This doesn't have anything to do with you and me."

"There is no you and me, Steven. So don't come to my room tonight." Lifting her chin she walked away from him, thinking this was a woman's worst nightmare come true. Here she was with no new man of her own, trapped with an old love and his new lady friend, and discovering the pain of loss was as fresh as yesterday. And discovering that Steven still had the power to turn her into jelly.

Trying to put him out of her mind, she approached James. "Where's Aunt Tilly? I thought she'd be downstairs by now."

James straightened behind a salver of scrambled eggs. "Madam has not come down yet." The frown he flicked toward the doorway expressed surprise and growing concern.

"That's strange." Meg looked toward the doorway, too. "It isn't like Aunt Tilly to sleep in. She prides herself on being an early riser. Perhaps someone should check?"

"As you wish, miss." James gave the buffet a quick glance, then hurried out of the dining room.

Meg glanced over her shoulder at Steven who was watching her, frowning over his coffee cup. Moving as far away from him as possible, she joined Dennis Parnham at the windows.

"At least the storm has ended," Dennis commented. Sipping his coffee, he watched a pale sun wage battle against an advancing bank of leaden clouds. "It finally stopped snowing at about five this morning. But it looks like more is on the way."

"You were awake at five?" Looking strangely naked without her jewels and plumes, Candida buttered a slice of raisin toast. For morning wear she had limited herself to one diamond ring on each hand. It wasn't the lavish display of last night, Meg noticed, but enough of a showing to remind onlookers they were dealing with a person of consequence.

"I'm surprised you have to ask," Howard commented in an acid voice. "Couldn't you just roll over and notice the empty space in your bed?"

"Don't start, Howard." Candida glared at him. "I can't deal with jealousy on an empty stomach. At least wait until after breakfast."

When Candida mentioned jealousy Meg felt another burst of heat in her cheeks and carefully avoided looking at Steven. Instead she studied Howard, who was clear eyed and steady of hand this morning. If Meg hadn't known better, she would have sworn he hadn't had a drink in weeks.

"For your information," Dennis snapped, turning toward the table. "I slept in my room and Candida slept in hers."

"Do you know that for a fact?" Howard drawled. "Maybe my wife slept in my room last night."

"Don't be silly." If Dennis's attempt to embarrass Howard was deliberate, it was also effective. An angry flush infused Howard's cheeks. Dennis's smile was nasty. "Everyone knows the two of you don't sleep together anymore. That's why Tillis assigned you separate rooms."

"That's enough, Dennis," Candida snapped before Howard could react. "You're mad at me. Don't take it out on Howard."

Steven seemed to reach a decision. He pushed away from the sideboard and walked toward Meg, bringing the scent of English soap and that damned sexy after-shave.

Before he could speak, Suzanne glided forward and slipped her hand through his arm. "I was so glad when the wind finally stopped. I hate windy weather, don't you?"

"It was still noisy last night. There seemed to be a lot of traffic in the corridor," Meg said, not looking at Steven. She glanced at Suzanne's hand possessively linked through Steven's arm and she escaped toward the buffet, blindly reaching for a plate. Although she never ate breakfast, she picked up the bacon tongs and selected two strips of bacon.

"Excuse me." James reappeared in the archway, his forehead pleated in worried lines. "Madam does not answer a knock at her door. I tried the latch, but the door is locked."

Meg dropped the bacon. "Why wouldn't Aunt Tilly respond to your knock?" Unless something was wrong. "Do you have a key?" she asked uneasily.

Reaching into his vest pocket, James produced a key ring. "I opened the lower lock, the actual door lock. What I should have explained, miss, is the upper bolt is in place. The door is bolted from the inside."

"And Aunt Tilly didn't respond when you called to her?"

"I'm a bit concerned, miss. I've never known Madam to sleep beyond six or to neglect her guests."

"Well, don't you get it?" Candida's bright laughter rang across the room and everyone turned to look at her. "The whole thing's clear now." She waved the slice of raisin toast. "This is a prank, of course. Tillis set us up last night. That was step one." Mimicking Tillis Morgan, she lowered her voice and announced in a dramatic tone, "Everyone here has a reason to want me dead."

"Oh. Yes, I see." Dennis Parnham smiled. "So now we're supposed to fly into a panic and think, *Tillis doesn't answer her door, therefore she must be dead. One of us took the bait and murdered her in her sleep.* Is that the idea?"

"Well, of course it is." Candida peered around the room. "Most likely the old sneak has hidden a tape recorder somewhere so she can play it back later to embarrass us. I imagine we're supposed to fly into a frenzy, then start hurtling accusations at one another." Opening her mouth, she munched into the raisin toast. "The woman is absolutely incorrigible. The rest of you can run off in panic if you wish, but I'm going to stay right here and enjoy my breakfast." She raised her voice to the corner of the room, speaking for the benefit of any hidden recorders. "You don't fool me, Tillis Morgan. This prank is as transparent as your silly books."

Steven moved up beside Meg. "How can we get into Tillis's room?" he asked James.

"There's a row of windows . . . I could fetch a ladder."

"You're certain the door is bolted from the inside."

"Yes, sir."

Tillis was Meg's aunt, Meg should take charge. And she needed to build confidence in her decisions. "Fetch the ladder at once, James," she said firmly. "Candida is probably correct. This sounds like a prank. But just in case . . ." They would most likely discover Aunt Tilly reading in bed, waiting for her "body" to be found, and very pleased by the uproar she had caused. Still, the situation was worrisome and unpleasant.

"Maybe she really is dead," Suzanne suggested.

Offended, Meg responded in a sharp voice. "You almost sound as if you'd be pleased if she was."

Smiling, Suzanne stepped to the coffee urn and freshened her cup. "Obviously we're supposed to think she is."

Disgusted, Meg followed Steven and James into the foyer where they pulled on caps and coats. Even though Meg knew in her heart this was just one of Aunt Tilly's silly pranks, she was feeling more nervous by the minute. Howard joined them, his expression as grim as her own.

He pressed Meg's shoulder. "How can I help?"

"I don't think we'll need you," Steven said. He turned to James. "If you'll hold the base of the ladder, I'll climb up." As Steven was by far the younger man, it seemed the most sensible suggestion. "Thanks anyway, Howard."

"I'll come along just in case."

James opened the front door. "I'll fetch the ladder from the garage, then meet you at the back of the house."

Steven met Meg's gaze as he tugged on his gloves. "Don't worry. This situation has all the earmarks of a prank."

"Of course it's just a prank." She wrung her hands and followed Steven to the door. "I . . . be careful. I'll wait upstairs. And after Aunt Tilly has her laugh, I plan to give her a tongue-lashing for scaring everyone half to death!"

She rushed up the staircase and hurried to the end of the corridor, halting before Aunt Tilly's door. "Aunt Tilly?" There wasn't a sound. Nothing but silence. Meg's knock sounded overloud in the deserted hallway. When she tried to open the door it caught against the interior bolt.

One by one the others appeared and Meg ceased pounding on Aunt Tilly's door. "I thought you were going to ignore the fuss," she said to Candida.

"Oh, if everyone else is willing to play along..." After tightening the sash of her bathrobe and flicking toast crumbs from her bosom, Candida cast a look of envy at Suzanne's coffee cup. "I wish I'd thought to bring my coffee, too."

Dennis gave Candida his cup, then patted his pockets. "I want a cigarette."

"Did you hear something?" Suzanne asked after several minutes had passed.

"Nothing. You're imagining things." Shoving back the fur-trimmed sleeve of her robe, Candida peered at a watch face surrounded by diamond chips. "What's taking so long?"

"What difference does it make? We're not going anywhere," Meg said, thinking of the drifts blocking the road and the mounds of snow Steven and James had to climb over to reach the back of the house.

Howard came up the staircase, his wet pant legs trailing clumps of snow. "It shouldn't be long now." He rapped hard on the door. "Tilly? You've had your joke, now open this door."

Following another silence they finally heard footsteps inside the bedroom, then the bolt scraped back and Steven filled the doorway.

"Aunt Tilly?" Meg tried to see around him, but Steven stepped in front of her. When she tried to push past, he caught her arm and blocked the entrance.

"Don't go inside, Meg." He drew a breath and touched her cheek. Now she noticed his face was ashen. "Tillis is dead."

Everyone froze, staring at him. Then Meg shook off his hand with a furious gesture.

"Stop it," she said angrily. "I don't know what instructions Aunt Tilly gave you, but this prank has gone far enough! It's over, do you understand?" Eyes flashing, she stared at him. "This isn't funny."

"I wish to God it was a prank, miss. But it's not." James appeared directly behind Steven. He, too, had climbed the ladder. Moisture glistened in his eyes, and his voice was thick and choked. "Madam is dead."

"Oh, the hell she is!" Elbowing forward, Candida pushed Steven aside and ducked under his arm. "I'll have to see her scrawny dead body with my own eyes before I— Oh, my God!"

Meg dashed inside behind her and halted when Candida did. A gasp sucked the breath from her chest and blindly she grabbed Candida's sleeve. Her fingernails dug into the dyed pink fur. "Oh, no. No!"

Tillis Morgan was dead. To Meg's horror, it was not a prank. Aunt Tilly was unmistakably dead. She lay sprawled on the floor in her black-and-white flannel nightgown almost directly beneath the window; a dusting of snow powdered her hair and forehead.

Turning blindly, Meg reached for Steven. When his arms closed around her, she pressed her face into the collar of his parka and released a sob.

Dennis Parnham stared at Tillis's still figure. "Oh, Jesus."

Swearing softly, Howard covered his face with his hand. After a moment he lowered his fingers and murmured. "Bless her heart. She put up a hell of a fight. Look at this room."

To say a struggle had ensued was to wildly understate the case. A large wing chair lay on its side. A side table and two lamps had toppled. Books had been knocked from the bookcase. The mattress was slightly askew. Loose papers littered the floor like confetti.

"I'm sorry, Meg," Steven murmured, his lips in her hair.

Embarrassed that she had automatically turned to him, Meg disengaged herself and, feeling sick, she watched James pull a sheet from the bed and gently draw it over Aunt Tilly's body.

Candida had bent to peer at something on the floor. "My, my." She pointed but didn't touch. She was too seasoned a mystery writer to disturb evidence. "What have we here? A broken ashtray, a broken cigarette and an ivory cigarette holder. Now who do you suppose these items belong to?"

Dennis flushed under the sudden unpleasant attention. He patted his jacket pockets as if searching for his cigarette holder.

"Obviously you were here last night," Howard accused. "Right in the thick of things from the look of it."

"Now wait just a minute. I stopped by for half an hour. I admit it. Damn it, stop looking at me like that. Tillis *asked* me to stop by. But I swear I don't know how that ashtray and cigarette got here. I didn't smoke while I was here. Tillis wouldn't permit it."

When Dennis realized this statement indicated he must have returned at a later time or that he was lying, he wet his lips. "No, wait. I...I did smoke. Yes, I had a cigarette. And I must have left my cigarette holder here. I wondered what happened to it." He spread his hands. "Why are you all staring at me? I did *not* kill Tillis! She was alive when I left this room!"

"It seems someone else was here, too," Suzanne said, kneeling beside Tillis's body. She directed their attention to a ruby-and-amethyst ring lying a few feet from Tillis Morgan's outflung hand. "Candida was wearing this ring last night."

"What?" Stepping forward, Candida stared down at the ring. "That's mine, but it's impossible! I swear I was not here last night. I've never been in this room until now!"

Dennis cocked an eyebrow and spoke in the same sarcastic tone Candida had used to point out the ivory cigarette holder. "I suppose your ring just walked in here."

"Don't give me that oily smile, Dennis Parnham!"

Suzanne lifted an eyebrow. "How do you explain your ring ending up a few feet from Tillis's dead body?"

"I have no idea how it got there." Extending her hands, Candida showed them how loose her rings were. "Maybe the ring dropped off when I ran in here just now. Then it rolled over—" she pointed but couldn't bring herself to look at Tillis's sheet-draped body "—over there."

"Nice try, but you weren't wearing this ring at breakfast," Suzanne pointed out. "Besides, there's snow on it from the window. This ring has been here as long as the body has."

"What the hell are you implying? I was not in this room last night! Wait—I know. Tillis came to my room, she must have stolen the ring off the bureau top or off my finger and—"

Steven interrupted. "Tillis didn't enter your room, Candida. I came up the staircase as she was talking to you in the corridor. Tillis never touched you. She didn't take your ring."

"Now look at that," Dennis said. "The broken glass near the brass lamp. Isn't that the glass Howard used last night?" Malicious pleasure curved his lips. "Howard was the only person using a monogrammed tumbler."

Meg gripped Steven's arm and leaned against him again. Tears flowed down her cheeks. "Please. Can we go downstairs?" she whispered. "It doesn't seem right to stand here arguing, not with Aunt Tilly..."

Suzanne stooped to pick up some of the loose papers scattered over the floor. "They're manuscript pages. From *First Guess,* one of Tillis's old books."

"Meg is right. We're disturbing evidence." Steven's arm tightened around her, then gently he nudged her toward the door. "Everyone out." No one had to be urged twice. "James, lock the door, then telephone the police."

"At once, sir." Bending, James pulled out his key ring, then turned a key in the bedroom lock.

"Before you do another thing, James," Howard said. "I need a drink. Either serve drinks or tell me where Tillis has put the liquor now."

"The liquor cabinet is concealed behind a panel in the dining room, Mr. Clancy. You'll notice a cherry-wood panel to the left of the sideboard. Slide it toward the windows."

"Trust Tillis to find different hiding places for the liquor," Howard grumbled. "She was a lovely woman in many, many ways, but she felt compelled to make a mystery out of damned near everything."

"Suddenly she's a 'lovely woman'?" Jealousy flared in Candida's eyes. "Last night she was a lousy cook, a neglectful wife, a harridan who dragged your name through months of tabloid mud and cost you your job and your pension. But now that a glass with your fingerprints all over it is found at the murder scene, she's a 'lovely woman.' You're so transparent, Howard."

"You know I didn't murder Tilly." First in to the dining room, Howard walked directly to the cherry-wood panel and slid it to one side. "Well, I'll be damned. It's a whole room. And nicely stocked, too." He emerged brandishing a bottle of vodka. "Bloody Marys anyone?"

Meg's stomach churned and she sat down abruptly. When Steven pushed a handkerchief in her hand, she accepted it gratefully.

"Are you all right?" he asked, pressing her shoulder.

"No. Aunt Tilly's dead!" She couldn't accept it. Slowly Meg looked around the room. "And someone here killed her."

Howard broke the silence that followed. "I'll admit there were times when I wanted to wring Tilly's neck." After pouring vodka into a tall glass, he added a splash of spiced tomato juice, then swallowed heavily. "Better." He sighed and blinked at them. "But the truth is, I'll miss the old girl. Tilly and I settled our differences way back when."

"Apparently Tillis didn't think so," Suzanne commented.

Howard narrowed his eyes. "I beg your pardon?"

"Last night Tillis indicated you were among those who wouldn't grieve much over her death."

"I've changed my mind. I would like a Bloody Mary, Howard." Meg hoped it would settle her nerves. Her hands trembled and tears continued to well in her eyes. When she could control the quiver in her voice, she raised her head and studied Suzanne. "Aunt Tilly said *everyone* at the table had a reason to want her dead. We haven't heard your reason, Suzanne."

Immediately Steven's fingers dug into Meg's shoulder. His meaning was plain. But if Steven hoped to spare his precious Suzanne any awkward questions, he was going to be disappointed.

Meg shook off his hand. "Well, Suzanne?"

"You know," Candida said, leaning back in one of the dining room chairs. She tilted her head in a thoughtful expression. "I believe Meg's right. Tell all, Suzanne. Why did you want Tillis dead?"

Suzanne shrugged her padded silk shoulders. "Tillis didn't include me in her accusations."

Dennis raised a hand. "Tillis said *everyone* at the table. For the sake of discussion, let's say Tillis did include you. So how do you benefit from her death?"

"The only possible reference is so thin and flimsy it isn't worth mentioning."

"Mention it anyway," Meg said. She gave Steven a defiant look, not caring that he looked angry.

Suzanne also glanced at Steven. "I suppose it's no secret that I was initially opposed to a book about my husband's murder. But as it seemed Tillis planned to write the book with or without my consent, I dropped my protest and cooperated in every way."

Dennis lit a cigarette. "But you object to having the book published?"

"I did in the beginning. I dreaded the fresh publicity the book would generate. I'd prefer to put all that ugliness behind me. Plus, it seemed a waste of time and effort. Tillis herself admitted there was no satisfactory ending for the book as the murderer was never apprehended."

"If I were writing that book," Candida said, thinking out loud, "I'd have been searching for the ending. I wouldn't have relied solely on the police investigation, I'd have conducted an investigation of my own. I'd have discovered who murdered your husband."

"I believe that was Tillis's intention. She was gathering evidence, sifting through paperwork, interviewing people..."

"And Tillis failed," Steven said, moving to stand beside Suzanne. "That's why she abandoned the project and destroyed her notes."

"Surely you of all people can't honestly believe Tillis destroyed her notes." Candida smiled. "Name one writer who ever destroyed his or her notes. It simply doesn't happen. All of us are secretly convinced our notes possess some kind of magic power. We regard our research as sacred. If the magic doesn't work for this book for whatever reason, it may work for the next. Every writer I know would rather run through Bloomingdale's stark naked than destroy a single jot that might form the basis for next year's bestseller. Every set of notes, every scrap of research that Tillis ever compiled is right here in this house."

Knots of frustration formed along Steven's jawline. "Thank you, Candida, for enlightening us." He clenched his teeth, then drew a breath. "However, Tillis insisted she destroyed her research on the case and I believe her."

"Maybe." Dennis blew smoke into the air. "Or maybe Tillis dug up some damaging scandal that Suzanne's afraid of."

"Well, well." Candida's eyes sparkled. "Could we be talking blackmail here?"

"Don't be stupid." Suzanne's expression turned to ice. "Do you really think Tillis Morgan was a blackmailer?"

Candida's sparkle faded into disappointment. "Tillis had a lot of disagreeable qualities, but, no—regrettably I can't visualize her as a blackmailer."

"There is no evidence to suggest I was in Tillis's room last night because I wasn't," Suzanne said. "Each one of you has a motive to kill Tillis Morgan. But I don't."

James returned then and one glance at his expression told Meg something else was terribly wrong.

"What's happened?" Steven asked.

"The telephones, sir. The wires have been ripped from the wall."

"You can't telephone the police?" Meg stood.

"No, miss. I can't telephone anyone. And there's more." James pressed his hands together. "It seems the cars have been disabled. The tires are flat."

"On *all* the cars?" Dennis stared.

"Do you have an air pump?"

"It appears to be missing, miss."

"Howard, you'd better fix me a Bloody Mary, too." Candida sighed. "I suppose it's silly to ask this considering the way things are going, but, James, did you reach anyone last night about plowing out our road?"

"Yes, madam, I did."

Everyone brightened.

"Jim at the service station promised he'd get to us as soon as he could. He predicted it wouldn't be before the day after tomorrow, though. And that's only if there's no more snow."

Meg's shoulders dropped. "Have you heard a weather report? Is more snow expected?"

"I'm afraid so, miss. The radio forecaster predicts scattered snow beginning this afternoon and continuing through the evening."

Steven carried his coffee cup to the windows and gazed up at the swollen gray sky. "It looks like we're going to be stuck here awhile." He gave Meg an I-have-to-talk-to-you look.

"With a dead body!" Candida shuddered.

"Oh, for heaven's sake." Dennis made a face. "You deal with dead bodies all the time. Why should one more disturb you?"

"Shut up, Dennis. The corpses I deal with are fictitious. This one is *real*. And it's personal! That's Tillis up there dead as a mackerel! I didn't like her, but... but I'm sorry she's dead." Candida dabbed her eyes with the sleeve of her robe. "I hate to admit this, but I'll miss the old fraud."

Dennis rolled his eyes. "If you believe that, ladies and gents... Come on, Candida. You've been jealous of Tillis for half your life. You were worried to death that she'd win the Macabre Series and you'd be seen as the has-been you are."

"You heard her, Dennis," Howard growled. "Shut up."

A wave of disgust overwhelmed Meg. "Aunt Tilly made the Parnham Agency a lot of money before she found a new agent who wouldn't steal her work. She made your reputation, Dennis. Can't you feel a little sympathy that she was murdered?"

"Parnham has never forgiven Tillis for leaving his agency," Steven said. "Plus, he's too busy anticipating the money he'll make from Tillis's first four books to waste any time on sympathy."

"Keep it up, Caldwell. I'm keeping track of every slanderous remark. Of course, you can afford a long court case, can't you? Now that you're half a million dollars richer and can buy back a million and a half dollars worth of company stock."

Meg touched her fingertips to her forehead. "I'm going upstairs to lie down. No one seems to care that Aunt Tilly was murdered, all you can think about is accusing one another. Candida's right—this isn't fiction. This is real. But none of you seem to care."

Steven followed her out of the room. "Meg, wait." He caught her arm and she told herself the resultant tremble she felt had nothing to do with him. "I'll go with you."

She raised her eyes to his wide mouth and to her shame she wanted his arms around her, wanted the comfort Steven could have given her. "Oh, Steven," she whispered, tears filling her eyes. "I wish things could have been different."

"Why can't you believe in yourself?" he asked softly, looking down into her eyes. His hands moved up her arms. "That's the root of the problem, isn't it?"

Immediately she stiffened. "Excuse me. I do want to lie down." She pushed his arms away. "And I need some time alone."

Meg felt his gaze on her as she walked up the staircase, felt his anger and frustration. She felt the same emotions, too. Plus confusion. She didn't understand the conflicting messages he was sending. And right now she was too upset to think about it.

JAMES KNOCKED at Meg's bedroom door about two o'clock, waking her from a fitful doze. "Sorry to disturb you, miss.

But Mr. Caldwell wants everyone downstairs in the living room."

Mr. Caldwell could go jump in Dillon Reservoir. Meg bit her lip and sighed. "I'll be along in a minute."

She found her shoes, splashed water over her face and pulled a comb through her unruly curls. Actually Steven was probably right; it was time for a meeting. They'd all had a few hours to consider the situation. There were things that needed to be said, questions that needed answers.

The others had already gathered when Meg entered the living room. A cheerful fire crackled in the grate. James had set out a light repast for anyone who wanted sandwiches or coffee. Steven sat at the card table with Candida beside him poised over a legal-size pad to take notes.

"Now that everyone's here," Steven said as Meg seated herself on the sofa between Dennis and Howard, "I want to bring the group up to speed on what James and I have been doing." Meg noticed that Suzanne had chosen Aunt Tilly's thronelike chair. "We need to discuss our situation and what happens next."

"Who appointed you our leader?" Dennis demanded.

"Someone needs to take charge. Do you want the job?"

"I was just asking, that's all."

"If no one else objects, we'll proceed." When no one spoke, Steven continued. "James and I have searched the house. We wanted to rule out the possibility of an intruder. There's no sign anyone was here last night except us."

"I doubt an intruder would have hung around to be discovered," Meg pointed out. "If he left after... after he did what he came to do, the snow would have covered his tracks."

"Possibly. But I don't think we're dealing with an intruder. However, you've raised an important point. I think we can agree the snow stopped about five o'clock. It's reasonable to assume it began to taper off about an hour earlier. Therefore, judging from the small amount of snow on Tillis's bedroom floor, I think we can infer she was killed between four and five this morning."

"We know Dennis was awake at five." Having flung this dagger, Candida noted the information on the pad of paper.

"I saw no intruder leaving the premises," Dennis said, choosing to misinterpret Candida's implication.

"James and I walked around the premises and we found no footprints in the snow other than those we made taking the ladder around the house." Steven looked at each person. "So. Who was the last person to see Tillis alive?" No one answered. "Come on folks, we're going to have to do better than this. We can try to figure it out, or we can wait for the police. Either way, we're going to need some answers. I saw Tillis about eleven, eleven-thirty. Did anyone see her after that?"

Howard waved his Scotch. "No one wants to admit being the last person to see Tilly."

"Let's put that question aside for a moment," Meg suggested. "There's something else puzzling me. Steven, you just mentioned the snow on Tilly's bedroom floor. How did it get there?" With an extraordinary effort, Meg kept anything personal out of her expression when she looked at him.

He did the same, answering in a forthright manner. "James and I probably scraped some snow inside when we came in the window. But that's not the entire answer. The window was open about four or five inches when we arrived. There was snow on the carpet beneath the window before I climbed through."

"Open?" Meg's eyebrows lifted. "That explains why the room was so cold. But why on earth would Aunt Tilly open the window during a blizzard? That doesn't make sense."

"The killer opened the window." They all looked at Howard. "The corridor door was bolted from the inside. So how did the killer leave? Obviously he went out the window."

"Don't be an idiot." Dennis spread his hands. "That's a two-and-a-half-story window. Anyone dropping out of that window would be injured. He'd break his neck."

"The snow would cushion his fall."

"But there's another problem," Meg said slowly. "If the killer opened the window wide enough to crawl through, then he somehow managed to lower it behind him. How?"

"How wide is the sill?" Candida asked.

"Not that wide," Steven replied. "Maybe three inches on the outside. Not large enough to stand on. Meg's right. No one going through the window could then lower it behind him."

"Therefore, the killer could not have escaped through the window," Meg concluded. "So how *did* he get out of the room?"

Steven met her eyes and she realized they were thinking in tandem, working together. For the moment at least, it felt like old times. And she saw in Steven's dark eyes that he recognized it, too.

"Everyone is referring to the murderer as a 'he,'" Suzanne observed from the depths of the thronelike chair. "But if I recall correctly, there are a couple of ladies present who wanted to see Tillis dead."

"Are you accusing me?" Candida demanded.

"If the shoe fits..."

"How dare you!" Candida sprang out of her chair and went for Suzanne.

Chapter Four

It took both Steven and Howard to wrestle Candida back into her chair, and several minutes passed before Candida calmed down enough that the discussion could continue. Meg decided she would have disliked Suzanne Halverson even if Steven were not involved with her.

When Candida stopped shouting, Meg asked Suzanne, "Why did Aunt Tilly invite you for the weekend? If she had abandoned the book, why did she need you here?"

"I wasn't invited. I came to Breckenridge to ski. Once I arrived, I decided to pay Tillis a call. Coming to Morgan's Manor was strictly an impulse. I had some questions about the book." She shrugged. "While I was discussing the book with Tillis, the rest of you arrived. At some point someone mentioned the road had become impassable. Shortly thereafter I discovered James had taken my luggage to a room and I assumed I was welcome to stay."

"When you and Tilly came out of her office, it looked as if you'd been arguing. You were both angry." Howard gestured with his drink. "What was that all about?"

"It's none of your business."

"The hell it isn't," Candida snapped. "There's been a murder here, and *you're* one of the suspects, too!"

Suzanne lifted a cool eyebrow. "Did anyone observe any blood? Any crushed bones? Are we absolutely certain that Tillis didn't die of natural causes?"

"If she did, it was a pretty damned violent natural cause." Dennis blew a smoke ring and made a sound of irritation. "Have you forgotten what her room looked like?"

"We can definitely rule out natural causes," Candida said with a look of disgust. "At the risk of being indelicate, we only saw one side of Tillis. There's a possibility that Tillis's down side is bashed in. The fireplace tools were scattered around. Maybe she was struck with the poker, but the damage won't be evident until she's moved. Or she might have been strangled, in which case there wouldn't be blood or obvious damage. There would be marks beneath her collar that we didn't observe. But we can state with absolute certainty that Tillis did *not* die of natural causes."

Meg stood abruptly and went to the buffet for a glass of ice water. Standing with her back to the others, she fought to get control of herself. Instinct told her that Tillis would have been the first to briskly advise her to put her emotions aside. Emotionalism impeded intellect. Aunt Tilly had said so a dozen times and Meg agreed. Aunt Tilly also would have expected her to approach the facts in a cool professional manner. Meg needed her wits about her. She couldn't afford to go queasy every time someone referred to the murder scene. She would never discover the murderer's identity unless she resolved to approach the puzzle with detachment.

"Are you all right?" Steven asked when she returned to the group. Genuine concern warmed his dark eyes.

"I had a bad moment, but I'm fine now. Where are we?"

"There's something else no one seems to have considered." Suzanne tented her long fingers beneath her chin. "There were *eight* people in the dining room when Tillis said everyone present had a reason to want her dead. She didn't say, 'Everyone here except James has a reason to want me dead.'"

Startled and hating to admit it, Meg had to concede Suzanne's point. Without speaking, Candida leaned to tug the pull rope and after a few minutes James appeared. Clearly uncomfortable, Steven explained the issue in question.

Meg sympathized with Steven's reluctance because it was apparent that James was shattered. Red-rimmed eyes suggested he had been weeping. He looked ancient and tired. And startled when he learned the nature of his summons.

"I didn't think Madam included...but I understand you must inquire." He straightened his shoulders and looked steadily out the back windows. His voice emerged sounding like the rattle of old parchment. "Madam gave me to understand that Hilda and I would be remembered in her will. That's all Madam said. I don't know if she intended a sum of money or a memento of some sort."

"Did you or Hilda go to Tillis's room last night?"

"I stopped by Madam's room about thirty minutes after Miss Meg returned from her walk outside. Madam and I spent about five minutes discussing the menus for today. Then my wife and I tidied the kitchen before we retired to our quarters on the third floor. We watched television and went to bed after the news."

Steven nodded, thanked James and told him that was all.

"I can't believe we did that," Meg murmured after James left. She shook her head. "That poor old man is devastated."

"And we are getting exactly nowhere," Candida stated. She drummed her fingernails on top of the legal pad. "Before we try to ferret out who did it, perhaps we should figure out how it was done. Agreed? What we have here is a classic locked-door mystery." Her bosom lifted in a tremulous sigh. "Tillis would have loved this, absolutely loved it. Well. We've all read or written locked-door murder mysteries. So how was this one done? How did the murderer get out of Tillis's room? That's the problem, isn't it?"

Dennis was first to offer a theory. "How about the old standby solution—the killer locked the bolt from outside the room."

Steven stroked his jaw and stared at Meg. "Maybe the killer doesn't get out. He hides in the room until the body is discovered, then he appears during the confusion arising at the body's discovery. It appears that he rushed into the room with everyone else."

Meg met his gaze. "Suppose the first person on the scene is the murderer. He commits the murder, then pretends the victim was dead when he found the body." She didn't flinch from Steven's startled frown. "It only appears like a locked-door murder."

"Maybe the killer is never in the room in the first place," Howard said when it was his turn. "I read this story once—I forget the exact details—but the killer shoots an icicle through the window. It looks like the victim was stabbed, but the police can't find a weapon because the icicle has melted."

Candida muttered under her breath. "That's so far out, Howard. And here's another long shot. The killer slips into Tillis's room through a secret door and leaves the same way. I used this idea in one of my books."

"It was one of her best," Howard informed them.

"I'm not an expert in murder like the rest of you," Suzanne said when Candida coldly inquired if she had a possible solution.

"So *you* say! Maybe you're more expert than anyone here."

When it appeared that Candida and Suzanne would go at it again, Steven held up a hand. "It's time we took a short break. Let's have some coffee and sandwiches, then we'll discuss each possibility and see if any of them fit the facts."

He followed Meg to the windows, away from the others, and handed her a cup of coffee. Outside, blue shadows crept through the snow-shrouded pines. Meg was thinking it would be dark soon when she spotted the first snowflake.

"Oh, no. It's snowing again!" Her heart dropped to her toes. And Steven was standing too near. She could smell the after-shave he always wore, and she remembered his arms holding her in Aunt Tilly's bedroom. She warned herself to keep the conversation impersonal. "We have to talk about who disabled the cars and the telephones. And the delay additional snow will cause in getting help."

"I doubt anyone is going to admit anything." Steven's sweater was the same chocolate shade as his eyes. Meg felt the disturbing tug of his solid athletic body. "For a minute, it felt like better days, didn't it? You and me thinking along the same lines."

"Why do you say things like that? It only makes it harder for both of us." Anger flashed in Meg's eyes. "Look, Steven. We tried to have a relationship, but it didn't work. I was too possessive, you were too uncommunicative. Nothing's changed. I can't tell you to go off and have a good time with Suzanne. And you're still talking about talking without saying anything."

"If it had been up to me, I would have told you everything from the beginning." He stared at her. "On second thought maybe that's not true. Maybe for once I wanted you to just trust me. Do you know what it feels like? When the person you care about doesn't trust you?"

"I *do* trust you. Or I did." It was just so damned confusing. Was there any rational way to explain jealousy? "I just... it's just that..." She threw out her hands, upset. "I can't explain it. I just cared so much." She wished to hell she hadn't admitted that.

Steven's face revealed a frustration as deep as her own. "You're one of those aggravating women who drive men crazy. I don't know whether to hurl you out a window or make love to you." His gaze focused on her lips and an electric tingle exploded down Meg's spine. Her stomach tightened. "I'd like to do both. Instead I'll try to talk to you. But it has to be in private, Meg. Tonight."

No other man affected Meg the way Steven Caldwell did. He could leave her weak-kneed and shaky inside with just a look. The realization left her feeling helpless and dejected.

"We're ready to resume," Candida called. She consulted her notes with a show of importance. "While the rest of you were eating sandwiches, I tested Dennis's theory about the murderer locking the door from outside Tillis's bedroom. There is absolutely no way to slide that inside bolt from outside the door. I tried it every possible way and it can't be done."

Steven took his seat at the card table. "To demolish another theory—we're agreed there was no intruder, and the rest of us were in the dining room. So no one could have been hiding in Tillis's room. Everyone is accounted for."

"And we can scratch Howard's dumb theory about someone firing a projectile into the room," Dennis said. "The killer would have to be perched at the top of a two-and-half-story pine in the middle of a blizzard. He'd have to hope that Tillis would open the window, then he would have to fire through a four-inch opening at the exact moment Tillis happened to pass by."

"That window bothers me," Meg said at the instant Steven said the same thing. She looked at him a moment, then dropped her gaze. "Regarding the theory of the first person in the room being the killer..." She drew a breath. "There wasn't time. Steven went up the ladder first, but James was right behind him. Plus, those of us waiting in the corridor would have heard the struggle and the furniture being overturned. For this theory to work, Steven would have had to murder Aunt Tilly and vandalize the bedroom before James appeared—in less than a minute. There's no way."

Flipping a page of the legal pad, Candida traced a red fingernail down her notes. "How about secret entrances? Did anyone ever hear Tillis mention a secret door?"

"Really, Candida," Dennis smiled. "You've been reading too many of your own novels."

"Pig." Sulky mouthed, Candida rang for James and put the question when he appeared.

A ghost of a smile appeared on James's lips. "I've worked here for twenty years and never discovered any secret passages."

"That doesn't mean there aren't any," Candida insisted stubbornly.

"I suppose there could be secret passages and I failed to notice." The ghost of a smile took on a little flesh.

"Aunt Tilly mentioned Morgan's Manor had secrets. Do you know what she meant by that?" Meg asked.

"Well, the liquor room is a secret unless you know about the sliding panel. And there's another room where we keep the silver and another where Madam stores her furs." James gave Meg a look that said he would show her the rooms later in private.

"There you are," Candida crowed. "Secret rooms! Is there another secret room opening off Tillis's bedroom?"

"I'd be most surprised if there were." When no one said anything further, he added, "What time will you be wanting dinner served, miss?"

It startled Meg that James deferred to her as the mistress of the house. Tears clogged her throat. "The sandwiches were . . . I think we'll dine late. About eight?" The others nodded. "Something light. Please tell Hilda not to go to any trouble."

"This is embarrassing." Dennis stubbed out a cigarette with an irritated gesture. "We havc two of the best mystery writers in the field today, the best agent working in mystery and a mystery publisher. And we can't come up with a workable scenario."

"Why would Aunt Tilly open the window?" Meg wondered aloud. She could see the same question was worrying Steven. "Why would the killer open it, for that matter? It's a frigid night, snow is blowing—but someone opened that window. Why?"

"The body is lying almost directly beneath the window," Steven said, thinking aloud. "Maybe someone wanted it to appear that Tillis had been dead longer than she really was."

Meg looked at Dennis. "You said you smoked a cigarette in Aunt Tilly's room. Did Aunt Tilly open the window when you lit up?"

"I really don't remember if I smoked or not. But I do know Tillis did not open the window while I was there."

Howard sighed. "I hate to admit this, but I saw Tillis after Dennis did and I didn't see an ashtray and the window was not open. But I think Dennis is the killer." His eyes narrowed. "I think you killed Tilly, Dennis, because you wanted to make sure she didn't win the Macabre Series. You want Candida or Meg to win so your agency will get a piece of the money."

"That's a damned lie! Maybe you killed Tillis so Candida would have a better chance at the Macabre Series! Your meal ticket's sales haven't been so fat lately, have they? You have a stake in who wins the Macabre Series, too!"

Steven stepped between them. "I know everyone is on edge and upset, but let's try to keep personal grievances out of this."

"Are you sure about the window, Howard?" Meg persisted. "You were drinking heavily last night. Can you trust your memory?"

"I drink too much, I admit it. But because I drink a lot, I have a high tolerance for liquor. Believe me, I wasn't so foxed that I'd fail to notice an open window."

"Dear Tillis had quite an evening, didn't she?" Candida sniffed. "Three men in her room. Saying your goodbyes, were you, gentlemen?"

The question stirred something deep in Meg's mind, but she couldn't pull the reference to the surface.

"I've had it, folks." Standing, Dennis placed his hands in the small of his back and scowled at Howard. "We've been at this for hours. It's six o'clock now. I'm in favor of taking a break until dinner."

Suzanne smothered a yawn. "This was a waste of time, wasn't it? About the only things we know for a fact are that Tillis is dead, no one could possibly have killed her, everyone is lying about being in her room and Steven was very likely the last person to see Tillis alive. Otherwise we've learned nothing."

"I am *not* lying, damn it!" Sparks blazed in Candida's eyes.

"Your ring got there by itself." Suzanne smiled as if at a private joke, then excused herself. Before she went upstairs, she asked Steven to accompany her. She wanted to talk to him.

Meg watched them go and felt her heart twist.

Candida promptly vanished, Howard headed for the hidden liquor room and Dennis settled himself in front of the television to watch the evening news.

"Tillis's death will make all the national channels," he commented to Meg. He was practically rubbing his hands together. "The media is going to eat this up with a spoon. Famous mystery writer murdered in secluded mansion surrounded by enemies old and new. A classic whodunit. I'd trample my grandmother to get to a telephone right now!"

"You really are a slime, Dennis. The minute I can get out of my agency contract, I'm gone."

"Sorry, darlin'. The agency agreement is ironclad. Meanwhile we're going to make a lot of money together. With Tillis out of the running, I predict you're a shoo-in for the Macabre Series. Candida's a has-been. She's lost it."

"You didn't think so a few days ago."

He shrugged and lit a cigarette. "Things change."

Because she couldn't stand spending another minute in the same room with Dennis Parnham, Meg marched out of the living room. Not until she stood in the foyer pulling on her cap and gloves did she realize where she was going.

The crisp frigid air outside was exactly what she needed. Closing her eyes, Meg stepped onto the veranda and drew a deep breath of icy, needle-sharp air and held it inside.

Last night's wind had swept the ground almost clear of snow along the front side of the house. After pushing her gloves into her parka pockets, Meg walked as far as she could before the drifts became too deep to negotiate.

The early-evening snow was lovely, falling in thick fat flakes that called to mind romantic skiing vacations. Tilting her head back, Meg caught a powdery snowflake on her tongue and tried not to remember the ski trip to Vermont. With Steven.

It wasn't as if she hadn't tried to forget him. She hadn't fallen into the trap of moping by the telephone for eight months. There had been other men, other enjoyable evenings.

But Steven was a tough act to follow. Many people didn't understand writers, but Steven did. He understood the stress and pressure of a looming deadline, didn't complain during those awful times when Meg ignored him and worked around the clock to finish a manuscript on time. He understood the spikes of despair when she was positive she would never have another salable idea, and he could tease her into laughing and admitting she was being silly. He sympathized with her bereft feeling when the manuscript was finally finished. And he understood the lump-in-the-throat joy she experienced when she stood in a bookstore and saw her book—*her* book!—in front of her on the shelf.

He knew her life history, had listened as she described growing up on a farm in Iowa, knew that she had followed her dream to New York City before she understood a writer didn't have to live near the presses to publish a book.

And he knew the intimate things. That she hated having freckles, that she wished she wore a larger bra size. He knew she never felt she was dressed right and that she turned shy meeting people for the first time. He knew about Mark Braden, the man she had almost married, and how it had shattered her when Mark eloped with her best friend. Steven knew she loathed Greek and Chinese food. He knew that kissing her breasts drove her wild.

Meg stared up at the snow tumbling out of the twilight sky and wished she was not thinking these things. But she was. And she knew Steven as well as he knew her.

She knew business compelled him to attend publishing parties that bored or irritated him, knew he had to entertain sulky writers at lunch and stroke their egos when what he really wanted was to shake some humility into them. She knew the panic and long hours a breakdown in scheduling could cause, or a foul-up in the artwork department. And she knew how he felt when he lost out in the auction of a book he loved and truly wanted to publish.

And she, too, knew some of the intimate things. She sensed that Steven still battled some lingering conflicts over following in his father's footsteps, that he didn't fully trust his judgment about choosing the right tie for the right suit. She knew he laughed at cornball jokes and was secretly addicted to sitcoms. She knew he sang in the shower and scattered wet towels everywhere.

She knew that she still loved him.

But she'd been hurt once by a man unworthy of trust, by a man who pretended to be open but wasn't. It struck her as ironic that she was in the same situation again. Mark had told her that she misunderstood his relationship with Sandra, just like Steven was telling her she misunderstood his relationship with Suzanne. Right up to the moment he eloped with Sandra, Mark was telling her she had no reason to be jealous.

A sigh sent white vapors spiraling among the snowflakes. It was almost dark. Time to return inside.

Shaking free of old and bitter memories, Meg gazed up at Morgan's Manor, now hers. What on earth would she do with it? Three odd-shaped stories of Gothic design. An anachronism. She started toward the veranda, then something occurred to her and she turned around.

Unless it was a trick of the fading light, it appeared the windows on the third floor were boarded from the inside. Surely James and Hilda had not boarded the windows in the servant's quarters. But that was what it looked like. She would have to remember to ask James.

When she returned inside and hung her parka and cap in the foyer, no one was around. The TV still blared in the living room; she thought she heard Steven and Howard talking in the dining room.

As she wasn't eager to run into Steven, she turned down the back corridor and ended before the door to Aunt Tilly's office. Feeling like an intruder, she hesitated, then pressed the latch and stepped inside.

"Oh. I'm sorry, I didn't realize anyone was in here."

Candida looked as startled as she did. "You scared me to death!" She fanned her face with the book in her hand, then pushed the book back on the shelf. "I wanted to see Tillis's research library. I didn't think anyone would mind."

"If you mean me—I wonder about other writers' resources, too."

Biting her lip, Candida stepped into the lamplight. "Meg, I want you to know—I didn't kill your aunt. There was a lot of bad blood between us, and it's true I want the Macabre Series and I'm a step closer with Tillis out of the running. It's also true I'm not crying my eyes out that she's gone. But... I've been thinking about what Tillis said last night. You know, about how much she enjoyed her enemies, and I understand what she meant. I'll miss Tillis. Life is going to be pretty damned dull without her. She was my favorite person to hate."

Meg sat on the arm of a chair. "May I ask you something personal? About you and Howard and Aunt Tilly?"

A smile curved Candida's full mouth. "You're wondering why Tillis and I both wanted a balding, rather overweight insurance salesman."

The color deepened in Meg's cheeks. "Something like that."

Candida shrugged. "Who can explain why one person falls in love with another person? I can tell you that once upon a time Howard didn't drink like he does today. And I can tell you that he's a genuinely nice man. It didn't bother me a bit to cuckold Tillis, but Howard went through agony. Howard is weak, but—" she spread her hands "—but he's—nice. I know that's a pallid word, but it's also the best description. Howard Clancy is a nice man. A thoughtful, loyal man. I was so damned jealous that he belonged to Tillis. And maybe she was jealous when I won him. I can't explain it any better than that."

"Jealousy," Meg said softly, covering her eyes. Then she looked at Candida again. "But you and Dennis...I'm sorry, this isn't any of my business."

"Sometimes nice isn't enough," Candida explained. "Sometimes we need drama and thunder and lightning.

Sometimes we can't help hurting nice people just because they are nice. Or maybe we feel compelled to push them to the limit until they can't be nice anymore, until they turn as mean and small as we secretly believe we are ourselves. Well." Candida cast a self-conscious look toward the door. "Enough of that. I think I'll join the others for cocktails. Are you coming?"

"You go ahead. I'll be along in a minute or two."

When Candida had gone, Meg looked around the room. There was something exceptionally intimate about a person's office. This was the room that held the greatest emotional charge. Here one triumphed or collapsed in defeat. This was the dream site, and this is where one came to lick wounds and hide from the slings and arrows of the world. This was the room that contained a writer's pulse beat.

Clasping her hands behind her back, Meg walked slowly along the bookcases, as interested as Candida had been to read the titles on the spines of Aunt Tilly's books. Meg owned many of the same volumes, but her library was not nearly as extensive as Aunt Tilly's.

When she reached the skeleton hanging from the coatrack she paused and smiled as she realized it had a rubber knife taped to its ribs. After examining the photos on top of the mantelpiece, she sampled the contents of the poison bottles and discovered they were indeed filled with bath salts. Finally, having circled the room, she gingerly sat on the chair behind Aunt Tilly's desk.

In daylight the view would be wonderful. The windows opened to a sweeping vista of pine and spruce and mossy mountainside.

For several minutes Meg sat quietly at the desk, her fingers folded on top of the blotter, her thoughts engaged in a moral battle. Should she open the desk drawers and inspect the contents?

It seemed an unforgivable violation to rifle Tillis's desk while the room so strongly bore Tillis's imprint. Meg would hate it if a stranger went through her desk drawers.

But she wasn't a stranger. This house, this room, were hers now. And certainly Tillis would expect her to search for clues.

Still it was with reluctance that she opened the top drawer. There was the usual paraphernalia, loose paper clips, staples, rubber bands, a roll of stamps. Two bankbooks Meg simply could not bring herself to open yet, and a pile of bills and receipts.

The death threats were in the third drawer. Hands shaking, Meg withdrew the envelopes and confirmed the New York City postmarks. The envelopes had been mailed about a week apart, the most recent being a week ago yesterday.

Each of the threats was pasted together from newspaper clippings, the words different sizes and different type sets. Each carried the same message.

If you don't stop poking your nose into ancient history, you will die. You know this is not a joke.

Meg could understand why Aunt Tilly had not taken the pages to the police. There wasn't enough information. "Ancient history" could refer to events far in the past, or it could be someone's idea of yesterday. Still, someone had taken the trouble to paste the threats and mail them.

And now Aunt Tilly was dead.

Gooseflesh rose on the back of her neck and on her upper arms. Hastily Meg folded the threats back into their envelopes and pushed them into the drawer. Then, standing, she rubbed her arms briskly and gave herself a shake.

All right, get serious she commanded herself. This is a real-life murder mystery, not a ghost story. She'd just take a peek into Aunt Tilly's supply room, then she'd hightail it back to a noisy room full of people. She would save further exploration of Aunt Tilly's office for a bright sunshiny day when every creak didn't sound so idiotically sinister.

Meg opened the door to the supply room and reached inside for the light switch. Then she sucked in a hard breath.

Every box of stationery and envelopes had been torn open and emptied on the floor. So had the envelopes of carbon paper. Reams of typing paper lay thick on the floor in front of the file cabinet. Every drawer of the cabinet was jerked open and files strewn helter-skelter atop the rest of the mess.

Bending—Meg refused to think of it as collapsing—she reached a shaking hand and picked up an empty file folder. The label read, *Death Drums*. Presumably the folder had held Aunt Tilly's notes for that book. She picked up and scanned a loose sheet, recognizing a page from an early draft of *The Conroy Case*. It was going to be a daunting task to reassemble the files. Who did this, she wondered, pushing upward on shaky legs. What were they looking for?

Candida's image rose in Meg's mind as she stared at the chaotic mess covering the supply room floor. She remembered the guilty look on Candida's face when Meg found her in Aunt Tilly's office. Shortly before she was discovered, had Candida been searching for a copy of Aunt Tilly's proposal for the Macabre Series?

Two weeks remained until the proposal cutoff date. Maybe Candida hadn't yet submitted her proposal. In that event, it would be enormously helpful to know what the competition had proposed. Even if the strongest competitor was now dead.

And that, of course, was the most helpful circumstance of all.

Chapter Five

Once again Meg found herself seated across from Steven at the dinner table, trying not to meet his eyes.

"Will it ever stop snowing?" Sighing heavily, Candida looked away from the dark windows and returned her attention to the apple pie. She pushed her plate aside. "I can't believe we're actually living the oldest cliché in the mystery-novel business. Trapped on an isolated mountain, cut off from all communication. There's a dead body upstairs and one of you is a murderer. If I wrote this, my editor would die laughing before she had time to scribble a rejection letter."

It was the first time anyone had spoken in several minutes.

"I'm sure you'd write it in such a fresh way that everyone would love the book and it would be a runaway best-seller."

"Oh, Howard." Candida sighed again. "You're always so loyal and so...so damned nice." She spread her palms in a gesture of helplessness. "Such a genuinely nice man. What's wrong with me that I hate it that you're so nice? Why do I always push you to be nasty? And you so seldom are."

"Oh, please." Suzanne pushed back in her chair. "We're all on edge here. Must you choose this moment to analyze your husband and yourself?"

"I was just making a comment, for God's sake. Why are you so edgy anyway? You aren't one of the invited enemies, you weren't in Tillis's room, you swear you had no reason to kill her. This is all according to you, of course. But if any of it is true, then what do you have to complain about? All you have to do is wait for the plow to rescue us, then you can waltz off and resume your skiing vacation."

"Frankly, the company is becoming tedious."

"Oh my heavens!" Meg sat up straight and blinked. "Skis."

Steven understood at once. "Why didn't we think of this earlier? Damn it."

Meg stared at him. "One of us could ski down to Breckenridge and get help!"

There was a beat of silence, then a rush of excited voices.

"Suzanne," Steven leaned forward, his pie forgotten. "Did you bring your skis? Are they in your rental car?"

"No. I decided to rent equipment here rather than go through the aggravation of checking everything on the plane, then having to collect it and—"

Candida flew out of her seat and jerked the velvet rope to summon James. "James! Are there any skis on the premises?"

"Skis?" Sudden understanding followed. "Of course. I should have thought of it at once. There are two sets in the garage."

Everyone at the table leaped up and ran for the coat closet. They all pulled on parkas and hurried out to the garage.

James halted in front of an empty rack against the back wall. He put his hand against the wall, blinked, then slowly turned. "The skis are gone."

"Gone? What do you mean they're gone?" Candida demanded. "How can they be gone?"

James shrugged helplessly. "I don't know, madam. There were two sets of skis here a day or two ago. Now they're gone."

"Were the skis in the rack when you came into the garage to get the ladder?" Steven asked finally.

"I don't remember." James wrung his hands. "I was worrying about Madam. All I could think about was fetching the ladder and hurrying. I didn't even notice the tires were flat on the cars. All I could think about—"

"So no one can say when the tires were flattened or when the skis vanished." Dennis made a sound of disgust. "Some detectives you are."

"Wait a minute," Meg said, watching her breath plume out before her. "Give me a second to think about this. Okay, let's assume the murderer punctured the tires, and the murderer took the skis, all right?"

"Who else?" Dennis flung out his hands.

"Why did he do it?"

"What an idiotic question! He did it to keep us here, of course. So he'd have a full complement of suspects to obscure his own activities."

Staring at Meg, Steven nodded his head. "I'm following you. And it's an excellent point. We knew early last evening that we were snowbound and marooned. No one was going anywhere."

Candida pursed her lips. "I see where you two are leading. Stealing the skis and disabling the cars seems redundant. It wasn't necessary because of the storm."

Stepping to Aunt Tilly's car, Steven inspected the flattened tires. "The murderer knew we couldn't go anywhere because of the drifts. By morning the murder had been committed so there was no reason to flatten the tires then. So why do it?"

"There has to be a reason," Meg said. "There must be some benefit to the killer to keep us here."

Candida nodded. "Maybe the killer has to delay the arrival of the police for some reason. He had to consider the possibility that maybe one of us could bash our car through the drifts last night or this morning. To make sure we can't, he flattens the tires. And to make doubly sure that no one can go for the authorities, he hides the skis."

"This is all fascinating speculation," Suzanne remarked, "but could we continue the discussion inside? It's freezing out here."

For an instant Meg met Steven's eyes, feeling the warmth of knowing they were sharing the same thoughts, that their ideas dovetailed beautifully. He smiled as if he were thinking the same thing before Meg hurried outside.

She fell into step beside James during the trek back to the house. "What are the chances that your friend at the service station will plow us out anytime soon?"

James frowned at the tumbling snowflakes. "Not encouraging, miss, I'm sorry to say. We haven't had a weekend storm this severe all season. The plows will be working around the clock, but we're at the bottom of the list."

"Surely this isn't the first time Morgan's Manor has been snowed in. Who usually plows out the road?"

"Jim or Ed from the service station. But when I spoke to Jim last night he already had two dozen calls. At that time, we weren't anticipating an emergency. Everyone planned to stay for the weekend, we had plenty of supplies...there was no urgency." James's breath released in a sigh. "I told Jim to put us last on his list."

It was a subdued group who gathered in the living room for coffee and brandy.

"Well? Now what?" Dennis brandished a cigarette and turned a brooding expression toward the fireplace. "Do we just sit here and wait to be rescued?"

"Do you have a better idea?" Candida grimaced. "All you've done is complain, Dennis. Too bad the killer didn't murder you while he was at it!"

"You would have liked that, wouldn't you?"

Candida narrowed her eyes. "Maybe I would!"

"Oh, spare us." Suzanne sighed, then wandered to the coffee urn. Tonight she wore a blue silk designer dress. The petal hem fluttered attractively against blue silk stockings.

It was the kind of dress Meg longed for in her heart, but would never have bought. She glanced down at her jeans and lemon-colored sweater. A small sigh lifted her breasts. Tomboys never thought to buy blue stockings.

"Is anyone up for a rubber of bridge?" Breaking the silence, Howard ran his fingertips over the surface of the card table.

"Bridge! How civilized. Having completed his work, the murderer now sits down to a relaxing game of bridge. Well, count me out." Dennis stood and placed his empty brandy snifter on a side table. "I'm going upstairs. I'd rather read a briefcase full of dreadful manuscripts than sit around playing card games with a murderer."

Meg's first impulse was to agree with Dennis. But on second thought, she decided bridge might be a good idea. It would give them something to concentrate on that wasn't connected to Aunt Tilly's murder. And at least they wouldn't be hurling accusations at one another.

"I'm game," she said, taking a seat at the card table. "Come on someone, Howard and I need two more players."

"Make that three more players," Howard said. "Now that I think about it, I've had too much to drink to make a decent partner for anyone. I believe I'll go upstairs, lie down awhile and finish Ludlum's latest thriller."

"Actually Dennis and Howard are doing us a favor," Candida announced, taking a seat at the card table. "Neither is a skilled player. Come on, Steven and Suzanne. There's nothing interesting on TV and you aren't doing anything else. Sit down and shuffle the deck. Although I don't like to play cards with a left-handed player," she said, squinting at Suzanne.

"It does *not* affect how I play," Suzanne snapped.

They played in silence, concentrating fiercely, playing a cutthroat game. No mercy offered; no prisoners taken. Meg and Steven were both strong players and they knew each other's game. Each was determined to beat the other. They had been playing for almost an hour when the front door slammed.

"Who was that?" Steven asked.

"Dennis." Suzanne looked up, then back down at her cards. She sat facing the archway that opened onto the foyer. "Bundled up like an Eskimo, but still smoking. I loathe smokers."

Meg shifted to see wisps of cigarette smoke slowly dissipating in the foyer beyond the archway. She glanced at the clock. "Where on earth is he going at this time of night?"

Steven shrugged and returned his attention to his hand. "Dennis is a big boy. He doesn't need us to watch over him."

"It is odd," Candida commented with a frown. "Dennis detests fresh air. He goes from office to taxi to his apartment with scarcely a breath of air that hasn't been heated, cooled or treated in some manner. I've never known Dennis Parnham to seek out fresh air of his own free will. As for—"

"Are you going to play that hand, or talk?" Scowling, Suzanne stifled a yawn. "It's hard enough to concentrate. This altitude makes me sleepy. If Candida will deign to finish that hand maybe we can all go to bed."

A few minutes later Meg lifted her head. "Did anyone besides me hear a noise?"

"Hear what? I don't hear anything but the stereo."

"I thought I heard something, too," Steven agreed, laying down his cards. As he started to rise from his chair Howard appeared from the direction of the staircase. "Oh, it was you."

"I thought you went to bed," Candida said. But Howard didn't look as if he had been to bed. He still wore the clothing he'd worn to dinner. A gray jacket, navy tie and dark slacks.

"I've been thinking," Howard said, studying Candida. "I don't like the idea of you being alone tonight." He shrugged an apology toward the others. "No offense, but there's a murderer among us. I'd feel better if you slept in my room tonight."

"That's just—" Then Candida's expression collapsed and her eyes filled with gratitude. "Thank you, Howard. I don't want to be alone, either." She managed a thin smile. "As Howard said, no offense but I don't want any of you murdering *me* tonight."

"It's ten-thirty. Are you ready to go upstairs?" Howard asked, looking at his watch.

Candida glanced at the scorecard, noticed she and Steven were lagging behind. "I think so. I'm tired, too."

Meg had an uncomfortable idea that if she hadn't been so tired and upset from everything that had happened today, she could have put her finger on something slightly askew. She couldn't bring the thought forward enough to identify it.

Then she did. Or maybe it was something else that was awry, but she suddenly realized if Howard and Candida went upstairs, she would be left alone with Steven and Suzanne. Quickly she pushed back her chair and stood. "I believe I'll call it a night, too."

"Steven, will you join me in a nightcap?" Suzanne asked, calling Steven back when it appeared he would follow Meg.

"I really don't... well, just a quick one."

Meg met his expressionless gaze, then glanced at Suzanne before she turned away. Judging from the predatory interest in Suzanne's cool eyes, Meg doubted Steven would turn up at her door tonight, after all. She tried to tell herself she didn't care.

WHEN A KNOCK SOUNDED at her door, she almost ran to answer it, surprised and embarrassed by how glad she was that Steven had remembered her, after all.

"Oh." She blinked at James, then hastily apologized for her look of disappointment. "I was expecting someone else."

"I came about tomorrow's menus, miss."

"Whatever you and Hilda decide will be fine. I'm sorry, James, I'm just not up to planning menus or making decisions about the house yet. I hope you understand. It's not that—"

"Quite so, miss. Hilda and I will manage."

"Before you go, there's something I've been wondering." She stepped into the corridor beside him. "How many telephones are in the house?"

"Five, miss." He listed their locations.

"I see." Meg hadn't guessed the existence of the phone on the third floor. "You're saying someone went into your quarters and jerked the phone wires out of the wall even there. But who knew about that telephone?"

"I can't say, miss. All Madam's guests have visited Morgan's Manor before except Mrs. Halverson." James's expression indicated he didn't hold Suzanne Halverson in high regard. "It's possible everyone knows where all the telephones are."

Obviously someone did. "You and Hilda were occupied downstairs most of yesterday, weren't you?" He nodded confirmation. "So someone could have disabled the telephones then?"

"Not in the afternoon, miss. The phones were in service after dinner when I phoned the service station about the plow."

"I'd forgotten that. So pulling out the wires had to happen later in the evening."

"As far as I know, the call to the service station was the last telephone call made and that was about nine o'clock. The vandalism could have happened anytime after that."

"There's something else I'm curious about. It appears most of the windows on the third floor are boarded up. Could that be true?"

The faintest smile touched James's lips. "Yes, miss."

As Meg's bedroom was nearest the landing, she saw Suzanne appear at the top of the stairs, and she stopped speaking until Suzanne had passed them in the corridor. Suzanne gave her a lengthy speculative look that Meg couldn't decipher.

"Don't the boarded windows make your apartment as dark as a cave?" she asked, returning her attention to James.

"Only the back half of our apartment lacks windows, miss. It was a bit strange at first, but in twenty years we've gotten accustomed to it. We don't spend much time in our quarters anyway, and when we're there, we're usually in the living room."

"But why were the windows covered over?"

"Years ago, before Hilda and I came to Morgan's Manor, Madam's father remodeled the servants' quarters and other parts of the house. As I understand it, the original servants' quarters were a collection of small sleeping rooms. Then, when modern conveniences made it possible to manage a large house without so many servants, Mr. Morgan tore out the sleeping rooms and remodeled the third floor into one apartment for a live-in couple. As Madam explained it, the original configuration didn't align with the new apartment. New walls ended smack in the middle of a window and so forth. So the windows were boarded over and the interior walls resurfaced. There are a few boarded windows on the second floor, too." James coughed into his hand and phrased the next sentence as tactfully as he could. "It's said Mr. Morgan always chose the least expensive way to do things."

"He was too cheap to do the job properly, is that it?"

"As you say, miss."

They smiled at each other.

"Thank you, James. Right now I'm seeing mysteries in everything."

"It's a terrible, terrible thing that's happened here," he said in a low voice. "Madam's loss will be keenly felt."

After James left, Meg walked to her window and gazed out at the falling snowflakes. Their intensity seemed to be diminishing. Lost in thought, she started when another knock sounded at her door.

"I didn't mean to frighten you," Steven said, stepping into her bedroom. "Had you forgotten our date?" Smiling, he carried a brandy bottle and two snifters to her bedside table.

"This is hardly a date." But his phrasing underscored the mistake she had made. Allowing Steven into her bedroom brought a rush of memories, and invited intimacies Meg did not wish to encourage. "I'm not sure this is a good idea."

"Are we going to start that again? I thought we agreed we had to talk."

"Look, *someone* murdered Aunt Tilly..."

"Good God." He straightened abruptly and turned to face her. "You mean you're afraid to be alone with... Meg—" his broad shoulders stiffened and his dark eyes stared into hers "—do you really suspect me? Can you honestly think I could murder anyone?"

"You seem to have been the last person to see Aunt Tilly alive." She stared at him, testing the thought. Then her shoulders dropped and she sighed. "No, of course not. The trouble is, I don't think the others are murderers, either. But someone is." After a pause, she looked up at him. "Who do you think the killer is?"

Before he answered, he handed her a snifter of brandy and sat down on the edge of her bed. "I think enough accusations have been tossed around, don't you?" He smiled when she walked away from the bed and took the chair by the window, tucking her feet up under her body.

"There's something you should know." Rolling the snifter between her palms, Meg related her conversation with James. "Did you know there was a telephone in the servants' quarters?"

"No. I didn't."

"I'd be willing to bet no one else did, either." Meg frowned. "I hate to say this, but I have an uneasy suspicion that James and Hilda are the only people who knew the location of all the telephones."

"Are you suggesting James or Hilda ripped the wires out of the wall?"

"I just can't believe that." Meg looked away from the lamplight playing over Steven's strong chin and jawline. His hair was rumpled and the suggestion of a new beard shadowed his cheeks. "But no one else has spent enough time in this house to know James and Hilda have a phone in their quarters."

"Meg, the reason I wanted to talk to you—"

"Wait. There's something else." She told him about the supply room in Aunt Tilly's office. "At first I thought Candida was the culprit, searching for Aunt Tilly's Macabre Series proposal. But on second thought, I'm not as convinced. It seems hard to believe that Candida would rip apart the supply room, then calmly start browsing through the library. But who else would be looking for something?''

Swearing softly, Steven bent forward and rested his elbows on his knees. He ran a hand over his face. ''I'll bet you a lobster dinner it wasn't Candida who tore through Tillis's files. It was Suzanne.''

Meg's eyebrows soared. ''Okay, Steven. You wanted to talk about Suzanne, so talk. After hearing that, I want to hear what you have to say.''

What she really wanted was to halt the flood of memories. Meg kept remembering the last time they had been in a bedroom together. With another man she would have felt shy and awkward about conducting a conversation in a bedroom. But not with Steven. It struck her as remarkable how quickly they had resumed old habits. Steven had pushed off his shoes, plumped up the pillows and stretched out on top of the quilt. She had kicked off her own shoes and curled into the corner of the wing chair. They had enjoyed a hundred stimulating conversations sitting in these exact positions. And afterward . . .

''Oh, God, where should I begin?'' he said.

''Tell me why you think Suzanne might have vandalized Aunt Tilly's supply room.''

''The story starts long before this weekend. You remember when Whitney Halverson was murdered. Whitney was found shot to death in his car while Suzanne was in Los Angeles. I started seeing Suzanne shortly afterward—as a friend,'' he added. His gaze challenged her to protest.

''It's your story. Tell it the way you see it. But I'll concede you started seeing Suzanne as a friend. In the beginning.''

Tilting his head, Steven studied the circles of color rising on her cheeks. "The relationship with Suzanne was never what you thought it was, Meg."

"Let's omit any personal references, okay?" Meg turned her face to the window. Her cheeks felt hot.

"That's impossible," he said bluntly. "You and I—our relationship—is twisted into the events of this weekend whether we like it or not."

"What are you talking about?"

"We're one of the triangles that make up this weekend, at least the way you see it, we are. You, me and Suzanne. Then there's Suzanne, me and Tillis—the Halverson book triangle. And there's Howard, Candida and Tillis—an old triangle that still vibrates. And there's Howard, Candida and Dennis—that triangle is sending off powerful signals. Then we have you, Tillis and Candida—the Macabre Series triangle. And we have Tillis, James and Hilda—the Morgan Manor triangle. Finally we have publisher, agent and writers—the industry triangle."

Meg stared. "All the triangles interlock," she whispered. "They each have a dynamic that's crashing up against another dynamic."

Steven nodded. "The triangle I want to talk to you about involves Suzanne, her maid and her husband—the basic elements in the Halverson case." He drew a breath and met Meg's eyes. "In the beginning I probably did spend too much time with Suzanne. I felt I owed something to her because of my friendship with Whitney. I felt he would have expected me to offer support to his widow. Plus, the story fascinated me. An older wealthy man, a beautiful younger wife, a violent death, the double tragedy of the maid dying shortly afterward. After a few weeks it occurred to me there was a book in Suzanne and Whitney's story. I asked Tillis if she would be interested in writing it."

"Aunt Tilly would have loved jumping into the middle of a real murder case."

"She accepted the offer at once."

Swinging his legs from the bed, Steven took the brandy bottle to Meg's chair and freshened her drink. His nearness made her feel dizzy and she didn't breathe again until he returned to the bed. A sinking feeling stole over her. He was so intense, so steady and solid. And she was so willing to believe whatever he told her.

"As Candida pointed out, any book about the Halverson case faced an insurmountable problem. It had no ending. While trying to find an ending, Tillis studied the police reports, the newspaper accounts, every scrap of evidence she could pry out of the authorities. And she managed to get copies of everything the police had. As you know, Tillis could be very persuasive. Plus, she conducted interviews with just about everyone who had known Whitney or Suzanne and she made hundreds of telephone calls tracking down loose ends."

An uneasy sensation opened in the pit of Meg's stomach. She leaned forward in her chair. "Did Aunt Tilly realize how dangerous conducting her own investigation might be?"

"To Tillis, the investigation was an exciting challenge. She and I agreed I would continue to see Suzanne on a social basis. My task was to try to discover if there was anything Suzanne hadn't told the police."

Meg put a growing suspicion into words. "Were you looking for clues—or did you and Aunt Tilly suspect Suzanne was somehow involved with Whitney's murder?"

A long minute passed before Steven answered. "In the beginning there seemed to be no question that Suzanne was in Los Angeles at the moment Whitney was shot. The airlines checked out. A woman answering Suzanne's description used her ticket to fly to Los Angeles, then checked into the Royal Palms Hotel."

"But?" Meg didn't take her eyes from his face.

"But Tillis discovered Suzanne failed to sign the hotel register. No sample of her handwriting proves it was actually Suzanne who checked into the Royal Palms, although the description matches. At least from what the hotel clerk could see of her."

Meg frowned. "What does that mean?"

"The woman who registered at the Royal Palms wore dark glasses, a slouch hat and a scarf. She was bundled up."

"In *Los Angeles?*"

He smiled. "It was enough to raise a question mark in Tillis's mind, too. Suzanne explained the muffling by saying she had a mild case of the flu, chills and so forth. Then I discovered Whitney had been planning a divorce. Suzanne confided he had spoken to his attorney. That's why she was upset about Whitney's murder but not devastated. As Whitney's widow, she inherited his considerable estate, as his ex-wife she would have inherited nothing."

"I'm starting to track this." Meg leaned forward again. "At some point, you and Aunt Tilly concluded Suzanne murdered her husband. You couldn't prove how she did it. But you had a theory."

"Right on target. And I have a feeling you can guess the theory."

"I think so, but tell me anyway."

"The theory didn't hold much water as Tillis couldn't produce a shred of supporting proof. She hoped Suzanne might let something slip to me. But aside from the information about the divorce, it didn't happen."

This was the kind of puzzle Meg loved. Her eyes sparkled as she thought it through. "For Suzanne to be the murderer, then she couldn't be the woman on the plane. She had to be in New York City when Whitney Halverson was shot."

"You're doing fine, keep going."

"It could have been the maid on the plane masquerading as Suzanne. Suzanne stays in New York, kills Whitney, then flies to California under an assumed name." Meg pulled her lower lip between her teeth. "This puts a new light on the maid's suicide. Did you and Aunt Tilly conclude that Suzanne covered her tracks by pushing the maid over the balcony?"

"There isn't an iota of proof. None. Just speculation on mine and Tillis's part. Except..."

Meg was starting to feel like a fool as the implications of the conversation filtered to a personal level. She had done Steven an injustice. His interest in Suzanne had been tied to a book and to discovering his friend's murderer. He thought it was possible Suzanne had murdered *two* people. And all this time Meg had believed it was a romantic entanglement. Shame colored her throat and cheeks. She had allowed her jealousy to poison her thoughts.

"Except what?" she asked, her head down.

"Except Tillis telephoned me a couple of days ago. She was very excited. She said she had found the ending to the book and she had enough proof to take to the authorities. She asked me to fly to Colorado and confirm what she had found. She didn't want to risk the material in the mails. Suzanne told the truth about how she arrived here. She wasn't invited. Tillis was definitely not expecting her."

"I think I owe you an apology."

"We'll return to that in a minute." He held her gaze for a long dizzying moment. "There's more you should know."

"Go on." Meg's hands were trembling and she felt as if a weight had lifted from her heart. It was as if she had stumbled around in the darkness for a very long time and suddenly emerged into the sunshine. He wasn't in love with Suzanne.

"Tillis said she and Suzanne had a terrible argument shortly after Suzanne arrived. Suzanne demanded that Tillis drop the book and stop prying into the murder. Maybe Tillis hinted that she knew who had committed the murder, I don't know. Tillis was vague on that point. But she admitted some regrettable things were said. Eventually Tillis realized the situation could be dangerous. She knew the storm was worsening and the roads were drifting over. She suddenly realized Suzanne might be unable to leave Morgan's Manor. Not knowing how dangerous Suzanne might become if she believed she was cornered, Tillis pretended to be persuaded. She told Suzanne she would abandon the book and had, in fact, already destroyed her research."

"But that was a lie."

"Absolutely. Tillis would not have asked me to fly to Colorado to examine her research if she had destroyed it."

"When you went to Aunt Tilly's room last night, did she show you the new evidence?"

"No," Steven said after a pause. "We discussed the material only as it applied to you."

Meg stared at him. "I remember now."

"Yes. At dinner Tillis announced you were her primary beneficiary and would inherit the notes and research for her new book. I made the situation worse by mentioning a new revelation in the case."

"Earlier, Aunt Tilly tells Suzanne the research has been destroyed," Meg said slowly. "Then at dinner she gives the very same research to me. And you announce there's explosive new material."

"If Tillis could prove Suzanne murdered her husband—which was the implication of the new material—then Tillis also understood she was in danger. By stating that you would inherit her research, she feared she had placed you in danger, too."

"And Candida kept insisting Tillis would never have destroyed her notes."

Steven nodded, his expression grim. "Now you tell me someone has rifled through Tillis's files."

"Suzanne." Meg stared at him. "The next question is did she find what she was looking for?"

"My guess is she didn't," Steven said after a pause. "Tillis said she hid the material. I doubt she hid it in as obvious a spot as her file cabinet." He studied Meg. "Tillis also said she told you how to find the material."

"What?" Meg straightened. "But that's... no, Steven, she didn't. Maybe she intended to and was murdered before she had a chance. But Aunt Tilly didn't talk about the Halverson case at all. No, wait a minute." Frowning, she tried to remember. "No, she never said a word about hiding something or where it could be found. I'm sure she didn't."

"Meg, try to remember. When I spoke to Tillis at eleven-thirty, she said you would know how to find the material if you needed to. She didn't exactly say she had revealed her hiding place, but she displayed no doubt that she had pointed you in the right direction. She felt confident you would know where to look."

"That's crazy." Meg spread her hands. "Steven, I don't have a clue!"

"Tillis agreed it was time you knew what she was working on. Her death makes it imperative that you know."

"Steven..." It had to be said. "Do you think Suzanne murdered Aunt Tilly?"

For a full minute he didn't speak. "I think Suzanne has the strongest motive," he said finally.

"Should we tell the others?" The minute Meg spoke, she knew she was wrong and she waved the words away. "No, we can't let Suzanne know what we suspect. Not while we're trapped here."

"I absolutely agree. Plus, we have to remember there isn't a shred of proof, nothing, Meg, until Tillis's notes are found. And the notes won't prove anything about Tillis's murder. But right now, the possibility that the research notes exist places *you* in danger. If Tillis was murdered because of those notes . . ."

"Then I'm next on the list," Meg whispered. Her hands started to shake and she held them out in front of her. "Oh my God. I don't think I'm as brave as I thought I was," she said in a small voice.

Steven knelt beside her and took both her hands in his. "I'm not going to let anything happen to you."

"Oh, Steven, I was wrong about everything. I'm sorry."

"You were wrong about Suzanne," he said, bringing her hands to his lips. He kissed her fingertips. "And you were wrong about my secretary, and that new writer, what's her name? Ellen Prather. Meg, you've been wrong about all of it."

Slowly Meg pulled her hands away. "You haven't helped much. You could have told me all this before. It would have spared me a lot of pain if you'd explained all this months ago."

He rocked back on his heels and examined her expression. "Is that true? If you had known I was seeing Suzanne because I was trying to learn more about Whitney's murder, can you honestly say you would have advised me to continue seeing her?"

"The point is, you didn't tell me." She drew back in the chair. "Just like you didn't tell me until we were arguing about it that there were problems with Ellen Prather's contract and that's why you had to keep seeing *her.* You could have spared us a lot of problems by communicating more openly."

Standing, Steven looked down at her and his brows met in a frown. "Communication isn't the problem. The problem is trust. For a relationship to work, both parties have to trust each other. You can't build a solid relationship by always assuming the worst."

She stood, too. "Aunt Tilly trusted Howard and he had an affair with Candida. Howard trusted Candida and she's openly sleeping with Dennis Parnham. I trusted Mark Braden and he eloped with my best friend."

"I'm not Mark Braden, damn it." Steven glared at her, his frustration evident. "How long do I have to continue paying for Mark Braden's sins?"

Meg drew back as if he had slapped her. "Is that what you think I'm doing? Punishing you because I can't punish Mark?"

"That's part of it, yes. Each time I spend time with a woman you decide a painful experience is about to be repeated. Finally, with Suzanne, you decided to reject me rather than wait for me to reject you, which is what you feared would happen again." He caught her by the shoulders and gave her a shake. "And damn it, Meg, that's exactly what might have happened. You can't expect me to go on being accused whenever I happen to smile at another woman. That's not realistic. There *are* other women in my life. My secretary, authors, friends I knew before I met you. Just like there are other men in *your* life. But I don't make you feel guilty about them."

"That's because I don't see them anymore. I don't rub your nose in other relationships." Meg twisted away from his hands.

He swore. "You're missing the point. I don't *care* if you see other men. If you want to have lunch with an old friend, fine. Do it. Because I *trust* you. I trust our relationship. At least, I did. You're the one who can't trust. And without trust, there can be no relationship!"

"And without communication, there can be no relationship!"

"If you'd open your eyes, you'd see that we communicate better than anyone else we know. But your idea of communication is having me explain and justify every word, every smile, directed to another female. And, Meg, I'm not going to do that."

"Fine. No one's asking you to. Because you and I don't have a relationship, not anymore!"

Meg realized they were shouting and she lowered her voice. The instant she did, they both heard voices in the corridor. The sounds in the hallway broke the tension flashing between them and gave Meg an excuse to move away from him. She tiptoed to the door and pressed her ear to the wood.

"It's Candida and Howard," she whispered.

Steven looked at her a moment, then joined her at the door.

They heard Candida's voice as clearly as if she were standing a foot away. "Honestly, Howard. You really should seek help. Go to AA or something."

"All I want is just one more, that's all. To help me sleep. I'll only be a minute. You stand here on the landing, right under the sconce."

"Why can't I wait in the bedroom?" Candida grumbled.

"Because if someone tried to murder you in the bedroom, I wouldn't hear you scream or get there in time to save you. This way, if you scream, I'll hear you and so will everyone else."

"How long is this going to take?"

"Just long enough for me to pour another Scotch. Not long. There were two bottles on the serving cart in the living room. I'll dash in, fill my glass and be back in two minutes. Now stand right here and don't move. I want the light shining on you. Okay?"

"Just hurry up, will you?"

Meg heard footsteps receding down the staircase. She gazed at Steven's dark head pressed to the door beside hers and suppressed an urge to giggle. "If we opened the door right now," she whispered, "we'd scare Candida out of her wits." Straightening, she rubbed her ear.

Her smile faded as she suddenly realized how close she and Steven were standing. Inches away, she could see the shadow of his new beard, responded to the electric warmth and excitement of his body near hers. An earthquake began in the pit of her stomach and trembled outward. She wanted to move away from him, but she couldn't. Helplessly she gazed up into his intense dark eyes and found he was staring at her mouth. A tremble began at her toes and swept upward.

And then he kissed her. One instant they were standing together looking into each other's eyes, the next instant Meg was in his arms crushed against his body. It was a hard angry kiss, a kiss explosive with the passion they had once shared. A kiss that punished and flamed with desire in the same moment.

Meg's lips opened and her fingernails dug into his shoulders. She felt his hands on her waist pulling her hard against his thighs, felt the heat of his need and passion. She felt her own nerves kindle and surge to the surface of her skin, was aware that her pulse raced and pounded in her ears.

When he released her, she stumbled backward, breathless and wide-eyed.

"Maybe someday I'll get over you," he said in a low voice, his eyes traveling hungrily over her face. "But it hasn't happened yet. Maybe our relationship isn't what it once was—but it's still a relationship whether you and I like it or not."

The door opened, and he was gone.

IN THE MORNING after a sleepless night of tossing and turning, Meg walked down the staircase and entered the dining room. "Good morning," she said, heading straight for the silver coffee urn.

"What's good about it?" Candida asked in a sour tone. Once again she wore the furry pink bathrobe. Strands of auburn hair dripped over her collar. "We're still trapped in this gloomy pile of stones and we still have a dead body upstairs." She turned brooding eyes to the windows.

Meg slid a wary look toward Steven, as confused now as she had been after he left her room. He looked as tired and out of sorts as she did. "Where's Dennis?" she asked, turning to James.

"Mr. Parnham hasn't come down yet, miss."

A terrible sense of déjà vu tightened Meg's skin. "The same man who was up at five o'clock yesterday morning isn't up yet at eight o'clock?"

Candida lowered her fork. "Oh, no," she whispered. "Surely you don't think..."

"Did anyone see Dennis return last night?" Steven asked, approaching the coffee urn as Meg left it.

"Return from where?" Howard asked. After Steven explained, Howard said, "Maybe he's still wandering around outside." He didn't sound upset by the suggestion.

"That isn't funny, Howard," Candida said sharply.

Steven touched Suzanne's shoulder. "What was Dennis wearing, do you remember?"

Pushing up from the table, Suzanne walked to the doorway and checked the coatrack in the foyer. "He came back inside. Dennis was wearing a blue parka and a ski cap. They're both hanging on the coatrack."

"Oh my God." Candida raised wide eyes. "He's dead. I just know the killer got Dennis, too."

After a moment of silence, everyone rushed for the staircase.

Chapter Six

Suzanne was the last person up the staircase, carrying a cup of coffee and a slice of buttered toast.

"God forbid that something as trivial as another murder should interfere with your breakfast!" Candida's contempt was magnificent to witness. Her bosom thrust forward, her chin pulled down, her upper lip curled.

"And how interesting, not to mention incriminating, that you automatically presume Dennis has been murdered," Suzanne replied. "May we assume you have prior knowledge?"

Candida narrowed her eyes and leaned forward. "You may assume I have a brain in my head since he was the only one missing from the breakfast table. However, I can't imagine why anyone would murder Tillis or Dennis when they could have the pleasure of murdering you!"

Suzanne's smile was so supremely superior that only Meg's intervention prevented Candida from slapping her. "Please, not now," she said, stepping between them.

"You publishing people are so dramatic and excitable," Suzanne murmured, continuing forward to stand behind Steven.

It occurred to Meg that although she spent most of her professional life creating murder mysteries, she had never been remotely connected to a real murder case. Until now.

A chilly ripple of unease and fascination swept over her as she watched Suzanne finish eating her toast.

Had Suzanne Halverson actually cold-bloodedly murdered her husband and her maid? In the dim corridor light Suzanne looked so normal, so reasonable. It didn't seem possible she could murder anyone.

But it didn't seem impossible, either. And maybe Suzanne hadn't stopped at two murders . . .

Steven pounded again on Dennis's bedroom door. "Dennis? Are you in there?"

"See if it's locked," Howard advised.

The door opened easily and swung inward. Someone gasped.

For one terrible moment no one uttered a word. They stood immobile in the doorway, staring inside the room at Dennis Parnham's slumped body.

"You see?" Candida whispered. She straightened to her full height. "What did I tell you! He's as dead as last year's bestseller. So now we have two dead bodies we're stuck with. This isn't just frightening, it's appalling!"

"Stay in the corridor," Steven ordered in a gruff voice. After passing a hand over his face, he shook his head, then straightened. "All right. This time we won't all go rushing into the scene. One person will enter the room. Suzanne?"

"Why Suzanne?" Meg asked, surprised.

"Suzanne is the only person here who did not know Dennis and presumably had no reason to kill him."

"I loathe smokers . . . but not enough to murder them," Suzanne drawled, smiling at Meg.

Placing his hand on Suzanne's waist, Steven guided her forward. "Do you have any objection to examining Dennis to determine if he's as dead as he looks?"

Suzanne answered with a shrug, then stepped into the room. Without hesitation she walked to the chair where

Dennis sat slumped, his silver head hanging to one side at an unnatural angle. She placed two fingers beneath his ear.

"No pulse. I'd say his neck is broken. He's cool to the touch as if he's been dead for a while."

Candida leaned into the room. "Stand right where you are. Don't touch anything. But take a look around. Do you see anything suspicious?"

"You can see for yourselves there's no evidence of a struggle. He's not wearing his jacket or tie, but otherwise it appears he's wearing the clothing he wore last night. White shirt, dark slacks." Bending, Suzanne examined the typewritten pages scattered around the base of the chair. "He was reading a manuscript titled *Death, Death, Death* by someone named—" she tilted her head "—Beth Poppins."

Candida rolled her eyes. "That's overkill, overkill, overkill. Beth Poppins, whom I've never heard of, is definitely a novice."

"You can see that his briefcase is open." Kneeling, Suzanne looked inside. "There are two or three more manuscripts, an expensive-looking pen set, business cards, what looks like a set of agency contracts and three unopened packages of cigarettes."

"That reminds me—check the table beside his chair," Meg called from the doorway. "The ashtray. Was Dennis smoking when he was killed?"

"What a peculiar question. If you have to know, there's one crushed butt in the ashtray. A couple of spent matches. Very little ash."

Meg frowned. "Is there another ashtray in the room?"

"None that I can see. Why, are you planning to take up smoking?"

Meg pressed her lips together. "Can you see if there's anything in the wastebasket?"

"It's empty."

"That helps with the timing," Steven nodded, following Meg's train of thought. To Suzanne he said, "Can you tell if he has any blood or tissue under his fingernails? Did he put up a fight?"

Suzanne bent beside Dennis's dangling hand. "Nothing unusual that I can see." She smiled. "I'd guess he knew his killer, probably trusted him. Or her."

"Thank you, madam detective, none of us would have thought of that," Candida snarled. "I'm going to get dressed, then I'll meet all of you downstairs." She leveled a grim look at Howard. "I'd like to have a Bloody Mary waiting. A strong one."

After beckoning Suzanne out of the room, Steven instructed James to lock the door. Without speaking everyone filed down the staircase and back into the dining room, glad for the bright sunshine falling past the heavy velvet curtains. Howard walked straight to the sliding cherry-wood panel, pushed it open, then emerged with vodka and spiced tomato juice. Howard mixed the drinks and James served them around the table.

Meg had an absurd idea everyone was waiting for someone to make a toast. Howard cleared his throat, opened his mouth, then he muttered something and swallowed half his drink. Meg tasted hers tentatively and was relieved to discover it wasn't as strong as she feared it would be.

"We can't just sit here any longer, waiting to be rescued," Steven said, his tone somber. "It's time we talked about someone walking down to Breckenridge."

James shook his head. "Forgive me for interrupting, sir, but that's a perilous idea. It's stopped snowing, but the wind has whipped up again. Taking the windchill factor into account, the temperature outside is minus fifteen. It could be fatally dangerous to attempt an eight-mile walk in this temperature and altitude."

Howard agreed. "I read a story once where a guy tried to do something like you're suggesting. He exhausted himself wading through drifts, then became delirious. Hypothermia, I imagine. Anyway, he wandered off the road, got lost, and they found his body in the spring. I don't think walking to town is an option."

James inclined his head in agreement. "I hope none of you will attempt it. I feel certain Jim will reach us with the plow by tomorrow."

"By *tomorrow?*" Candida came into the dining room and flung herself into a chair, then downed half her Bloody Mary. "By tomorrow someone else could be dead! The murderer is picking us off like ducks in a shooting gallery. One per night. So what are we supposed to do? Just sit here and wait until we're all dead?"

"If anyone has any ideas, now's the time to speak up." Frustration tightened Steven's jaw. He drummed his fingertips on the tabletop. No one spoke. "If the plow isn't here by noon tomorrow, I'll walk into Breckenridge to get help. Regardless of the weather. We can't wait much longer, we have to take the risk."

Howard's reference to hypothermia continued to reverberate in Meg's mind. She looked at Steven, picturing him delirious and freezing and her chest tightened. Clenching her teeth, she carried her drink to the windows. "At least it's stopped snowing." The sky was clear and cold, so dazzlingly blue it hurt her eyes to look up. Wind teased long tails of snow off the top of the mountain peaks in the distance, but there were no clouds.

"Whichever one of you is the killer," Suzanne said, "*you* should have to make the walk into Breckenridge. Any volunteers?"

Candida's glare threw off sparks. "Whichever one of you is murdering people, would you do everyone a favor and kill that smug bitch next?"

"Oh, dear, now I've made you angry." Suzanne smiled, then gave Candida a thoughtful look. "First, you want Tillis dead and—what do you know?—Tillis dies. Then you mention it's a shame the killer didn't murder Dennis—and how lucky can you get?—Dennis turns up dead. Does anyone recognize a pattern developing here?"

Howard grabbed Candida as she started around the table, her fingernails reaching. With effort he wrestled her back into her chair.

"Let's all calm down," Steven cautioned. "Insults and accusations won't get us anywhere."

Meg discovered her shoulders were tight, her chest constricted. Drawing a breath, she held it, then expelled the tension. "Should we discuss Dennis's murder?" she asked Steven. "Assuming we can do so in a rational manner?"

"We can try," Steven said, glancing at the others.

"There are certain facts we probably can agree on," Meg began.

Candida nodded, still glaring at Suzanne. "The bed wasn't slept in. Dennis was wearing the same clothing he wore to dinner. We can reasonably assume he was murdered last night."

"We can also assume he was murdered relatively early in the evening."

"Because of the cigarette," Steven agreed. Once again he and Meg were thinking along the same lines.

She nodded. "Dennis was a heavy smoker. But there's only one cigarette butt in the ashtray. And that's not because he emptied his ashtray. Suzanne reported there was nothing in the wastebasket."

"I see." Grudging admiration lit Candida's eyes. "If Dennis had been sitting there reading for any length of time, there would have been several cigarette butts in the ashtray."

"Wait a minute," Howard interrupted. "I don't like the direction this conversation is heading. You're suggesting that Dennis was murdered almost immediately after he went upstairs. That means you're saying I did it. All of you were downstairs watching each other and playing bridge. Except me. I went upstairs right after Dennis did. And no one saw him alive after that."

"Don't be silly, Howard. You couldn't murder anyone." Candida made a face. "Plus, Suzanne *did* see Dennis after you went upstairs. Dennis returned downstairs and went outside. He was outside when you came down to get me for bed."

Howard looked puzzled. "I still don't get it. Why did he go outside?"

Standing, Suzanne went to the sideboard and refilled her coffee cup. "He didn't stop to chat. We don't know why he went out."

Howard followed her. "Are you sure it was Dennis?"

"Who else could it have been?" Suzanne spoke with exaggerated patience. "Steven was with us, you appeared a few minutes later. That leaves Dennis. Of course it was him."

"If Dennis was killed shortly after he returned inside, then the question becomes, 'When did he return?'" Steven looked toward the breakfast buffet. "Did anyone see Dennis after he went out? James?"

"No, sir. I wasn't aware that anyone went out after we returned from the garage."

"I didn't hear him come in," Candida said. "Howard and I read for a while, then we went to sleep around midnight. Dennis Parnham was a slug and whoever killed him did the world a favor. But it wasn't me and it wasn't Howard. We were never out of each other's sight."

"I didn't see him return, either," Steven said without looking at Meg. "I had a brandy with Suzanne, then went to my room."

Meg waited. When Steven didn't mention going to her room, she released a tiny sigh of relief. Eventually the police would have to know the truth, but for the moment Suzanne didn't have to know.

"James came by my room to discuss today's menus and we stood in the corridor. But I didn't see Dennis return."

James jogged her memory. "You mentioned you were expecting someone, miss."

"Did I?" A fistful of butterflies were released in her stomach. "I can't think why I'd say something like that. I wasn't expecting anyone."

When she glanced up, Steven was watching her with a frown. She gave a tiny shrug of her shoulders and looked away from him.

"Someone isn't telling the truth here," Suzanne commented.

Meg felt her cheeks turn pink and knew she sounded suspicious as hell. "If James says I said that, I must have." Flustered and trying to look innocent, she spread her hands. "I don't remember. But I don't know why I would have said I was expecting someone when I wasn't." Feeling guilty for lying, she didn't dare glance at James.

"It occurs to me that everyone who had a motive to kill Tillis also had a motive to kill Dennis," Steven mentioned. Meg appreciated his effort to take the attention away from her.

"Which leaves me out," Suzanne observed.

In Meg's mind Suzanne was the most likely candidate to have murdered Aunt Tilly, although she couldn't figure out how Suzanne had done it. But she couldn't think of any reason why Suzanne might want to murder Dennis Parnham.

"It's obvious whoever murdered Tillis also murdered Dennis. Surely no one imagines it's a coincidence that Tillis and Dennis just happened to be murdered at the same house on the same weekend surrounded by the same suspects." Candida uttered a snort of exasperation.

"Well, that takes us off the list of suspects," Howard announced cheerfully, pouring another Bloody Mary. "Candida and I were together when someone broke Dennis's neck. We can alibi each other."

"But you weren't together every minute," Meg objected. "I happened to overhear the two of you in the corridor last night. Candida waited on the upstairs landing while you went downstairs."

"Oh, for heaven's sake. Howard was only gone two minutes."

"Out of curiosity I stood on the landing under the sconce before I came down to breakfast," Meg persisted. "From that particular spot you can't see the bottom of the staircase. So you don't really know where Howard went or what he did."

"He went downstairs to get a drink. He returned two minutes later with a drink." Candida lifted her shoulders in a shrug. "Where's the mystery? Besides, Dennis wasn't murdered downstairs, he was killed in his bedroom."

Suzanne smiled at Candida. "I believe the point Meg is trying to make is that you two were *not* together every minute. If you'd lie about that, what else are you lying about?"

"We're not lying about anything," Howard said, placing his hand on Candida's shoulder to keep her in her seat. "Besides, didn't we agree that Dennis was killed early in the evening?"

"At a time when no one could have killed him." Steven pushed a hand through his hair. "We seem to have two murders that no one could have committed."

"But someone did," Meg replied quietly. "The question is—what do we do now?"

No one had an answer.

THE AIR WAS FRESH, cold and wonderful, perfumed by the strong tangy scent of pine. Meg stepped off the veranda and drew the crisp air deep into her lungs.

When she opened her eyes she noticed a movement about sixty yards from where she stood and turned to discover a liquid-eyed deer poised as still as a statue, watching her.

"Oh, Steven, look!" Then Meg remembered she was alone and felt foolish. A sigh lifted her chest as she realized how deeply Steven was ingrained in her life and thoughts.

In less time than it would have taken to describe her delight, the deer whirled and darted through a stand of pine, then disappeared into a shallow gully. After a moment Meg spotted him again, bounding up the rise on the far side of the gully.

She watched with pleasure, glad to be reminded that lovely things still inhabited the world. A few miles from where she stood, laughing vacationers zipped down crowded ski slopes. Couples were ice skating, frolicking in condominium hot tubs, enjoying a leisurely lunch inside one of the trendy restaurants lining Breckenridge's main street. Elsewhere in the world, and not that far from here, business proceeded as usual.

Responding to the needle-sharp wind, Meg tugged her cap down over her ears, then glanced back at the house, relieved to be free of the oppressive atmosphere inside. Then she ducked her head and walked around the house until she stood nearly beneath Dennis's window. She didn't approach close enough to disturb any possible evidence beneath the window, but close enough to observe there probably wasn't any evidence.

Disappointment altered her expression. She had half expected to discover the murderer had emptied Dennis's ashtray out the window. That would have suggested the murder occurred later than they assumed it did. But the snow beneath the window was as clean as a flow of marshmallow sauce.

Next, she trudged around the house to stand beneath Aunt Tilly's window where she gazed up at the gigantic fat icicles hanging from the eaves beneath the stone sill of the window.

Why had Aunt Tilly opened the window the night she was murdered? Meg felt positive the opened window was significant. But in what way? No answer came to mind.

Frustrated, she directed her attention to the ground directly beneath the window. Yesterday's snow had not been thick enough to obscure signs of activity. She could see where the ladder had been, where Steven and James had trampled the drifts. In front of the ladder marks were holes in the snow where icicles had fallen from the roof. The holes ran the length of the house, some with broken icicles still protruding above the surface.

If there were clues here, Meg couldn't spot them. Keeping her head down against the piercing wind, she started back toward the veranda, reluctant to return inside.

If she hadn't paused to look at the mountainside in the hope of spying the deer again, she would have been seriously injured.

An enormous thick icicle shot past her shoulder like a dagger and buried itself in the snow at her feet with a heavy sound.

Heart pounding, Meg gaped at the shattered pieces a moment, realizing if she had taken one more step the icicle would have struck her head or her back. Howard's story about using an icicle as a murder weapon flashed through her mind and she quickly raised her head.

Sunlight skittered across one of the second-floor windowpanes.

An icy chill constricted Meg's flesh. Light flashed across the pane because the window moved. Someone had just closed it. Her gaze fastened on the stump of an icicle beneath the stone sill and her stomach did a slow roll.

She was willing to wager everything she owned that the window opened into Suzanne Halverson's room. And she had a blood-freezing suspicion that the hurtling dagger of ice had been no accident.

The upsetting icicle incident unnerved Meg enough that she almost missed noticing something peculiar when she passed the windows to Aunt Tilly's office. Here the tracks made by Steven and James widened and curved beneath the windows. One of the stone sills seemed to have accumulated less snow on the ledge than the others. As she watched, a flurry of wind swirled more snow off the ledges.

Shaking her head, she continued toward the veranda. Sinister implications popped up everywhere, probably meaningless.

But she had not imagined the daggerlike icicle.

PASSING CANDIDA on the sofa, Meg proceeded directly to the coffee service and poured a cup with unsteady hands before she returned to warm herself in front of the fireplace. "Where is everyone?"

"What happened to you?" Candida tossed aside the book she was reading and studied Meg's pale expression. "You look like you've seen a ghost." A mirthless smile curved her mouth. "It wouldn't surprise me if we have a few ghosts around here."

"Candida, if you weren't in Aunt Tilly's room, how did your ring get in there?"

Candida dug her fingers into the twist of auburn hair arranged on top of her head. Nature had never created that particular shade of auburn. "I've thought about that a hundred times and I can't come up with an answer. I could swear I put that ring on the top of the bureau with the others."

"Could the murderer have come into your room while you were sleeping and stolen the ring?"

"I wish I could say yes. That would explain the mystery. But I locked the inside bolt before I went to bed. Unless our murderer can walk through walls, he couldn't have taken the ring while I was sleeping."

Still tense, Meg sat down and sipped her coffee, letting the heat warm her. "There are too many incidents in this situation that defy explanation," she muttered.

"At least one mystery is solved." When Meg raised an eyebrow, Candida explained, pleased to have figured it out first. "Now we know why the tires were flattened and the phones disabled."

"We do?"

"Obviously it was done to prevent us from summoning help and from leaving the premises. Because..." She paused dramatically. "The killer had to keep us trapped here because he wasn't finished! Dennis was still alive."

"Good God," Meg whispered. "Yes. Of course."

"If I were you, I'd sleep with one eye open tonight. I know I'm very glad to have Howard. I don't want to be alone in this house after the sun sets. It's fatal." After looking over her shoulder, she leaned forward and spoke in a conspiratorial whisper. "On another subject—what's going on between you and Steven? I thought that was over."

"I beg your pardon?"

"Oh, come on. We're mystery writers. We notice things. I'd have to be blind and a fool not to notice the tension between you two. The air quivers with it when you're both in the same room."

"I think you're exaggerating, don't you?"

"Hardly. I'm not exactly a stranger to this kind of awkward situation." Candida smiled. "Look, this isn't any of my business—"

"That's right."

"But during the past two days I've come to respect you. At least a little. So I'm going to say this. When we arrived at Morgan's Manor, you and Steven were circling each other like bulldogs. Now something's changed. You're still circling, but the hostility has disappeared. I'd say you've progressed to wary but warm."

"Candida, I really don't want to discuss this."

"Whenever a man does that kind of turnaround, you have to ask yourself why. What changed? If I were you, and thank God I'm not, I'd be asking myself what have I got that Steven Caldwell has suddenly decided he wants? Or that his great and good friend, Suzanne the snow queen, wants."

Ice accumulated in Meg's veins. She stared at Candida without seeing her, but Candida's words rose like glaciers in her mind. It hadn't entered Meg's thoughts that Steven might have an ulterior motive. She hadn't asked herself if he wanted something from her.

And of course he did. Steven had told her up front what he wanted. And what Suzanne wanted.

They both wanted to find Aunt Tilly's research notes.

And it appeared they both believed that Meg knew where the material was hidden.

"Did I strike a nerve?" Candida purred, observing Meg's expression.

"I don't know what to think anymore." Rising abruptly, Meg turned her hot face to the fire. Was it possible that Steven was toying with her, hoping she would lead him to Aunt Tilly's notes? Closing her eyes, confused, she pressed a hand to her mouth.

Maybe Steven was so bewitched by Suzanne that he didn't care anymore that Suzanne might have murdered Whitney.

Maybe he wanted to find Aunt Tilly's notes and destroy them to protect Suzanne. Maybe...

She bit her lip hard. No, she was letting the jealousy interfere again, letting it rule her thinking. Steven wasn't like that. He was a good man, an honest man. He wouldn't protect a murderer. But love did strange things to people.

"Stop it!" she whispered, shaking her head. "You have to trust."

"I couldn't disagree more." Candida sniffed. "You can't trust anyone. Trust at your own peril, that's what I always say. By the way, has anyone found the alleged death threats Tillis claimed she received?"

"I found them." Gazing into the fire, Meg repeated the message pasted on the threats. "The part about ancient history could refer to anything."

"Not really. Let's think this through. A love triangle could be ancient history. Howard, Tillis and myself. But that particular piece of ancient history was put to bed long ago. So to speak. That can't be the reference. Did Tillis have any ancient history with Dennis?"

"I think we can rule out Dennis since he was murdered, too."

"How about Steven?" Candida asked. "Any ancient history there?"

Steven. Meg's stomach hurt when she thought about him. "I don't think so."

"Which brings us to Suzanne." Candida's eyes gleamed. "Ancient history—murdered husband. Poking about—researching a book. Plus the threat says 'You know this isn't a joke.' How would Tillis know the threats aren't a joke unless she knew that whoever wrote the threats had committed murder before and was capable of doing so again? Maybe whoever murdered Suzanne's husband discovered Tillis was investigating the case. If we knew who the suspects were in the Halverson case, we'd probably have a good idea who sent the death threats."

"I know a little about the Halverson case," Meg said quickly, hating herself that she was about to jump in and turn suspicion away from Suzanne. "If you're thinking Suzanne is on the Halverson suspect list, she's not. She was in Los Angeles when Whitney was murdered."

"Of course I was thinking about her," Candida said bluntly. "If I know Tillis, the thought crossed her mind, too. Maybe Dennis wasn't so far offtrack when he suggested Tillis had dug up something embarrassing to Suzanne. Murdering your husband would be considered embarrassing in some circles."

Meg's expression was sober. "You're building a scenario out of whole cloth, you know that, don't you? There's no evidence connecting Suzanne to her husband's murder." Not yet. "And how about Dennis? If the same killer murdered both Aunt Tilly and Dennis . . ."

"Dennis is a problem. But you know what a sleaze he was. Maybe Dennis found out something about the Halverson case and was blackmailing Suzanne, so she broke his rotten neck."

"Candida, that's absolute fiction. You're getting worked up over thin air. Personally, I'd love to agree with you. But there isn't a whisper of evidence to support anything you've said. The police did not implicate Suzanne in any way. And she didn't know Dennis Parnham. You're speculating based on personal dislike."

"You're right." A sigh lifted Candida's bosom. "It's just that I'd enjoy it immensely if Suzanne turned out to be the killer. I want it to be her."

So did Meg, but she couldn't believe Suzanne had killed Dennis.

"Everyone had a motive to kill Tillis," Candida said, pacing beside the sofa. "Don't look at me like that. It's true.

Except maybe—*maybe* Suzanne. And Howard, his motive is thin on Tillis's murder. Dennis is the problem. It's too bad Tillis is dead. She would have been a damned good suspect. She hated Dennis for years." Candida stopped and her eyes widened. "Oh my God."

"What's wrong?" Meg asked. Candida's face had turned a snowy color, then flashed crimson. She swayed on her feet. Alarmed, Meg stepped forward, but Candida shoved her aside.

"I've figured this out!" Her voice spiraled upward toward hysteria. "Didn't you read Agatha Christie's *Ten Little Indians?* Of course you did. Everyone's read that book. Remember? The host is the first person killed, only he isn't really dead. He fakes his death so he can murder everyone else without suspicion. No one suspects him because they all believe he was the first victim!" Trembling shook Candida's body and her voice rose to a shout. "So he goes around killing all the enemies that he's invited to his isolated island!"

"Candida, please. Calm down. You're worrying me."

"Don't you get it? Don't you see? Tillis invites all her enemies up here for the weekend, just like in Christie's book. And now Dennis is dead! Tonight, she'll get another one of us!" Candida's voice had risen to a shriek.

"What's going on in here?" Steven asked from the doorway.

"Am I glad to see you! Candida is hysterical. She thinks—" Howard appeared in the doorway behind Steven, looked into the room, then rushed to his agitated wife's side.

Whirling, Candida beat her fists against Howard's chest. "Tillis is alive. *She's* the murderer! Tillis is killing us off one by one!"

"Sweetheart, that isn't possible." Catching her fists, holding her, Howard spoke in a low soothing voice. He tried to stroke Candida's forehead, her heaving shoulders. "You saw Tillis, honey. She was dead."

"No! No, she isn't! I tell you, it's the same as Christie's book. She's going to kill us off one by one!" Great sobs racked Candida's body. She spoke in shuddering gasps.

"Meg?" Speaking quietly, Steven touched her arm. "What happened here?"

"I don't know," Meg answered helplessly. "We were talking and she got more and more worked up, then suddenly...she's convinced Aunt Tilly isn't dead."

In mounting consternation, they watched as Candida went out of control. She screamed, she wept, she shouted and cursed. She insisted that Tillis was alive and the thought terrified her.

"Why won't you believe me?" Mascara flowed down her wet cheeks. "You're setting us up for another murder! Oh, God! It's like that book. Tillis could be creeping around right now setting up tonight's murder! And you won't do anything! You're going to let her murder me!"

"What do you want me to do, sweetheart?" Tense with anxiety, Howard followed her frantic pacing, trying to calm her. "What will help you?"

"Go see if she's still dead!" The scream seemed to deplete Candida's energy. Collapsing on the sofa, she curled into a ball and sobbed. The fright and desperation in her weeping set everyone's nerves on edge.

"Steven?" Howard looked at him and cleared his throat. "I think we should...I don't know what else to do..."

Incredulous, Meg also turned to Steven. "Surely you aren't considering...Steven, that's crazy!"

"Meg, look at her," Steven said quietly, nodding toward the sofa. "She's hysterical and frightened out of her wits. If this is a performance, it's a convincing one." Leaning, he pulled the rope to summon James, then instructed James to accompany them upstairs and open Tillis's room. "Howard, if this shock treatment is going to work, Candida has to see for herself."

Without a word, Howard scooped Candida off the sofa and carried her toward the staircase.

"Meg?" Steven asked, his expression grim. "Are you coming?"

A shudder convulsed her shoulders. "No."

When they returned fifteen minutes later, neither Howard nor Steven spoke a word. They walked directly to the serving cart and poured tumblers of straight Scotch. Ten minutes later Candida returned to the living room. She had washed her face, combed her hair and donned a subdued wool jersey dress for dinner.

"I apologize," she said stiffly. Crimson burned on her cheeks. After a brief hesitation, she accepted the drink Howard silently offered. "I don't know what came over me. I just..."

"We understand," Meg said gently. "This situation has placed everyone under an unbearable strain. If we can just hold out until tomorrow..."

Above Candida's shoulder, Meg exchanged a long look with Steven. Earlier she had objected to his decision to walk into Breckenridge to summon help. Now she thought of the icicle incident and Candida's breakdown of nerves. She thought about Howard's steady drinking and how she herself had doubted Steven's integrity. She met his gaze and tried to signal that she supported his decision. They needed help. They needed to be rescued before someone else died.

They looked at each other for a full minute and Meg wondered what he was thinking. She had an idea Steven was trying to tell her something, too.

"I think I'll go upstairs and change for dinner," she said, dropping her gaze. Trying to read minds was futile. Once upon a time she had believed she could guess what Steven was thinking, but she wasn't sure anymore. Too much water had passed under the bridge.

As she walked up the staircase she thought about what had happened to Candida. And although Meg wouldn't have admitted it to a soul, for one terrible minute Candida's belief that Aunt Tilly was alive had made a crazy kind of sense. Everyone at Morgan's Manor hovered on the edge of hysteria.

MEG CHANGED into a navy-and-crimson sweater dress and freshened her lipstick, but she didn't return downstairs at once. Sitting beside the window, which she had opened a crack, hands folded in her lap, she watched the sunset flare into icy streaks of orange, then fade to lavender. She made herself think about Steven.

She forced herself to examine the worst possibilities. That Steven was in love with Suzanne and was conspiring to help her. That what he really wanted was Aunt Tilly's research notes. She made herself take a long speculative look at the two murders and she asked herself if Steven Caldwell could have committed either one.

The answer to all the questions was yes. All Meg's worst suspicions *could* be true. But were they?

"Trust," she whispered. In her heart she knew that Steven's statement about trust being the foundation of a relationship was true.

But trusting was so hard, it didn't come naturally to her. Ashamed of what she had been thinking, Meg was glad she had kept her thoughts to herself. Steven Caldwell could not be guilty of deceit, conspiracy or murder. It wasn't possible.

A tiny residual of doubt surprised her. But then she was new at trusting. Still, she had to begin somewhere.

Feeling a little better, she checked her hair in the mirror, then stepped into the dim corridor and closed her bedroom door. At the landing, she paused, looking up at the sconce Candida had stood beneath last night. There was something troubling about the incident . . .

Footsteps rushed over the carpet behind her. Before Meg could turn to see who was running toward her, a hand flattened against her back. And brutally shoved her forward.

Arms pinwheeling, she pitched down the dark staircase. The last thing she heard was a woman's scream. The voice sounded like her own.

Chapter Seven

Regaining consciousness, Meg found she was lying on the living room sofa, surrounded by anxious faces. She struggled to sit up, but the movement unleashed galloping horses in her head. The room spun in front of her eyes. Gingerly reaching a hand to her forehead, she eased back on the pillows. "What... what happened?" she whispered.

"Hold still," Steven instructed firmly. Now she felt his strong hands moving gently over her ankle. She knew she wasn't injured too severely because his touch sent a tingle though her body. "I don't think it's broken," he said.

Meg managed to open one eye and saw James hovering over her holding a tray of bandages. Everyone had gathered around to watch.

"This may hurt a bit, Meg. I'm going to tape your ankle." Steven's dark eyes met hers. "I think it's sprained."

The genuine concern in his gaze confused her and she lay back and closed her eyes. She no longer knew what the relationship between them was, or what it meant. Nothing was clear-cut anymore, except the chemistry that still operated in full force. His touch affected her like an atomic reaction. Even now.

"You have a cut on your forehead, miss," James said, kneeling beside her. Gently he bathed a spot near her hairline, then applied antiseptic and a padded bandage. When

Meg moved her arm, she discovered her elbow had been bandaged, too.

"A scrape, miss."

"May I have an aspirin?" she requested. "My head is pounding."

"I'm not surprised," Steven said in a level voice, glancing up from the end of the sofa. His hand was warm on her leg, almost a caress. "You took a header down the staircase. You gave everyone a bad scare."

"I thought you were dead," Candida announced with an elaborate shudder. "You were just laying there, all crumpled up and not moving."

"For once Candida's prediction was wrong," Suzanne commented. "But of course the evening is young yet." Sipping coffee, she watched Steven wind tape around Meg's ankle. "It's swelling a little. That's going to hurt."

"I can't believe I was so clumsy." There was something about the fall that Meg felt she should remember, and that she wanted to remember, but she couldn't pull the memory through the headache banging the inside of her skull. "This is so embarrassing. I haven't fallen down a flight of stairs since I was a toddler."

"It was your high heels," Candida guessed, nodding toward the navy pumps someone had retrieved and placed on the coffee table. "Writers don't wear heels to work. We get out of the habit of walking in them. Believe it or not, I've tripped a dozen times on my stilettos."

Even if her head hadn't felt as if the top were ready to fly off, Meg could not have imagined Candida Ripley working in sneakers as Meg did.

"Is the aspirin helping, miss?"

"I think so. Thank you, James." This time she managed to sit up, and after a moment the room steadied. She ached all over.

Steven kept his hand on her leg even after he secured the tape around her ankle and lower leg. "You cut your forehead, banged up your elbow, scraped your knees and I think your ankle is probably sprained. I imagine you have a dozen bumps and bruises we don't know about, but nothing seems to be broken."

"That's nothing for a tomboy like me," Meg said, managing a wobbly smile.

Steven's answering smile didn't reach his eyes. "When you wake up tomorrow morning, you're going to feel like you were run over by a truck." He glanced at James. "You mentioned a cane?"

"I'll fetch it at once."

Steven went to the bar for a drink. "That does it. We have two dead bodies and a person who requires medical attention." He glanced toward the darkness pressing against the windowpanes. "At first light, I'll walk to Breckenridge."

"I don't like the idea, but I think you're right. Let's hope you're alive to do it," Candida muttered.

"We can't wait any longer for the plow to get here," Howard agreed.

"Perhaps we should discuss what we're going to say after we're rescued," Suzanne suggested, moving away from the sofa to the thronelike chair.

"What is there to discuss?" Howard shrugged. "We just tell the police what happened."

"Suzanne has a point," Steven said, still watching Meg. His gaze lingered on her taped leg, then traveled up her body and settled on her face. "Tillis's murder will make the national news. Swarms of reporters are going to descend on Breckenridge. And on us."

"We aren't going to be permitted to leave," Candida said, thinking out loud. "The police are going to insist that we remain in the area."

When he realized he was staring, Steven moved away from Meg and stood in front of the fireplace. Thoughtfully he studied the faces in front of him. "The media is going to hound us for statements, for the inside story. A lot of accusations have been flung about in the past couple of days. I think Suzanne has raised a legitimate question. Are we going to use the media to continue insulting and accusing one another?"

"I'd hate to have that happen," Howard mentioned.

Candida broke the ensuing silence. "Despite everything that's been said here, about motives and who wanted to kill whom, there's something about each murder that makes it impossible for any of us to have done it. Someone here *did* murder Tillis and Dennis. But the truth is—based on what we know right now—none of us can point a finger and say with any certainty, 'You did it.'"

"Much as I hate to agree with anything you say," Suzanne murmured, "I do agree."

"Then can we also agree that we'll let the police make any necessary accusations and we will refrain from doing so?" Steven's glance told Meg that he hoped she would keep their speculation about Aunt Tilly's notes confidential until they had the evidence in hand. "If a reporter asks our opinion about what happened here, we'll merely say the police are investigating."

Everyone pledged to honor the agreement.

"I've found Madam's walking stick," James said, placing the cane within Meg's reach. "When would you like dinner served, miss?"

"I imagine dinner is ready now, isn't it?" When James nodded, Meg reached for the cane, let her head settle, then with Steven's assistance she stood. The walls bounced forward and back before her vision steadied. "The rest of you go ahead. I think I'll have a tray in my room. Maybe soup and something cold to drink if it isn't too much trouble, James."

Before she could protest, assuming she would have, Steven swept her into his arms. "I don't want you placing any weight on that foot," he said, his mouth inches from hers.

Meg suspected the dizziness that overwhelmed her had little to do with her ankle. Steven's arms felt safe and good. Hesitating only briefly, Meg wound her arms around his neck and rested her head on his wide shoulder. Usually she didn't feel comfortable surrendering her problems to someone else, but right now it was a relief to have Steven take charge. She closed her eyes and relaxed in his strong arms.

"How heroic," Suzanne commented, watching Steven carry Meg effortlessly toward the stairs. "Will you dress her in her jammies, too?"

"I'll do that," Candida announced firmly, following Steven up the staircase.

After Steven placed Meg on her bed, he leaned over her and gently touched his fingertips to her cheek. "How are you feeling? Honestly."

"I feel like hell. Honestly."

"I thought so." He smiled. "I'll stop in later." With reluctance, he moved toward the door.

"Oh, go on, get out of here." Candida made a shooing motion with her hands. "The best thing for her right now is rest. And she isn't going to rest with you looking at her like that."

At the door Steven gave her a thumbs-up sign. "Hang in a little longer. Help will be on the way soon."

"Looks like things are heating up," Candida commented when Steven had gone. "Is that wise?"

"I don't know." Biting her lip, Meg sat up and carefully swung her legs over the side of the bed. "For the moment, everything personal is on hold."

"Good. I hate to be negative, but *everyone* is a suspect until these murders are solved." Fists on hips, Candida gazed at Meg. "Steven's right about one thing. Tomorrow you're going to ache every time you move."

"I can't believe I was so clumsy."

"Well, let's get you out of that dress and into your nightgown." Sitting beside Meg on the bed, Candida carefully unzipped the back of the sweater dress, then gingerly helped Meg ease it over her head. Candida stared. "You're covered with bruises." She shook her head, dislodging an auburn curl. "You're damned lucky you didn't break your neck."

Like Dennis. That disturbing thought tumbled through Meg's mind nudging other thoughts that frustrated her in their elusiveness.

"Flannel," Candida noticed, commenting on her nightgown. A smile curved her lips. "That answers one question. You didn't come here looking to patch things up with Steven."

"Steven likes..." But Meg didn't finish the sentence. A blush warmed her cheeks and she looked away. Once she was settled under the quilt against a mound of pillows, she swallowed another aspirin and urged Candida to join the others for dinner. "I'll be fine."

"I hate to leave you alone," Candida said uncertainly. "Someone could—" She bit off the words.

"I'd say the excitement is over for tonight," Meg insisted, hoping she was right.

A few minutes after Candida departed, a knock sounded and Howard pushed the door open with his shoulder. He was carrying a bed tray.

"Dinner is served," he announced in a cheerful voice, "and I've come to keep you company."

Meg inspected the tray after he placed it over her lap. The soup smelled heavenly, but she had no appetite. "The

Scotch must be yours," she said, smiling at Howard who had pulled a chair close to the bed. Because she knew she should eat something and because Howard urged her, she tasted a spoonful of the soup. "Are you really here to keep me company, or did Candida send you to protect me?"

"A little of both."

She did feel better having him with her. "Thank you."

Before lapsing into companionable silence, they spoke of inconsequential safe topics. Books they had enjoyed, films they wanted to see, Colorado versus New York weather.

After a while Howard told her that he remembered Meg as a little girl. Meg apologized that she retained no memory of him.

"Don't know why you should. It was a long time ago. You were just a cute little kid wearing pigtails and braces. Tillis and I stopped by your folks' farm on the way to New York City." He smiled at the memory. "It wasn't all fussing and fighting the way the tabloids made it sound. Tillis and I had our good times, too."

"I'm sure you did."

A sigh lifted Howard's chest. "But Tilly drove me crazy with her jealousy."

Meg started and the soup spilled across the bed tray. "Aunt Tilly was jealous?"

Howard laughed. "Lord, yes. You wouldn't think she would be, would you? Considering her enormous ego. But she was. Oh, yes." He looked into his Scotch. "After a while, a man starts thinking if he's going to be blamed for something, he might as well do it."

Dropping her head back on the pillows, Meg closed her eyes. When Aunt Tilly said jealousy was poison, she had known what she was talking about. But she hadn't told Meg how to make the feelings go away.

"Do you ever feel jealous?" Meg asked. Immediately she thought of Dennis and regretted the question.

"I suppose anyone in love experiences flashes of jealousy," Howard said slowly. "The immediate urge is to lash out at the people who are hurting you. But I can tell you that doesn't work. It only makes the situation far worse for everyone." He poked at the ice in his glass. "I guess the best solution is to be honest. Tell the person you love that you need reassurance. If you think about it, she doesn't know she's hurting you unless you tell her. If she knew you needed reassurance, she might give it and then you wouldn't feel so wild inside when she smiled at another man."

The conversation had passed from general to personal and Meg shifted uncomfortably. "I miss Aunt Tilly," she said softly.

Howard emerged from his personal reverie. "Who do you think killed her, Meg? I go over and over it in my mind, trying to figure it out, and I can't. I know enough about mystery writing from having lived with two mystery writers that the killer ought to be someone who did *not* leave something behind in Tilly's room. That's how it would unfold in a novel."

"I suppose." Then Meg grasped the implications of what he was saying. "You mean you think Steven, Suzanne or I murdered Aunt Tilly?"

"That's how it would be resolved in a novel. But I like you and Steven. I don't much care for that Suzanne person, but I can't think she killed anyone, either. We've got an unsolved murder and no reasonable suspects."

"Two unsolved murders," Meg reminded him with a sigh.

There was another knock on the door, and Steven entered. Howard stood and stretched, then picked up Meg's tray. "Well, I enjoyed our visit. Try to get some rest."

Meg tilted her head and raised an eyebrow. "Did Candida send you, too?" she asked Steven. "Are you the next shift?"

"I thought I'd check in on you before you went to sleep," he said, taking the chair Howard had vacated. "Are the aspirins helping?"

"You know, I keep thinking there's something about this tumble that I'm not remembering, something hovering around the edge of memory." Lifting a hand, she touched the bandage on her forehead and tried to concentrate. "I came out of my room. I walked to the landing. I paused to look at the sconce that Candida stood under last night. Then..." Meg's eyes widened and she sat up so suddenly that her head reeled. "Steven! I remember now. Someone pushed me!"

He stared. "Meg—are you sure?"

"Yes! I heard footsteps, but before I could turn around...where was everyone when you found me? Who was upstairs?"

"I didn't find you, Candida did." He frowned, trying to remember. "I think everyone was upstairs dressing for dinner. If you were pushed—it could have been anyone."

"What do you mean, *if* I was pushed?" Meg asked after a minute.

Taking her hand, he stroked it between his fingers. "Please don't be offended by what I'm about to say." Meg agreed, but she was already bristling, having guessed where this was leading. "We've all been under tremendous strain." Glancing up at her, he frowned uncomfortably. "You remember what happened to Candida this afternoon. For a short while she honestly believed that Tillis was still alive. When we were upstairs she swore she glimpsed Tillis sneaking through a doorway. Candida genuinely did not believe she was imagining anything."

"Are you claiming that I imagined someone pushed me down the staircase?"

"I'm not claiming anything, Meg. I'm merely suggesting it wouldn't be surprising if you did imagine something.

We're all nervous and on edge, seeing suspicious shadows where there may or may not be shadows."

"There's something else," she said in a tight voice, then she told him about the icicle incident. Even as she spoke, Meg realized how farfetched the whole thing sounded. That someone might try to injure her by flinging an icicle. Narrowing her eyes, feeling defensive, she stared at him, searching for signs of amusement or outright dismissal. "It was a huge icicle. Shaped like a dagger. Steven, it could have killed me."

"You didn't actually see a person at the window?"

She studied him another minute, searching for any hint that he thought she was exaggerating or overreacting. But he kept his face carefully expressionless. "No, I didn't," she answered reluctantly.

"So you can't say for certain that Suzanne threw the icicle. Or that she was even in her room at the time it happened."

Meg stared at him. "Why are you defending her?"

"I'm not. I'm just pointing out how the mind can play tricks when people are laboring under a great deal of stress. Maybe the window was open, or maybe you only thought it moved when the sun came out from behind a cloud and flashed across the pane. Maybe someone broke off the icicle and hurled it at you. Or maybe it broke off and fell of its own accord. It's possible there's a natural explanation for what happened. That's all I'm suggesting."

"You're saying that I'm imagining things."

"Meg, that *isn't* what I'm saying." He dropped her hand. "But it's possible, isn't it?"

With an effort Meg erased the scowl from her brow. "All right. I concede it's *possible* that I let my imagination run away with me." She opened her eyes and examined his expression. "But I don't believe it, Steven. I know what happened."

"Look, I don't want to argue with you." Standing, he leaned to kiss her forehead. "I'll let you get some rest now." His fingertips brushed her lips, then lingered on her cheek. "The next time I see you, I'll have a policeman and a medic right behind me."

"Be careful," she whispered, meeting his dark eyes. "I wish you didn't have to walk down the mountain. I wish there was some other way." Suddenly she couldn't imagine her life without Steven. She hadn't seen much of him during the past eight months, but at least she had known he was alive. And in some dim corner of her mind, she had hoped that maybe someday...

"I'll be fine. Don't worry." But she saw that her anxiety on his behalf pleased him. He paused at the doorway and smiled. "By the way, did I mention how sexy that nightgown is?"

Meg's laugh made her head ache and she touched the bandage on her forehead with a moan. "You're the only man I know who thinks flannel nighties are sexy."

His steady gaze held hers. "Good," he said quietly.

Good heavens. Was it possible that Steven occasionally felt a twinge of jealousy? Before she could say anything, he touched his fingertips to his lips and blew her a kiss, then he closed the door behind him.

Meg stared at the door for a few minutes, then she carefully climbed out of bed, gripped the cane and hobbled forward. She locked the inside bolt, then wincing and grinding her teeth against the pain, she returned to bed and collapsed against the pillows and closed her eyes, forcing herself to concentrate on what happened.

Damn it. She hadn't imagined a single thing. Someone had thrown the icicle at her. And someone had shoved her down the staircase.

IN THE MORNING, Meg felt as stiff as a poker. Every muscle in her body ached and protested when she tried to move. Her head was no longer throbbing and aching, but everything else was.

Groaning, she glanced at the morning sunshine, then dragged herself out of bed. It took forty-five minutes to dress, put on some makeup and do her hair. The effort exhausted her. She was secretly glad when Howard appeared, swept aside her halfhearted objections, then lifted her in his arms and carried her downstairs to the dining room.

"Thank God," Candida breathed. "We sent Howard up to see if you were alive. When you didn't come downstairs..."

As soon as Meg was seated, she scanned the faces in the room.

"All present and accounted for," Candida announced. "No new murders."

"Did Steven leave for Breckenridge?"

"James said he set out at dawn," Suzanne answered. "How's the ankle this morning?"

"Sore. But I'll live." She didn't look at Suzanne when she answered. If Suzanne didn't want her alive to find Aunt Tilly's notes, then Suzanne might have pushed her down the stairs. But then Candida might have done it, too. With Meg out of the way, Candida would win the Macabre Series by default.

After breakfast Howard insisted on carrying Meg into the living room and settling her on the sofa in front of the fire. Candida snapped on the television and they watched the morning soaps. No one was really interested in the soaps, but no one felt like talking, either.

They waited. Minds drifting, the television merely a focal distraction, they waited, straining to hear the sound of an engine in the driveway. Meg wished Howard hadn't told them the story of the man who had succumbed to hypothermia and died in the snowdrifts.

"WAKE UP," Candida said, shaking Meg's shoulder. "They're here!"

Blinking, Meg pushed up on the sofa. After rubbing her eyes, she leaned forward to peer through the living room windows. An enormous orange plow filled the driveway. As she watched, both doors opened on the plow's cab and Steven emerged. Relief raced through her body and now she let herself realize how worried she had been. A half-dozen police cars turned into the driveway behind the plow.

The ordeal had ended.

Within minutes two dozen people filled the house. A stream of uniformed men flowed up and down the staircase. Others spread throughout the house. Someone retaped Meg's ankle and examined the cut on her forehead and elbow. James laid out a buffet with coffee, sandwiches and small finger food. The sheriff's department arrived, then the Colorado Bureau of Investigation. A photographer dashed up the staircase followed by a fingerprinting crew. After a long while, two collapsible gurneys came down the staircase. Aunt Tilly and Dennis Parnham were carried outside.

Meg watched through the windows as the coroner's wagon slowly pulled out of the driveway and turned down the road to Breckenridge. Tears glistened in her eyes.

One of the sheriff's deputies took Howard into the dining room to record his statement; Candida went to Aunt Tilly's library. Steven gave his statement upstairs; someone took Suzanne into the kitchen. Meg gave her statement from the sofa in the living room. Twenty minutes later Sheriff Conner came into the living room and sat on the thronelike chair across from her.

"I knew your aunt, Miss Sandler. Tillis was our local celebrity. I'm confident I speak for the entire community when I say we'll all miss her."

If Meg had met Sheriff Conner out of uniform, she would not have guessed his profession. He was a large man, raw boned, with a ruddy, benign face. Only his eyes gave him away, intelligent blue eyes that missed nothing.

As she returned Sheriff Conner's smile, it suddenly occurred to Meg that she faced a daunting task ahead. There were arrangements to be made, people to be notified, a dozen things to do, all of them unpleasant. She reached a trembling hand to the bandage on her elbow, wondering how she would find the energy to proceed. Now that the terrible weekend had finally ended, she felt drained and tired.

"I've read over your statement, Miss Sandler, and there are a few points I'd like to clarify."

"I want to help in any way I can."

"To your knowledge, did anyone besides yourself actually see the death threats?"

"I doubt it, Sheriff. Unless someone searched Aunt Tilly's desk." She shrugged. "You saw the supply room. It's possible the same person who trashed the supply room also rifled through Aunt Tilly's desk."

"The person who vandalized the supply room—what do you think he or she was looking for?"

A flush of color tinted Meg's cheeks. "I don't know."

He studied her expression. "Deputy Merrit didn't find the death threats. We have only your word that they existed."

"What?" She sat up straight and blinked. "The threats were in the third desk drawer!"

"They aren't there now, Miss Sandler."

"Then whoever sent them must have taken them out of the desk and destroyed them," Meg said, speaking slowly. Turning her head, she glanced at the fireplace. The envelopes would have burned to ash in an instant. "But I promise you, Sheriff. The threats did exist. And the wording was exactly as I reported in my statement."

Sheriff Conner indicated her taped leg and focused a pointed glance on the bandage on her forehead. "What happened to you?" When she finished explaining, he studied her in silence. "You're absolutely sure that's how it happened, Miss Sandler? You lost your footing on your high heels and fell?"

She hadn't mentioned that she was pushed. After thinking about Steven's reaction, she was no longer absolutely certain about anything. Maybe Steven was right. Maybe her nerves were in such a state that she had only imagined a hand against her back. The memory had begun to blur. As for the icicle incident, Meg had learned her lesson. She'd heard how farfetched and outlandish the story sounded.

"The thing is, Miss Sandler—we've got two dead bodies here. And an accident, if you will, which could have had serious consequences. You're damned lucky it didn't. If I understand this correctly, you came within an inch or two of being body number three."

"I..." She bit her lip. "I'm sure it was just an accident."

Sheriff Conner didn't look persuaded. One bushy eyebrow lifted. "Is there anything you want to tell me?" he asked gently.

Oh, yes. Meg wanted to tell him about the icicle and about the hand shoving her down the staircase. But she would have felt foolish mentioning either when she had absolutely no proof that either incident was anything more than an overwrought imagination.

And she yearned to tell him about Suzanne Halverson, that Suzanne had murdered her husband and probably her maid. But Meg had no proof of that accusation, either. All she had was Steven's belief that such proof *might* exist. But maybe it didn't. Maybe it never had, or maybe the research material was lost forever.

Probably she should tell the sheriff that only James and Hilda knew where all the telephones were located. But she didn't because she didn't believe James or Hilda had disabled the phones despite that damning piece of information. She didn't want to point the authorities in the wrong direction.

Finally, she wanted to discuss all the vague formless thoughts floating in disconnected strands through her mind. She longed to discuss everything with someone whom she could trust. But it was pointless until she made sense of her thoughts herself. And until she had proof.

"No," she said at length, feeling the color deepen on her cheeks. Which Sheriff Conner's sharp eyes did not miss. "There's nothing else at this time."

"If you change your mind," he said quietly, "if you think of anything you might have forgotten..." He placed his card on the sofa beside her and Meg picked it up, turning it between her fingers.

"Sheriff..." She bit her lip and made herself say the words. "About Aunt Tilly..."

Sheriff Conner anticipated the necessary questions. "Breckenridge is a small town. We don't get many murders here. Therefore, both bodies will be taken to Denver to be autopsied." When he observed Meg's grimace, he added in a gentler tone, "An autopsy is standard procedure in a murder case."

"I know. It's just...how long...?"

"There's no way to guess. It will depend on the medical examiner's caseload, on a half dozen things that are outside our control. Some families hold a memorial service in these circumstances instead of a funeral. Some just wait. Sometimes a delay isn't all that bad."

Meg nodded, thinking about the reporters that would soon descend. Perhaps it was a good idea to delay the funeral until the sensationalism had abated.

"That about does it for now," Sheriff Conner said, standing. "We've notified the telephone company about the telephones. They'll get someone out here this afternoon. We'd appreciate it if you wouldn't leave the county without letting our office know where you're going." He didn't say she had to request permission, but his expression made it explicit. To soften the implication, he smiled. "Standard procedure."

"I understand." Meg shook his hand. "Thank you."

By four o'clock only one police car remained in the driveway. The plow had departed hours ago. Jim from the service station had repaired the flattened tires. A repairman was upstairs working on the telephones. James served coffee to those assembled in the living room.

"No thank you," Howard said, declining coffee. "No offense, but Candida and I are eager to get out of here." He smiled at Meg and shrugged. "We'll be staying at Hunter's Lodge if anyone needs to contact us."

"I hope that's not where you're staying," Candida said to Suzanne.

"I haven't decided yet."

Candida's auburn eyebrows soared. "You came here at the height of the ski season without making reservations? One might be tempted to think you never intended to ski at all, that you planned all along to visit Tillis, murder her, then get out of town."

"What a pity that your gift for fiction doesn't translate to your novels."

When Steven stepped between them, Meg watched with gratitude. She lacked the energy to play hostess or peacemaker. Aside from his ruddy, wind-burned cheeks, Steven appeared to have suffered no ill effects from the trek down the mountainside. He wore a tweed jacket over a white turtleneck and Meg decided he had never looked more handsome.

For a brief instant she considered asking Steven to stay at Morgan's Manor. Then she decided against it. She needed to be alone for a while. Plus, she wasn't sure if they had resolved anything in their relationship, if it could be called that at this point, or if they were back to square one.

Suzanne glanced at the staircase. "Well. If James will bring down my luggage, I'll say goodbye to you people. I can't say it hasn't been entertaining..." She tossed back a wave of blond hair and raised an eyebrow in Steven's direction. "You arrived by shuttle, didn't you? Can I give you a lift into town?"

He looked at Meg as if waiting for her to say something. When she didn't, he asked, "Do you need any help notifying relatives? Making arrangements?"

"I don't know yet. But thank you." Conflicting emotions pulled her in different directions. She wasn't ready for personal confrontations. But she hated to watch him go off with Suzanne.

"I'll phone you," he said. There was disappointment in his tone as if Meg had somehow let him down.

An awkward silence opened and deepened. In different circumstances they would have shaken hands, perhaps embraced, would have murmured polite goodbyes and promised to get together soon. But no one knew the proper etiquette for parting from fellow suspects, one of whom was a killer.

"We never held the MAIMS board meeting," Candida said, glancing at her wristwatch. "Now don't look at me like that, Meg. Life goes on, you know. That's why we came here, after all."

"Maybe in a day or two." Suddenly Meg was eager to see them go. Yesterday she had felt as if she and Candida might develop a friendship in spite of being competitors for the Macabre Series. Today, everything had changed. The distance had reappeared in Candida's cool gaze. She looked at Meg and saw a rival, a young upstart.

Steven was last to depart. Before he followed Suzanne to her rental car, he paused on the veranda and placed his hands on Meg's shoulders. She pretended his touch didn't send her heart crashing against her rib cage.

"I'll phone you as soon as I know where I'll be staying." He looked into her eyes. "Let's have lunch tomorrow. I think it would be good for you to get out of here for a while, too."

"I . . . call first. Let's see how I'm feeling then."

Suddenly she felt awkward with him. They could no longer avoid discussing personal issues by concentrating solely on the circumstances at Morgan's Manor. The moment was rapidly approaching when they would have to confront the changes this weekend had brought. They would have to decide where they went from here, backward or forward. Meg wasn't sure she was ready for that confrontation.

For an instant, she thought Steven intended to kiss her. His fingers tightened on her shoulders, his gaze traveled to her parted lips and lingered. Then Suzanne leaned on the horn, and his hands dropped to his sides.

"I'll see you tomorrow," he said as he turned down the steps.

Meg stayed on the veranda, leaning on her cane and watching until Suzanne's car curved out of sight, then James helped her across an icy patch and back into the house.

Writers not only work in solitude, eventually they learn to appreciate and almost crave solitude. Meg stood in the foyer, her eyes closed, enjoying the silence in the house and the knowledge that she was alone. Too long a time had passed in the company of people and she looked forward to a few hours all to herself.

Then she remembered the calls that had to be placed. Someone—herself—had to notify Aunt Tilly's agent about Aunt Tilly's death. And she had to telephone her mother and father. And Aunt Tilly's attorney and accountant. And all the friends listed in Aunt Tilly's thick address book. The dreaded task would not become less onerous by delaying it.

After asking James to serve a fresh coffee tray, she gripped the handle of the cane and limped toward the telephone in Aunt Tilly's office.

But no matter what she did or how she occupied herself, there was no escaping the question that dominated every thought.

Which of them had murdered Dennis and Aunt Tilly?

Chapter Eight

The next day was cold but bright and invigorating. A brilliant blue sky curved overhead; winter sunlight sparkled across the snowfields. The spruce and pine looked as if they had been dipped in sugar frosting.

Even Morgan's Manor possessed a storybook quality today, Meg thought, looking back at the house through the rear windshield of Steven's rental car. Icicles draped the eaves like a crystal necklace. Snow hugged the rooftops and sills in picturesque folds. Frost glittered on the stones as if the house had been strewn with diamond chips.

"This was a good idea," she said, turning on the seat to smile at Steven. "Thank you for inviting me."

Today Steven appeared well rested and relaxed. A wave of dark hair swept his forehead above his dark aviator glasses. He wore a cream-colored sweater over a chocolate turtleneck and dark slacks. The lines between his eyes had faded. No one seeing Steven or Meg would have guessed they had endured a nightmarish weekend. Realizing this, Meg flexed her shoulders and let the last remnants of tension drain away, determined to enjoy the outing. And the pleasure of having Steven all to herself.

"I'm sorry to have phoned so late," Steven apologized, smiling at her, then looking back at the road. With the snow banked high on both sides, the road reminded Meg of a broad sled run. "I tried to call last night but your line was continually busy. This morning I had to rent a car, telephone my office... I called as soon as I could."

"I know my phone has been tied up. I've been notifying people of Aunt Tilly's death."

The hardest call she'd had to make had been to her parents. Meg's mother, Aunt Tilly's sister, had been at a Friends of the Library meeting and had not been home. But informing her father about Aunt Tilly's murder had been almost as upsetting as speaking to her mother would have been. His shock and grief had been palpable. Next she telephoned Aunt Tilly's agent, Marcella Brass, and that, too, had been an extremely difficult conversation. Aunt Tilly and Marcella had been friends as well as business associates. Then came the names in Aunt Tilly's address book. Meg hadn't finished until after eleven o'clock.

"Where are you staying?" she asked, changing the subject.

"Good timing," Steven said, pointing to the Poles, a hotel complex at the bottom of Aunt Tilly's road. "I'm staying there."

Meg studied the sprawling complex and warned herself not to say a word. But the question came anyway despite an effort to bite back the words. "Is Suzanne staying at the Poles, too?"

"Suzanne rented a unit on the first floor. I took one on the fourth floor," Steven said. He didn't look away from the road.

"I see." Her old enemy, the green-eyed monster, gripped her chest and squeezed. Instantly Meg pictured Steven and Suzanne checking in together, and later sitting head to head over a candlelit dinner, laughing, gazing into each other's eyes, fingers intertwining. Don't do this to yourself, she pleaded silently, don't think about it. But the image of Steven and Suzanne flickered in front of her mind.

Steven's hands tightened on the wheel. "Look, Meg. Suzanne gave me a ride into town. She was looking for a place to stay. I was looking for a place to stay. What was I supposed to do? Tell her, yes, there are several vacancies at the Poles, but you can't stay here. You'll have to find another place because...I don't know the reason, Meg, you fill in the blanks."

"Of course you couldn't say that." Dots of hot color rose in Meg's cheeks. Hearing it stated that way made her feel foolish. "You don't have to explain anything."

"The hell I don't." Anger tightened his expression when he glanced at her. "Did you hear your tone of voice? It's the same old thing. Explain this, justify that. I told you why I was seeing Suzanne, I explained there's no romantic involvement, but that doesn't mean anything to you, does it? Either you haven't been listening, or you don't believe me. Neither possibility is very pleasant."

"Steven, I'm sorry."

She was more sorry than he knew. In an instant the rapport between them had changed to anger and defensiveness. And Meg was to blame. Closing her eyes, she tried to remember how many times she had done this. How many times had she taken a nice moment and let her jealousy turn it into something unpleasant? A feeling of helplessness overwhelmed her.

Neither of them spoke again until Steven parked in the lot across from the Bell Tower Mall and helped her out of the car. "I feel so silly about my foot," she murmured, leaning on her cane and hoping to start over with an uncontroversial subject. The swelling around her ankle had diminished considerably, but she still couldn't wear a shoe comfortably. To accommodate going outside, she had pulled a pair of James's wool socks over her house slipper.

Steven made an effort, too. He smiled and took her arm. "This is a ski town, remember? Here a banged-up leg is a badge of honor. Everyone will assume you earned it while executing a fantastic maneuver on the area's most wicked slope."

"Actually, the sprain isn't as severe as we first thought. The medic said I'll be as good as new in a couple of days."

But Steven had guessed right. Nearly everyone who passed gave her a good-natured, knowing grin. A few murmured, "Better luck next time" or "Hope that happened at the end of your vacation and not on your first day here."

The hostess at the Horseshoe II on Main Street seated them near the window at a table where no one would accidentally bump Meg's foot. Meg glanced at the restaurant's brass-and-tulip-glass appointments, the stylish mauve-and-emerald color scheme, then she leaned forward in her chair to watch the steady flow of vacationers streaming past the large front windows. It was wonderful to observe flushed cheeks, bright eyes, laughing happy people who weren't involved in a sensational double murder, people whose only thoughts were to enjoy themselves.

"How soon do you think the reporters will begin to arrive?" she asked after she and Steven had been served steaming mugs of hot mulled wine. They sat close together in order to hear above the laughter and conversation in the room, close enough that Meg was aware of Steven's breath on her cheek, his mouth inches from her own. She tried to concentrate on what he was saying, finding the task difficult.

"The story made the Denver TV channels last night," Steven replied. "The details were sketchy, but the reporters played up the sensationalism. Life imitates fiction, famous mystery writer murdered in classic locked-door case—that kind of thing. I imagine the national media will arrive by this afternoon."

Sunlight streamed through the window, teasing red highlights from Steven's hair. When he looked at her, he did so with his characteristic intensity, focusing his full attention. Anyone watching might have guessed they were lovers without a care in the world, totally absorbed in each other. Looking at him, Meg thought how handsome he was, how self-assured and at ease wherever he was. And how incredible it was to realize they were both involved in a murder case.

She also realized their conversation had trickled away like sand out of an hourglass. Steven was looking at her, but she recognized that shuttered expression. He was turning something over in his mind, examining it, approaching a difficult decision.

"A penny for your thoughts," she said softly. Instantly she regretted speaking. An uneasy feeling warned her that she didn't really want to know what he was thinking.

For a moment it appeared he hadn't heard, then he said, "I was thinking how beautiful you are. I like the way you're wearing your hair now. Short and curly. And red is a wonderful color on you."

Meg glanced at her red sweater and dark slacks. Nothing fancy. But her taste didn't lean toward designer items. An unreformed tomboy, her choices were as simple and as practical as she was. Sometimes, like today, she wished she could be different. It would have been nice to open her closet and find something special to wear to her lunch with Steven. Instead she had tried on and discarded three slacks outfits before deciding on this one.

"I appreciate the compliments," she said, telling herself to stop right there. But her mouth wasn't obeying her mind today. "That isn't really what you were thinking, was it?"

He hesitated. "Let's not spoil today by getting into problem areas, okay?"

Everything sensible warned her to accept what he was saying and change the subject. But the same undefinable impulse that drew people to disaster sites pulled her forward. "I thought you said you weren't uncommunicative..."

Steven frowned at his wine, moving the mug in tight damp circles on the tabletop. "All right. That's a fair comment."

Hating herself for not letting it drop, Meg watched him with a powerless feeling that she had stepped on a roller coaster of her own creation and it was too late to step off.

Lifting his head, Steven stared out the window as if gathering his thoughts. "Look, Meg, when I agreed to come to Morgan's Manor for this weekend, I didn't know Suzanne would be there. But I knew you would be. I didn't know if you were involved with someone else or not. I hoped you weren't. I had a half-baked idea that we would talk, that we'd discover we missed each other and recognize that what we had together was something special. I thought maybe things had changed during the time we were apart, enough that..." He met her eyes. "But they haven't. You're still possessive, you still make me feel guilty as hell over nothing."

At the back of her mind, Meg heard Howard's wistful voice saying that if a man is continually accused of something, after a while he starts thinking he might as well do it.

But this was a scene they had played before and Meg dropped into her role with habitual helplessness. The best defense was an offense, and she fell into it automatically. "If you had only told me what you were doing with Suzanne, that it was business, I would have handled the situation better. But the way you chose—anyone would have felt jealous."

"I'm sorry, Meg, but I don't believe that. The point is, Suzanne isn't the problem. If you weren't jealous about Suzanne, you'd be jealous about someone else. The problem isn't me being uncommunicative." He spread his hands. "I don't know how I could be more open than I have been.

I've been trying. The problem is your possessiveness, your jealousy. And I don't know how to deal with it."

Being with Steven this week had been upsetting in the beginning, but it had also been exciting and wonderful. The closeness of sharing common dangers, common problems, the joy of discovering they still thought along the same lines, the physical attraction that hadn't diminished. Now Meg looked at him and her heart constricted. She was doing it again. She was driving him away, and with him went the only future she had ever really wanted.

The man she wanted was rejecting her. She was causing it to happen and she didn't know how to stop it.

"You don't know how terrible this jealousy is from my end," she said in a low voice, looking down at her salad. "I wind up feeling so small and petty and ugly. But I see you with someone else and the world falls out from under me. Then I look in a mirror and see nothing but flaws, real or imagined. I tell myself if I were prettier, or if I didn't have freckles, or...it's self-destructive and awful. I can't concentrate on writing or anything else. I keep seeing you and someone else in my mind, and it's torture." Lifting her head, she looked at him with misery-filled eyes.

Frustration tightened Steven's jaw. "I can't understand it, Meg. You're a beautiful woman, you have a successful career, lots of friends, a man who would love you the rest of his life—if you would just let it happen. But you make a relationship impossible!"

He had never mentioned love before. Hearing it now, in this context, was like a dagger to Meg's heart. "I know, I know," she whispered. Leaning forward, she covered her eyes. "Oh, Steven, don't you think I'd change if I could?"

"Then why don't you? Meg, no one can change for you. This is something you have to do yourself. Put this crazy jealousy out of your life! You're tearing yourself apart for no reason."

"I want to! Do you think I *like* torturing myself? I hate it. But damn it, Steven, you could help by—"

He stared at her, then shook his head. "No, Meg. Trust doesn't come with strings attached—I'll trust you if you'll explain every smile, every little nuance. I won't do that, not anymore. It doesn't work. And it doesn't solve the problem." He leaned back in his chair, away from her, his body language closing her out.

"Maybe this isn't the right time to be discussing personal issues," Meg said. She heard the hint of despair in her voice, felt herself grabbing at straws. And she felt the approach of an inevitability that she couldn't bear to think about. "We've just been through an intense and highly emotional ordeal, maybe we're—"

"The part that's so hard to accept," he said, interrupting, "is how right we are for each other in so many ways. We have the same sense of humor, the same view of the world. We're both in publishing, we like the same books, the same things."

"Except for Greek food," she said automatically. Suddenly Meg felt a lump rise in her throat and recognized the sting of tears behind her eyelids. He was saying goodbye.

A brief smile touched his lips. "Remember the first time I took you to a Greek restaurant? What a surprise it was to discover a passion we didn't share?"

"I remember everything," she whispered. "Coffee and brioche in bed surrounded by the Sunday *Times*...burnt hot dogs and the sunset at the beach house." She closed her lashes, hoping to conceal the moisture welling in her eyes.

"Arguing about the book reviews...you slaving over a hot word processor while I read manuscripts or worked on contracts."

"You laughing at *Murphy Brown*...fixing dinner together on Sunday nights...the long phone calls during the week."

Neither of them mentioned the times Meg had quizzed him about his secretary, or about a pretty new author. They didn't bring up the imagined hurts, the angry explanations.

They lapsed into silence, remembering the past, increasingly aware there would be no future.

"Let's get out of here," Steven said in a gruff voice.

Fumbling behind her, Meg found her cane, then Steven helped her into her parka and to the door. They didn't speak again until he stopped the car in front of the veranda at Morgan's Manor.

Meg stared at a point in space, hoping she could hold back the tears until she got inside. This time the relationship was truly over. There would be no more second chances. Meg realized she hadn't genuinely believed it before. Somewhere in a secret corner of her mind, she had believed they would work out their problems someday and she and Steven would be together again. A magic wand would slay the green-eyed monster and everything would be all right.

Now, sitting so close to Steven that she could feel the magnetic warmth of his thigh next to hers, could smell the tweedy scent of his jacket and the intoxicating fragrance of his after-shave, she tried to tell herself that she would probably never again be alone with him. Would never again melt into his body as he took her in his arms and kissed her. Would never again awaken to his dark head on the pillow next to hers. Tears glistened in her eyes as she reached for the door handle.

"Meg." His fingertips touched her shoulder, then fell away. "We still have some unfinished business. After we leave here I won't be seeing Suzanne again. That's a dead end. But I still want to see the Halverson book completed. Have you given any thought to where Tillis might have hidden her research material?"

Steven spoke in his publisher's voice. Nothing in his tone hinted that Meg meant anything more to him than any other author or business associate.

"I'll start searching for the notes tomorrow," she answered without looking at him. She watched her fingers clasping and unclasping her purse.

"I'd like to help," Steven said. When Meg didn't speak, he added, "It's a big house, I imagine you could use a hand. You don't object, do you?"

"Is that a good idea?" she asked around the lump in her throat.

"Why not? We're friends, aren't we? And I'm your publisher." He smiled, moving firmly into his publisher-encourages-the-author role. "I'm going to publish your next bestseller..."

So that's how the future would be. Friends. Business associates. Meg hurt inside, she felt herself dying by inches.

"I'm going to beat this, Steven," she said in a low grim voice, speaking between her teeth. "I'm not going to live the rest of my life driving away the people I love."

"Good," he said finally. For an instant his business facade cracked and she heard pain in his voice, too. "I hope you do. I don't see how you can have a successful relationship until you learn to believe in your own worth, Meg."

She squeezed her eyes shut. "I don't know how or when, but I'll recognize the moment when it happens. One day the jealousy will be—gone." Please God, let the sick helpless feelings go away. "And I'll be free."

"I hope you're right." He cleared his throat. "Well. I'll see you in the morning, then."

The awkwardness of the moment hurt as much as the words still ringing in her ears. She and Steven had never felt awkward with each other before. There had never been uncomfortable silences between them. Until now.

Blindly Meg reached for the door handle, then drew back as a shadow darted toward the window. A flashbulb exploded in her eyes, then another.

The reporters had arrived.

MEG WATCHED through the living room windows as another media truck skidded to a halt in front of the house. A dozen photographers milled about in the driveway and on the veranda steps. Those who had been camped out on the veranda the longest looked cold and red cheeked and uncomfortable. Meg considered sending James out with coffee or hot cider, then decided the idea was crazy. Making them comfortable would only encourage them to prolong their siege.

And that's what it was, she thought as a photographer spied her at the window and dashed forward to snap her photograph before she jerked the draperies shut. A siege, an invasion. Trucks and cars jammed the driveway; people pounded at the door; the telephone hadn't stopped ringing since Steven brought her home from their disastrous lunch.

When James appeared to inquire if she wanted coffee or tea, his tie was askew and a sprig of grey hair stood up at the back of his head. A dozen shouting, pushy reporters had managed to accomplish what two murders had not. James looked harried and out of sync with himself.

He pressed his fingers together and drew a breath. "I've put the phone messages on Madam's desk, miss. News stations are calling from all over the country. One from England. I'm telling everyone we have no comment. Is that correct, miss?" After she nodded, he drew another breath. "I phoned Sheriff Conner as you requested, miss. He said we may clean Madam's and Mr. Parnham's rooms if we wish. But I haven't done anything yet."

"Thank you, James." Meg thought about it a moment. "I'd rather we didn't disturb either room until tomorrow."

"As you wish, miss." They both ignored the persistent pounding at the front door and the nonstop ring of the telephone. "They're at the kitchen door, too."

"Make sure the windows are locked and the draperies are drawn," Meg said, but she felt confident James had already secured the premises.

They discussed strategy, then James withdrew and Meg was left with the evening stretching before her. She warmed her hands in front of the fireplace, listening to the pounding at the door and the voices shouting in front of the house. Then, because she couldn't bear to think about the conversation with Steven, in spite of the fact that it kept intruding on her thoughts, she straightened her shoulders and walked toward the staircase.

Curiosity drew her upstairs and carried her to Aunt Tilly's bedroom door. For a long uncertain moment she stood in the dim corridor with her hand on the latch, asking herself if she really wanted to step inside, if she was ready for this. Finally she exhaled slowly, then depressed the latch and entered the room.

The first thing she saw was the outline chalked on the carpet beneath the window. A gasp caught in her throat. Then, blinking at the tears welling in her eyes, she made herself look at the chalky outline until it no longer possessed the power to upset her. That wasn't Aunt Tilly. Aunt Tilly was the vibrant woman dressed in the spider gown whose bright eyes had twinkled and flashed with impish pleasure. That was how Meg was determined to remember Aunt Tilly, not as she had seen her last.

When her nerves steadied again, she inspected the rest of the room, not hurrying. Candida's ring, Howard's smashed liquor glass and Dennis's cigarette holder were gone. The police had taken them as evidence. The poker was missing, too, and other items that might have served as a weapon.

Here and there she spotted traces of graphite where the fingerprinting crew had performed a haphazard cleanup.

The manuscript pages of Aunt Tilly's novel, *First Guess,* were also gone. If Meg remembered correctly, the plot was based on a trick premise. There hadn't been a murder at all; the victim in the novel had died of natural causes. Now Meg recalled seeing Suzanne inspecting the pages on the floor. And now she understood why Suzanne had suggested Aunt Tilly might have died from a heart attack or a seizure. Apparently Suzanne had also read *First Guess,* and scanning the loose pages had triggered her memory.

For several minutes Meg stood in the center of the littered bedroom, slowly gazing around her, remembering how the scene had looked when she first saw it.

There were so many questions.

How had Candida's ring, Howard's glass and Dennis's cigarette holder gotten into this room? Why were pages from *First Guess* scattered about the carpet? She didn't understand why Aunt Tilly had the dead copy of an early novel in her bedroom in the first place. The dead copies of her books were in the supply room downstairs.

Why hadn't anyone overheard the struggle that took place in this room? Meg examined the overturned lamp and side table, the toppled chair. The chair especially would have made a tremendous crash when it fell over. Why hadn't anyone heard the noise?

And why had the window been opened a few inches?

Meg had asked herself these questions a hundred times. Closing her eyes in frustration, she raised her fingertips and massaged her temples. "Help me, Aunt Tilly," she whispered. "I have a feeling everything would make sense if I just looked at it the right way." Now was the most conducive moment. Finally she was alone, unhurried and able to concentrate.

As clearly as if Aunt Tilly stood beside her, she heard Tillis Morgan's voice. *Never overlook the obvious.*

Rubbing her arms, Meg walked to the window and stared down at the latch until her eyes began to water and smart. The open window was the key. Logic and intuition told her so. What was the *obvious* reason why someone would open a window in a blizzard?

Think, she commanded herself. Start with the premise that Aunt Tilly opened the window. Why?

All right. Pretend it's you. You're in this room; you're alone and dressed for bed. You think someone in this house wants to kill you. You pace awhile, maybe you think about dying. Then you walk to the window and you open it because... Meg rubbed her eyes, swore softly under her breath and tried again and then again. You open it because...

Because...

And then she had it. Suddenly the obvious answer was right in front of her. Of course. Eyes widening, Meg continued to stare at the panes as a sad smile touched her lips. Yes, that had to be the reason for the opened window.

Turning, she surveyed the room, seeking other obvious answers to test the theory slowly coming together in her mind.

Why had Candida, Howard and Dennis lied about leaving the ring, the glass and the cigarette holder in this room? The obvious answer? They hadn't lied. Why had Candida lied about being in this room? Obvious answer? She hadn't lied; Candida was never here.

Why had no one heard the terrible struggle erupting in Aunt Tilly's room? Obvious answer? No struggle occurred. It didn't happen.

And finally, the biggest mystery of all—how had the killer escaped from the locked room? The obvious answer? He hadn't.

"Oh, Aunt Tilly," Meg whispered, smiling through a shine of sad tears. "I wish I'd known you better. You and I could have been such good friends. I would have enjoyed you so much." After wiping her eyes, Meg glanced at the chalked outline on the carpet. "But didn't you know you'd be found out?" The question was foolish. Of course Aunt Tilly had known she would be caught.

When James spoke from the doorway, Meg jumped.

"I didn't mean to startle you, miss. Mr. Caldwell is on the telephone. He says it's urgent."

"Thank you. I'll take it in here." After James withdrew, Meg sat gingerly on Aunt Tilly's quilt and picked up the bedside telephone.

"I know why the window was open," Steven said without preamble. "I just figured it out."

"So did I." Leaning forward, Meg covered her eyes with her hand. Once again she and Steven were thinking along a parallel track. "Tell me why you think it was open." When he finished speaking, she nodded. "That's what I think, too. I don't know what we'll find yet, but I can guess."

"Are the reporters still there?" Steven asked. Impatience deepened his voice.

"I'm afraid so. I won't be able to verify our theory until morning. But I can go through Aunt Tilly's statements and receipts."

"Meg, I want to be there when you check this out."

She nodded and looked at the dark windows. "We'd better plan on doing it at dawn. Some of these media people are early risers."

Again an awkward silence opened between them. There was nothing more to say, but neither of them wanted to say goodbye. Meg thought about asking where he had gone to dinner, but she didn't. Steven would interpret the question as, "Who did you have dinner with?" And maybe he wouldn't be wrong.

"Well. I'll see you in the morning," she said softly, sadly. After she hung up, she looked at the telephone a minute, then closed her eyes. But before she left Aunt Tilly's bedroom, she lifted the phone again and dialed Adell, Iowa.

Her father picked up on the second ring. "I know your mother wants to talk to you, honey, but she's resting now. We were up late last night talking, then up early this morning to watch the news reports."

"Don't disturb her, I know she must be terribly upset. But please tell her I need to speak to her when she feels up to it. I have some questions I think Mom may be able to answer."

"Helen's upset," her father agreed. "She's sad, of course. And furious and, believe it or not, amused. She's feeling all the confusing things Tilly must have known she would."

"Amused," Meg repeated. So she was on the right track. The obvious answer.

"Your Aunt Tilly sure was something." Her father paused to blow his nose, then she heard a moist chuckle. "She'll be missed. Tilly Morgan was one of a kind. There will never be another like her. She just couldn't pass up a good prank."

"There may have been another reason none of us knew about," Meg said carefully.

She didn't know if her father hadn't heard or if he chose to ignore her comment.

"All the news stories have picked up on *Murder at Eight*. I'll bet Tilly's books are selling like hotcakes. She would have loved it, wouldn't she? All the publicity, the speculation, the mysterious circumstances, all the book sales." Something that sounded like a strangled laugh came over the wires. "And don't you know Tilly had a grand time setting up Candida Ripley as one of the suspects. Yes sir, I'll bet she enjoyed that part the most. It's a hell of a prank."

"One of the awful things is that Aunt Tilly isn't here to enjoy the fuss she's causing."

"We'll have to enjoy it on her behalf, honey. You know that's what she would have wanted. Like all the speculation about Candida's ring being in the locked room. Tilly had a wicked sense of humor, didn't she?"

"That's one of the reasons I'm calling." Meg drew a breath. "How *did* the ring and the other items get into Aunt Tilly's bedroom? I have a feeling you and Mom know the answer."

"Honey, I can't help you. But maybe your mother can. She's been sworn to secrecy for years. Maybe it's time her secret came out—but she's the one to tell you. It's her and Tilly's secret. I'll have your mother phone you tomorrow."

Meg agreed because there was no other choice. It was frustrating not to have the answers right now this minute, but the pieces were beginning to fall into place. And she could guess what the missing pieces were. If the situation hadn't been so serious and so sad, if she hadn't felt so furious with Aunt Tilly, she would have laughed out loud.

Chapter Nine

A frosty glow lit the dawn sky when Meg's alarm rang beside her pillow. Yawning and rubbing her eyes, she slipped out from under the quilt. She swiftly found the clothing she had laid out the night before and pulled on her jeans and a thick sweater. She eased a pair of wool socks over her sore foot, then quietly hurried downstairs to the foyer for her cap, parka and gloves.

When she heard the crunch of car tires rolling over the brittle morning snow, she peeked outside to make sure it was Steven and not an early-bird reporter, then stepped out onto the veranda.

"Hi," she said, handing him a mug of hot coffee. The steam rose between them.

"Thanks." He accepted the cup with a look of gratitude.

"How did you figure it out?" Meg asked. She was determined not to allow any unpleasant silences. "About the window?" They started around the house, following the trail originally made by Steven and James, widened by the police inspectors. They didn't stop until they stood directly beneath Aunt Tilly's window.

"I'm not sure," Steven said, looking up. "Maybe it was getting away from everyone. The idea just came to me, and then everything fell into place." He tasted his coffee. "Did you check the records in Tillis's desk?"

Meg leaned on her cane and looked up as sunlight shot over the mountain peaks and lit Aunt Tilly's windowsill. Following an imaginary line down the two-and-a-half story wall, she drew her gaze to the ground.

"I found the statements. But it was too late to verify anything. No one would have been in their office. I'll do it after we finish here. If we're right."

But she saw what she was looking for, and so did Steven.

Holes made by falling icicles ran in a snowy line parallel to the foundation of the house. But here, almost at Steven's feet, one of the holes was out of line, positioned nearer the foundation instead of directly beneath the eaves. The snowfall on the day Dennis was killed had partially filled the hole, and two days of sunshine had melted the sides inward. It was more a dimple on the surface of the snow than an actual hole at this point. But it was what Meg had expected to find.

With Steven's assistance, she kneeled in the snow beside the dimple and examined it for a long moment through the silvery haze created by her breath. Everything hinged on this hole. If Meg was wrong about this, then she was wrong about all the rest, too.

"We'll know in a minute," Steven said, watching her. He spoke in a quiet voice, going through it again. "Why would someone open a window during a blizzard?"

"There's only one reason that makes sense. To throw something out," Meg answered. It seemed so obvious now. "Something Tillis didn't want to be found in the room later."

"I can think of only one thing that could be."

Steven met her eyes. "Go ahead. Let's find out."

After expelling a long frosty breath, Meg plunged her glove into the dimple and immediately her fingers struck an object. "It's here," she said to Steven.

Slowly she removed a brown plastic medicine bottle from the hole and brushed away the loose snow, then tilted the label toward the sunlight. Although some of the writing had smeared, she could read Tillis Morgan's name and make out the date of Aunt Tilly's last dinner party.

"She had the prescription filled the day she died." Sadness clashed with the exhilaration of being correct.

Taking the bottle from her hand, Steven removed the cap and looked inside. "It's three-quarters full of lead shot. I guess she wanted to make sure the bottle sank in the snow and didn't bounce over the drifts, then come to rest where it could be easily found."

"What was the medication?"

Steven squinted at the smeared label and read it aloud. The name of the medication meant nothing to Meg. However, she could guess the nature of the original contents, and knew how to confirm her conjecture.

Although snow was melting through the knees of her jeans and she had started to shiver with cold, Meg didn't immediately push to her feet. She took the weighted bottle from Steven and held it in her glove, thinking about Aunt Tilly's last evening. About the outrageous spider gown, the startling dinner conversation, the people Aunt Tilly had chosen to spend her last night with. She remembered Aunt Tilly's laughter and bright eyes, her obvious pleasure in her final dinner party. Finally Meg tilted her head back to see Aunt Tilly's window. She laughed out loud.

"She really was one of a kind. I still can't believe she did this."

Steven smiled, too. "When someone, maybe you, writes Tillis's biography, this is going to make a hell of a finish."

He helped Meg to her feet, and it seemed so natural to step into his arms. For a moment they stood together in silence, holding each other and thinking about Tillis Morgan. Then Meg became aware of Steven's arms around her and felt her heartbeat accelerate. She stepped away self-consciously and dusted her gloves together after she checked to make sure the bottle was in her pocket. "I think James has breakfast waiting."

After breakfast, they went to Aunt Tilly's office and Meg opened the top drawer of the desk. Removing the pile of bills and receipts she had separated last night, she withdrew two receipts. She then placed a call to Dr. Li at the Vail Valley Medical Center and followed it with a call to Presbyterian Hospital in Denver, finding the names and phone numbers on the medical receipts.

"It's all coming together," she said to Steven when she finished the telephone calls. He stood at the window, drinking coffee and waiting. "We were right."

"We have to call Sheriff Conner," Steven said, turning to face her.

Meg sighed. "I guess so." Reluctantly she reached for the telephone as it rang beneath her hand. She lifted the receiver and eavesdropped as James answered and stubbornly repeated, "No comment," to the excited reporter on the other end. The instant Meg hung up, the telephone rang again. The sun was up and so were the news hounds.

Leaning back in the desk chair, Meg pushed a hand through her hair and glanced at the TV Steven had snapped on when they entered the room. One of the Denver stations was delivering an hourly update on the locked-door murder case. As far as Meg could tell, there wasn't any new information.

But the sensational aspects of the case had captured America's interest. Every commentator across the country had developed a theory to explain how Aunt Tilly's murder had been committed and speculated on the list of suspects.

The reporters dredged up the old scandal about Tilly, Candida and Howard. Suzanne's past was rehashed. Dennis's famous clients were mentioned. Caldwell Publishing's stock repurchase agreement was dissected. Meg was named as Tillis's heir.

And through all the excited speculation, Tillis Morgan held center stage. She was the undisputed star of the nightly news; she was America's current sensation. Everyone tried to solve the locked-door mystery and phoned their theory in to talk-show hosts. Aunt Tilly would have been the first to clap her hands and crow about what fun it was.

Meg released a breath and looked at Steven. "What if we don't call Sheriff Conner?" she asked. "What if we just let him discover the truth for himself? And he will. He'll know as soon as he gets the medical examiner's report."

Steven was watching a television reporter demonstrate how an interior bolt might have been locked from outside the door. The demonstration was unsuccessful. "You mean just let the prank play out?"

Meg nodded. "I have this fanciful notion that Aunt Tilly is perched on the edge of a cloud somewhere, looking down and thoroughly enjoying the hullabaloo she's caused."

"Sheriff Conner will be furious when he discovers we knew about this and didn't call him immediately." Steven studied her over his coffee cup. "But it's your decision. I'll go along with whatever you want to do."

"Then we'll let Aunt Tilly enjoy her last moment in the limelight," Meg said softly.

Steven nodded. "I had an idea that's what you'd decide." They smiled at each other, enjoying this moment of accord. Steven set his coffee cup on the tray and cleared his throat. "Well. How do you want to organize the search for Tillis's research material. Any suggestions?"

Meg turned to face the window and bit her lip. Why couldn't it always be like this? She and Steven working together, thinking the same things, sharing the same feelings? Why did the outside world have to intrude? With a grimace, she realized she was copping out. The outside world wasn't the problem. Meg Sandler was the problem.

This line of thought depressed her. And it was pointless. The moment had passed for what-ifs and might-have-beens. Suppressing a sigh, Meg tried to decide on a plan for today that would keep them in different parts of the house. When she was near Steven all she could think about was the touch of his strong hands, the taste of his lips . . . She didn't need that kind of distraction. Or that pain.

"I'll take the attic," she said finally. "You start with the basement."

A look of relief crossed his expression as if he had been remembering, too, as if being together was as difficult for him as it was for her. "Sounds good. Maybe we'll get lucky and find the file before lunch."

But they didn't get lucky. At six o'clock they called a halt for the day.

"Would you like to stay for dinner?" Meg asked when they met for a glass of wine in the living room. She was tired, dusty and out of sorts. After spending the entire day in the attic going through trunks and boxes and rows of ancient files, she was convinced Aunt Tilly had been a pack rat. Aunt Tilly hadn't disposed of anything. What couldn't be crammed into the attic went down to the basement. Steven hadn't finished there until thirty minutes ago.

"Thanks, but I'll take a rain check. What I want right now is a hot shower," Steven said, stretching his neck against his hand. "You wouldn't believe the stuff that's down there. Old encyclopedias, boxes of clothing that must have belonged to your grandparents, broken garden equipment, furniture that's now being used by mice and chipmunks."

"Everything but the Halverson file," Meg said glumly, putting her feet up on the coffee table. She wasn't using her cane today and her foot had begun to ache. She also had a headache brought on by wondering what she would do with the items in the attic and the basement once she officially inherited them.

"The file is here somewhere," Steven said. He sounded tired. "We'll try again tomorrow." He glanced at his watch and Meg wondered if he was meeting someone for dinner. She bit her lip hard and didn't say anything. "Don't get up, you look tired," Steven said. "I know my way to the door."

"If there's something you'd rather be doing tomorrow, I can finish the search," Meg said in a tight voice.

He was standing behind her so she couldn't see his expression. But she imagined it. And she silently berated herself for asking to be hurt.

"I'll see you in the morning. Bright and early," Steven said finally. There was resignation in his tone. And somehow that was worse than anger would have been.

Meg stared into the fireplace and finished her wine. A tear rolled down her cheek.

STEVEN AND Sheriff Conner arrived at the same time, just as Meg was finishing breakfast. They elbowed a path through the shouting reporters and James let them in, then quickly shut the door behind them.

Steven stamped the snow from his boots and nodded at Meg's foot. "You're wearing shoes. That's great."

His hair, like hers, was still damp from a shower. He smelled like soap and frosty air.

Sheriff Conner removed his hat. "This won't take long, Miss Sandler. I've heard from the medical examiner and—"

"And Aunt Tilly's murder is a hoax," Meg finished. Sadness deepened the color of her eyes. "Aunt Tilly committed suicide."

The sheriff stared at her. "You could have saved everyone a lot of trouble, Miss Sandler, if you had told the truth the day I interviewed you."

"Steven and I didn't know the truth until yesterday. Not for certain." Meg led them into the living room and asked James to serve coffee. James leaned against the archway, a shocked expression pinching his mouth. Frowning, Meg placed a hand on his sleeve. "I thought you knew."

"In fact, we thought you were part of the prank," Steven added.

James stumbled forward and sank into a chair. He passed a hand over his eyes. "Good God, no. This is the first..." He swallowed hard and shook his head. "A suicide!"

"But the telephones. That had to be your work. You and Hilda were the only ones who knew where all..." Then it came to her. James and Hilda were not the only people who knew the location of all the telephones.

"Tillis," Steven said softly, following her thought. "Tillis knew where the phones were located."

"She must have disabled them." Meg stared at him. "No one suspected it was her. But of course it was."

"Okay, folks." Sheriff Conner pointed to the sofa. "Sit yourselves down. You've figured out the telephones. And the locked bolt isn't a mystery anymore. What else can we clear up here?"

Meg's thigh brushed Steven's and a tingle shot to the roots of her hair. Startled, she eased away from him. But the unexpected contact had rattled her thoughts. She looked at the sheriff and heard herself babbling.

"In retrospect, the whole thing seems so obvious that it's hard to see how we missed it. Aunt Tilly scattered clues everywhere. Do you remember the little speech she made in the living room after dinner?" She directed the question to Steven because she didn't want him to know that his nearness affected her. But it did.

He was studying her with a distracted expression. "What did you say?" After she repeated her question, he nodded. "I agree. I think Tillis was saying goodbye, but none of us realized it at the time." His eyes dropped to Meg's lips. "Later she also managed to speak to each of us individually. She told me how much she had enjoyed being published by Caldwell, that she knew Caldwell would flourish under my stewardship, that kind of thing. It was a private goodbye, I think."

"That's how it was when she spoke to me," Meg said. Knowing Steven was watching her mouth made her lips feel funny. It occurred to her that Steven's sweater was the same dark caramel color as his eyes. She found it increasingly difficult to concentrate on what she was saying. "I think Aunt Tilly couldn't resist leaving clues. She could have closed the window, but she didn't. I think she left it open to nudge us toward the truth. That's also probably why she scattered pages of *First Guess* around the room, to suggest that no murder had occurred."

"When I saw her alone, she mentioned she had a headache." Steven moved slightly closer to Meg as he spoke. His hand was less than an inch from her sensitive thigh. "Did she say anything about headaches to you?"

"Now that I think of it...yes." Meg could have sworn she felt the heat of his hand on her skin. Responding to the near touch of his fingertips confused her. This sort of reaction shouldn't happen.

Sheriff Conner cleared his throat again and Meg gave herself a tiny shake. She had forgotten him. Sheriff Conner accepted a cup of coffee from the tray James offered before he withdrew, still white faced and distracted.

"What I want to know is how Miss Ripley's ring and the other items got inside Miss Morgan's bedroom," the sheriff said. "Miss Ripley and Mr. Clancy aren't budging off their story. They say they did not leave a ring or a glass in that room. So—how did those items get there?"

"I don't know," Meg replied, frowning. "I think my mother may have the answer, but I haven't spoken to her yet."

"Your mother?" Steven looked surprised. He glanced at Meg's shoulder, then withdrew his hand from the seat of the sofa.

"The ring and the other items aren't important anymore now that we're dealing with a suicide instead of a murder," the sheriff said. "But they're still a mystery. I'd like to hear your solution if and when you figure it out." He leaned forward and placed his cup on the coffee table. "There's no doubt that Tillis Morgan died of a massive overdose of prescription painkiller. We've checked with Presbyterian and her doctor there confirmed it was her medication."

"Steven, I think you'd better tell Sheriff Conner about the bottle we found." After Steven finished explaining, Meg added, "I kept the bottle for you. We were both wearing gloves so Aunt Tilly's fingerprints should be the only prints."

"Well, that's it, then. Your bottle is the last loose end. I'd say we've got this one wrapped up."

"Sheriff..." Some questions were difficult to ask; some truths difficult to hear. But Meg needed to know. "Is it true that Aunt Tilly had less than a year to live?"

"That was the medical examiner's best guess." Sympathy softened Sheriff Conner's expression. "Your aunt had an inoperable tumor at the base of her skull. The cancer had begun to spread to other parts of her body."

When Meg leaned forward and covered her eyes, Steven placed his hand on her back. "Why didn't Tillis opt for chemotherapy?"

"She could have," the sheriff answered. "But her doctors weren't optimistic. You and Miss Sandler probably know that the dangers and painful difficulties associated with chemo keep it from being a real cure. Miss Morgan chose to forgo that route. But without treatment, her deterioration would have been rapid. Your aunt faced a painful and unpleasant set of choices, Miss Sandler."

"And a painful and unpleasant future no matter what she did," Meg said in a low voice.

Seeing her distress, Steven caressed her shoulder. "But that didn't happen. Tillis left the world in the same way she lived in it. In high spirits and with a smile on her lips."

"Apparently so." Sheriff Conner didn't look happy. "The whole murder setup was a prank. And most of America fell for it."

"Candida was right all along," Steven added. "The setup was simply too good to be true. The business about being marooned, the dramatic announcement that everyone present had a reason to want her dead. All of it. From the very beginning the weekend read like a mystery novel. Tillis was setting us up."

"If Aunt Tilly's cancer had run its course, Aunt Tilly would have died quietly and in great pain. Her death would have merited a couple of inches in the newsmagazines and maybe a column in the book section of the major newspapers." Meg looked at him, but she was seeing Aunt Tilly in her mind. "That isn't what she wanted. She wanted to end with a big splash."

"Well, she managed that all right," Sheriff Conner said with a grimace. "Miss Morgan had her little joke. But the prank backfired. Someone used the opportunity your aunt created to commit a real murder. Dennis Parnham didn't fake breaking his neck. Someone did it for him."

Meg swallowed hard. In the exhilaration of solving Aunt Tilly's "murder," she hadn't forgotten Dennis Parnham, but she hadn't given him much thought, either. Focused on

Aunt Tilly, she had vacillated between sadness and amusement. Now the smile faded from her lips.

"Yes. Dennis," she said uncomfortably.

"Either of you folks have any theories about that one?"

Steven leaned forward, his elbows on his knees. "I don't think the body was moved. I think Dennis was killed in his chair, right where we found him."

Meg nodded thoughtfully. "It seems obvious he was killed from behind."

Steven turned to look at her. "If someone tried to assault Dennis from the front, he would have put up a struggle. Is that how you see it?"

Meg nodded, then glanced at Sheriff Conner. "Are we on the right track?"

Suddenly Meg had the uncomfortable feeling that she and Steven were *too* close to the truth. She imagined Sheriff Conner was studying them suspiciously. "So how do you experts account for the fact that the medical examiner places Parnham's death as happening between ten and eleven o'clock? Probably closer to ten than eleven. A time when you people swear it could not have happened because Parnham was outside wandering around in a snowstorm."

"I don't know," Steven said. Meg spread her hands in agreement.

The sheriff lifted one heavy eyebrow. "As near as I can figure it, Parnham has a window of about seven minutes during which he had to reenter the house, hang up his cap and parka, go upstairs, start reading, then admit his killer into the room and get his neck broken."

Neither Meg nor Steven spoke.

"The time window narrows even further when you consider the traffic in the corridor that night. Miss Sandler, you're in the hallway talking to James. After leaving you, James fetched a bottle of aspirin for Mrs. Halverson, so he's in the hallway. Then you, Mr. Caldwell, come upstairs and stop by Mrs. Halverson's room for a moment, then you go to Miss Sandler's room, so you're in and out of the hallway. Then Mr. Clancy and Miss Ripley are out there. Everyone was wandering around, but no one saw Parnham return inside, or noticed him upstairs."

Meg slid a look toward Steven. She hadn't known he had stopped by Suzanne's room before he came to hers.

Steven read her mind. He spread his hands and frowned. "Suzanne left her scarf downstairs. I returned it to her."

"I didn't say anything," Meg said in a tight voice.

Sheriff Conner examined Steven's expression. "If Parnham had acted on his threat to withdraw the authors he represented from Caldwell Publishing, you would have lost six of your top-selling authors. The loss would have dealt a blow to your company."

"It was an empty threat," Steven explained. "Those authors are under contract. But it's true Dennis could have caused a problem. Maybe some of his authors would have acted on his advice and reneged on their contractual obligations. Maybe they would have taken their next books somewhere else." He shrugged. "I would have been upset, but it wouldn't have ruined the company."

"Then you aren't having financial difficulties?"

"Hell, no." Steven frowned. "My bottom line isn't as strong as I'd like it to be. What company's is? But Caldwell Publishing is a healthy business. You're welcome to audit the books if this is an issue. I didn't kill Dennis Parnham. Your own timetable ought to tell you that."

"That's what makes this case so interesting," Sheriff Conner said, pushing to his feet. He settled his hat over a close-cropped head of sandy hair. "No one could have murdered Mr. Parnham. But someone did—didn't they?"

Meg and Steven followed him to the front door. "I think we've figured out that Aunt Tilly disabled the telephones,"

Meg said, "but what about the skis? Did Aunt Tilly hide the skis and flatten the tires, too?"

"I'm guessing your aunt disabled the telephones to heighten the immediate effect of the prank." Sheriff Conner peered out the side window at the reporters milling about the driveway. "But there wasn't any compelling reason to delay informing the authorities. In fact a delay might have caused the prank to fizzle. Therefore, I don't believe Tillis Morgan hid the skis or flattened the tires."

"You know," Steven said, leaning against the archway. "It occurs to me that killing Dennis required surprise, not strength."

"So the killer could have been a woman." A humorless smile lifted Sheriff Conner's mouth. "That's occurred to us. We aren't ruling anyone out, Mr. Caldwell."

Meg's eyebrows soared, then settled into a frown. She kept forgetting that she, too, was a suspect in Dennis's murder. Sheriff Conner's glance reminded her.

Sheriff Conner reached for the door latch. "I'm holding a press conference in about an hour to announce Miss Morgan's suicide." He raised his chin to the window indicating the noise outside. "I imagine most of the excitement will die down once the reporters understand there was no locked-door murder. No whodunit for America to solve."

"What about Dennis's murder?" Steven asked.

"With respect to Mr. Parnham, he wasn't a famous or eccentric mystery writer, and—there's no tactful way to say this—his murder is ordinary run-of-the-mill stuff." A shrug lifted Sheriff Conner's uniform. Then his gaze narrowed on Meg and Steven. "I'm guessing the reporters will be gone by supper time. But I'm not going anywhere. I'll be keeping an eye on everyone until Parnham's murder is solved."

Meg didn't like the way he was looking at them. Drawing a breath she stepped forward and gave him Aunt Tilly's medication bottle. "Thank you for stopping by."

"If you come up with anything else, or if you find any more evidence—" his gaze steadied on her face "—you don't wait for me to drop by, understand? You telephone immediately."

Color rose in her cheeks. "I will."

Meg watched through the draperies as Sheriff Conner crossed to the top step of the veranda and addressed the reporters, announcing his press conference. A few of the reporters spun to look at the house, their expressions drawn with indecision. Then most of them jumped into their cars and vans and followed the sheriff's car down the driveway.

When she turned from the window, Steven was watching her. "Are you going to make an issue out of Suzanne's scarf?"

"It seems peculiar that you didn't mention it," she said, passing him on her way back into the living room.

"Come on, Meg. It was a small thing. It never entered my mind that mentioning it was important." Thrusting his hands into his pockets, he walked to the windows and frowned at the departing cars and vans.

Meg walked to the fireplace and held her hands out to the flames. "I don't know what it is about Suzanne that brings out the worst in me," she said quietly. "She's just so damned beautiful, so perfect. When I think about her I feel dull and inadequate. I guess I had trouble believing you weren't involved with her because I couldn't imagine why you'd want me when you could have Suzanne."

Steven continued to gaze out the windows. He didn't turn to look at her. "You've met Suzanne. You've spent time with her. You have to recognize there's something inside Suzanne that doesn't connect. Okay, she's beautiful. But so are you." He paused, then turned toward her. "Look, Meg, I'm not the writer here, not as good with words as you are. But I can promise you there will always be someone out there who is prettier, smarter, richer or more successful than you are. And there are also plenty who are not as beautiful, not as smart, not as rich or as successful. If you want to, you can focus solely on the first group and make yourself miserable."

Meg lowered her head and covered her eyes. "I hate this," she whispered. "I hate it that I'm so damned insecure. Please, Steven, stop. Don't say anything more."

The irony was she had believed she had her feelings in check. Then she arrived at Morgan's Manor and was confronted with Steven and Suzanne. And all the old insecurities had flared to life. Suddenly Meg tumbled backward in time and was once again the devastated girl whose fiancé had eloped with her best friend, leaving her to face the humiliation of explaining to her family and friends what had happened. And, just as suddenly, she was flashing back on Steven and all the anxious moments she had experienced thinking the same thing was happening again.

"I *will* beat this," she whispered, feeling raw and vulnerable, needing reassurance that pride wouldn't let her request.

When she lifted her head, Steven had moved to stand beside her. The room seemed to spin as she stared into his brown eyes, eyes that reflected sympathy and regret.

"Oh, Steven." Her own gaze filled with helpless sorrow. "I'm so sorry. I ruined everything, and—"

Gently he took her into his arms and kissed her. This was not the angry passionate kiss they had shared a few days ago. His kiss was soft, almost tender. His arms closed around her and drew her close, cradling her against him as if she were too fragile to risk crushing.

When his mouth released hers, he continued to hold her, resting his chin lightly on top of her head. "I'm sorry, too, Meg. I wish things had worked out differently. There are hurts and regrets on both sides." In the following silence, Meg heard his heart beating against her ear. She swallowed the tears clogging her throat. "Well," he said finally, easing her away from him. "We have a full day ahead. Where do we search today?"

With all her heart Meg wished Candida had never said, "Ask yourself what you suddenly have that Steven wants." That statement cast a veil of doubt. Would Steven have been so gentle if they had the Halverson file in their hands? Would the sympathy and regret still soften his gaze?

What difference did it make? File or no file, their relationship was over.

"Please don't kiss me again," she said quietly, backing away from him. Anger flashed in her eyes. He should have known his kiss would only make it harder. Only make her want him more. Was he playing with her? Either the relationship was over, or it wasn't.

"You're right," he said. "I apologize. I shouldn't have done that."

"No. You shouldn't have."

Lifting her head, she marched out of the living room feeling confused, angry and utterly miserable.

Chapter Ten

Sheriff Conner was correct. The reporters didn't reappear at Morgan's Manor after Sheriff Conner's press conference on the courthouse steps. The emphasis in the case had shifted.

When Steven and Meg gave up the search for the day and met, frustrated, in the living room for a drink, they switched on the TV to watch the five o'clock news. It was preferable to talking.

The lead story on all the channels featured the hoax. In the excitement generated by this sensational development, no one appeared to remember Dennis Parnham or recall that a genuine murder had actually occurred.

"I didn't like Dennis," Meg murmured, "but there's something a little sad in seeing him dismissed so indifferently."

"Sheriff Conner isn't forgetting Dennis." Steven rested his head on the back of the sofa, crossed his ankles on top of the coffee table. "I had no idea there were so many rooms in this place. We've been searching for two solid days and I feel like we've only scratched the surface." He ran a hand over his face.

After switching off the TV, Meg resumed pacing in front of the fireplace. "There's something about that night that we aren't seeing. Something as obvious as the solution to the opened window."

"If there is, no one's spotted it. And all the evidence is in." Steven rolled his head to one side to look at her. "Everybody's spent hours puzzling over Dennis's murder. And everyone's coming up blank. Are you seeing something no one else is seeing?"

"No...it's just a feeling."

Meg couldn't pin down her intuition. But she felt certain there was something odd connected to breaking up the bridge game that night, something wrong. Something so obvious and ordinary that she couldn't isolate it. Thinking out loud, she replayed the scene for Steven, hearing the conversation that night, seeing the people.

She pulled off her bandana and pushed a hand through her hair. "It's so frustrating. I have a feeling that I'm right on the verge of seeing it."

"Seeing what?"

"Whatever is wrong with that scene. And there *is* something wrong." But the tiny wisp of memory flickered enticingly, then swirled away. It wouldn't be pinned down.

"And there's something about that incident in the corridor with Candida and Howard." There, too, something didn't ring true. Meg had sensed it from the beginning. That's why she had been so interested in the sconce Candida stood beneath.

That thought led to the memory of being pushed down the staircase. Concentrating, Meg tried to remember the exact moment when she had felt a hand against her back. But too much time had elapsed for her to be absolutely certain that she had indeed felt a hand on her back or that someone had really shoved her.

She cast a quick look at Steven and decided against sharing her thoughts. By now it embarrassed her even to think about the icicle incident. The icicle incident was a good lesson to remind her how jangled nerves could affect reason.

"I'm too tired to speculate over who killed Dennis Parnham," Steven said. "I shoved around more furniture today than a professional mover."

"And we aren't making any progress," Meg agreed, taking the thronelike chair across from him. Whatever she was sensing about the night Dennis was murdered would have to wait. In time it would surface.

"At least you got the supply room put back together."

Though Meg had known it was a foolish wish, she had hoped the Halverson file would appear in the mess covering the supply room floor. But of course it hadn't.

She found files of clippings, files of scribbled ideas for future books, files for books already published, files of press releases and promotional material, letter files and agent files, and papers that didn't appear to belong in any file. But nothing even remotely connected to the Halverson case had surfaced out of the chaos.

"So why wasn't the file in the supply room?" she asked, glancing at Steven. Already he had the shadow of a new beard. Once she would have teased him about it. "That's where the file should have been. Nothing else seems to be missing."

"Okay, let's work it through." Sitting up, Steven freshened his drink, raised an eyebrow at Meg. She shook her head and declined another Scotch and water. "We know the file existed. Tillis asked me to come here and review it."

"In the meantime Suzanne unexpectedly appears. It's safe to assume the file was intact at that time. And it was probably in Aunt Tilly's office. That's where she would have been working on it."

Standing, Steven moved to the fireplace. "Suzanne and Tillis argue in Tillis's office until they're interrupted by the arrival of everyone else. During that time Tillis tells Suzanne the notes are destroyed. Later she indicates to me that the notes are intact. She's hidden them and pointed you toward their location."

Meg rubbed her temples. "Aunt Tilly didn't leave the house, so the notes have to be hidden inside. What rooms did she go into? Can you remember? Did she leave her guests for any length of time?"

"Not that I noticed. My best guess is the file is in Tillis's office or her bedroom."

"We'll tackle those rooms tomorrow. My guess was the wall safe, or the concealed rooms where she kept the silver and her furs." But Meg had been wrong.

The silver and fur storage rooms had, however, solved a small mystery. The concealed storage rooms had been added long after the original house was built, and from the first, those rooms had been intended as secret hiding places for valuables. Creating space for the secret rooms had required reducing in size several adjoining rooms. Thus a few of the uncommonly small-sized rooms were explained. Plus, Meg had run across a few more windows that appeared to be boarded from the inside. The secret storage rooms supplied the explanation. Once again her grandfather had done his remodeling the cheapest way, building interior walls over windows. Slowly Meg was unraveling the mysteries of Morgan Manor.

"The mystery of the missing file is going to look so simple once we solve it," Meg said, frustrated. She looked up with a frown. "Steven—do you think it's possible that Suzanne found the Halverson file? Maybe we're wasting our time. Maybe the file is gone."

James appeared in the archway. "Sorry to disturb you, but your mother is on the telephone, miss."

"Finally. I was beginning to think she'd forgotten." Standing, Meg turned to Steven. "I really do need to take this call..."

"No problem, I was leaving anyway." He met her eyes. "Meg, about this morning..."

"There's nothing to talk about." Heat flooded her face. "Look, I overreacted. I'm sorry."

"I was out of line. I apologize."

Oh, God. He was apologizing for kissing her. It occurred to Meg this was a new low in their relationship. Wincing, she tried not to think about it. "We're friends, aren't we?" she said, her voice falsely bright. "Occasionally friends exchange a friendly kiss or a friendly hug. It seems I forgot that for a moment or two."

He looked as if he wanted to say more, but James was waiting at the archway. They were both aware Meg's mother was holding on the telephone.

"I'll see you in the morning," Steven said, lifting his hand in a wave.

Meg watched him pull on his parka and gloves, then she walked into Aunt Tilly's office to take her mother's call.

"I'm sorry I haven't reached you before," her mother apologized. "I've tried to phone, but your line was constantly busy, I couldn't get through."

Meg explained the media siege. "The calls didn't begin to taper off until about an hour ago. But now that the hoax has been exposed I expect things will quiet down."

"I know this whole experience has been terrible for you, honey. Believing Tilly had been murdered, then following that shock, Dennis's murder."

They discussed the weekend ordeal, exchanged condolences, talked about the arrangements, spoke of the hoax with a mixture of sadness and fond amusement.

"Did you know about Aunt Tilly's cancer?" Meg asked.

"No." A muffled sniffle sounded on the end of the phone line. "In retrospect, I think Tilly phoned to tell me one night, then changed her mind."

"She said you were always able to see through her. She said you could always spot her pranks."

"Yes," her mother confirmed in a soft voice. "Your father and I spied the makings of a prank as soon as we heard the news reports."

Meg leaned over the desktop and drew a breath. "Mother, Aunt Tilly made a point of directing me toward you." When her mother didn't comment, she continued. "I think Aunt Tilly was telling me that you would be able to answer a few questions that no one else can."

Her mother didn't deny the possibility or seem surprised. She merely said, "I see."

Meg continued. "The only unanswered questions left are—"

"How did Candida's ring and the other phony evidence get into Tilly's bedroom?"

"Yes! Plus there's a missing file I'm hoping you can shed some light on." Excitement charged Meg's voice. Until now she had wondered if she were wrong about her mother having the answers she needed. If she was building something out of nothing. But it seemed her instinct was correct. "Mother? Are you still there?"

"Honey, there's nothing I can tell you."

Disappointment drained the sparkle from Meg's expression. "Mother! If you know how those items got into Aunt Tilly's room..."

"I can guess. But if I'm right—well, it's a secret Tillis and I agreed never to reveal. We made a promise to each other years ago when we were children." A soft chuckle sounded in Meg's ear. "If Tillis wanted you to know the secret, she would have told you herself, at least she would have given you a hint."

"But she did hint. She referred to secrets. And she talked about you. I believe Aunt Tilly wanted me to know the secrets of Morgan's Manor, and she expected you to tell me."

"I'm beginning to understand. That rascal, Tilly, sent you to me instead of telling you anything herself so I'd be the one to break our promise. A last prank on me. Well, Tilly was wrong. I won't break our promise, either."

Meg hunched forward and covered her eyes with her hand. "Mother, please listen. You're thinking Candida's ring and the other items aren't important anymore. And—" she hated to weaken her position by admitting it "—I suppose you're right. How those items got into Aunt Tilly's bedroom is still a mystery, but no longer important to anyone but me. I think the sheriff has dismissed the items by just assuming everyone lied."

"Maybe they did."

"Maybe. But if I understand what you're hinting at, there's another explanation. Even if it isn't vital to the case anymore, I need to *know*. Can you understand?" Meg tried to sound persuasive. "I think I became a mystery writer because I don't like mysteries. When I write them myself there is no mystery, I know the answers before I put a word on paper. But these mysteries are real. And, Mom, they're driving me crazy. If you know how those items got into Aunt Tilly's room, if you know where a file might be hidden... well, I believe Aunt Tilly expected you—wanted you—to tell me."

"I don't know anything about a hidden file." Her mother hesitated, then spoke in a gentle voice. "Honey, isn't figuring out the answers part of the fun and the satisfaction of writing mysteries? Didn't you feel a thrill of discovery when you figured out Tilly's murder was a hoax?"

Meg frowned at the darkness pressing against the office windows. "Yes," she admitted at length. "But, Mother, I can't even guess what your secret is. Whatever promise you and Aunt Tilly made so long ago, surely the deal's off now. I need your help."

Another silence developed.

Finally her mother sighed, then spoke. "Once upon a time two young girls lived in a stone house on the side of a Colorado mountain. The two sisters were very close because all they really had was each other. They didn't have a happy family." Meg heard her mother exhale slowly. "Their father was a brooding, obsessively jealous man who spied on his wife and family. His jealousy poisoned whatever happiness the family might have enjoyed."

Meg drew a sharp breath between her teeth. No wonder Aunt Tilly had said jealousy was poison, using almost the same words Meg's mother had used.

"Their mother wept constantly and spent most of her time in her bedroom, choosing to become a recluse rather than incite her husband or subject her friends to his insane jealousy. The two sisters seldom saw their parents. It was difficult and ugly when they did."

"Oh, God. I'm sorry. I didn't know," Meg said quietly, covering her eyes.

"One day the two sisters were playing where they weren't allowed. When the housekeeper appeared they hid, knowing they shouldn't have been in that room. After the housekeeper departed, the two sisters fought over who was to blame for their almost getting caught. While they were pushing and shoving, they made a discovery about the extent of their father's sick jealousy. They made a pact never to reveal the secret to anyone. Three years later both parents were dead."

"What did they discover?" Meg whispered.

"That is the end of the story, honey."

Frustration wrinkled her brow. "Mother—this isn't fair."

Her mother's sad chuckle sounded as if she were standing in the room beside Meg. "I know. If Tilly had actually been murdered, and if I believed our secret played a role in her murder, of course I would break my promise."

"Mother—"

"Meg, the secret has nothing to do with Tilly's death or with Dennis's. The secret has to do with mental instability. Tilly and I agreed to keep our discovery secret because revealing it would have embarrassed the family. Do you see? It was a matter of family pride."

Meg blinked at the bookcases lining the office walls. "No, I don't understand." Determination entered her voice. "But I promise, if the secret still exists, I'll find it."

Her mother laughed. "It still exists. And I hope you do discover it. Morgan's Manor belongs to you now. It's right that you should learn its secrets. Both Tilly and I have given you plenty of clues."

"If you agree I should know, then—"

"I wouldn't dream of cheating you out of the pleasure of discovering the secrets of Morgan's Manor for yourself...without me having to break a promise that's older than you are."

Meg sighed. She'd been right to sense that her mother had some of the answers. But it had never entered her mind that her mother would balk at revealing them.

"Mother—may I ask you something?" She hesitated, then plunged ahead. "Jealousy ruined the life of your parents. And it sounds like jealousy created a situation that eventually drove Howard to have an affair with Candida, which led to the breakup of Aunt Tilly's marriage." She tried to keep her voice light. "Is jealousy a family curse?"

"It doesn't have to be," her mother said after a minute. The line fairly quivered with a mother-daughter pause.

Meg resisted the invitation to explain. "Haven't you ever felt jealous?" she asked.

"Everyone feels jealous at one time or another," her mother answered. "Whenever I feel jealous about some woman paying too much attention to your father, I remember my parents' marriage and what jealousy did to their lives. I remind myself that I'm strong enough to handle the pain if something happened to my marriage. And finally I tell myself that if your father can find a woman who's better for him than I am—then she deserves him. But she better want him poor, because that's how she'll get him."

Meg laughed. "Have you told Dad any of this?" She couldn't imagine her parents discussing divorce. They were the most loving couple she knew.

"Never," her mother said promptly. "That's the speech I give myself, not your father. As far as your father is aware, I think it's terrific that Virginia Mason thinks he's as handsome as Don Ameche. And part of me really does think it's terrific. Virginia reminds me not to take your father for granted, to appreciate him and the life we've built together."

Long after Meg hung up the telephone, she continued to sit at Aunt Tilly's desk, thinking about her grandparents, her parents, Aunt Tilly and herself. And Steven.

WHEN THE TELEPHONE RANG the next morning, Meg was in Aunt Tilly's bedroom, systematically searching the room for an unknown secret, hot on the trail of a wild guess. She didn't know exactly what she was searching for, but she thought it might be a false drawer or a hidden safe large enough to hold the Halverson file.

She had assigned Aunt Tilly's office to Steven. She felt a little guilty about it, but after speaking to her mother last night Meg thought the best hiding place was probably in the bedroom.

Children weren't supposed to play in their parents' bedroom. And Aunt Tilly's bedroom had once belonged to Meg's grandparents. At any rate, that was her guess. But she wasn't optimistic about finding something the police had not found after going over the room practically with a magnifying glass. Or finding a secret hiding place that

James had failed to discover after twenty years of cleaning this room.

Steven appeared in the doorway. "That's Candida on the telephone. She wants to speak to you, too."

"What about?"

"About a MAIMS meeting."

Meg sighed and picked up the telephone beside Aunt Tilly's bed. "Yes?" She listened a minute, then expelled a breath of irritation. "You insist on having a board meeting in the middle of a murder investigation?" She rolled her eyes at Steven and he grinned.

Candida's grating voice lifted in Meg's ear. "I've been in touch with the election committee and they're getting nervous that the election is looming on the horizon and we still don't have a slate of proposed offices. The bylaws can't be altered merely to suit our convenience. And the committee can't throw together an election at the last minute."

"Two of our board members are dead." Meg didn't apologize for her tone. "I'm sorry if that 'inconveniences' anyone, but that's how matters stand."

Candida's reply was as sharp as Meg's. "There are alternatives to allowing the organization to fall apart. We can appoint Steven to take my seat until after the election and the board can appoint me to fill out the remainder of Tillis's term."

"At the moment, you and I are the only living members of this board to do all this appointing."

An annoyed sigh sounded in Meg's ear. "What's the problem here?" Candida asked. "Why are you being difficult?"

Aware that Steven was watching her from the doorway, Meg bit her tongue and stared at the carpet. James had cleaned the room, but she imagined she could still see the chalked outline. "Right now I don't care about MAIMS. I have other things on my mind."

"I regret that you have 'things' on your mind, but so does the election committee. When you accepted a seat on the board of directors, you accepted the obligations that came with it."

"I'm in no mood for a lecture, Candida." Anger pinched her expression. From the corner of her eye, she saw Steven's grin widen.

"Well, maybe you need a lecture. Look, Steven has agreed to accept an interim seat on the board and he's agreed to an immediate board meeting. You seem to be the only problem here."

"He has?" she asked, swinging around to stare at Steven. He shrugged.

"There's a meeting room off the lobby at the Poles. Where Steven and Suzanne are staying," Candida added. When Meg didn't react, she continued in a brisk tone, "I'll expect you to be there at two o'clock. We have the room for an hour."

Feeling outflanked, Meg hung up the telephone and glared at Steven. "Why did you agree to this?"

"Why not? We aren't making any progress here. I thought we could use a break. If you agree, we could go out for lunch, then stop by the Poles for the board meeting."

Suddenly the idea of getting way from Morgan's Manor even for a short while sounded appealing. But Meg was uneasy about the idea of having lunch with Steven. There were a lot of things she hadn't yet sorted out. One of them was how to be "just friends" with a man who made her feel weak inside whenever she looked at him.

"I'll pass on lunch," she decided, pulling off her bandanna. "I still have some things to do here. You go ahead and I'll meet you at the board meeting."

He studied her expression. "Having a bad day?"

"I've had better." Hands on hips, she gazed around Aunt Tilly's bedroom. "Aren't you getting a little discouraged, too? We're running out of places to search."

"The truth? I'm starting to seriously wonder about what you said yesterday. I'm starting to wonder if someone else found the file first."

Suzanne's unspoken name hung between them. Then Steven left, and Meg returned to her room to do something with her hair and stare into her closet in hopes of finding something she hadn't already worn a dozen times since her arrival.

BEFORE MEG LEFT for the Poles, she gave James and Hilda the afternoon off and apologized that she hadn't thought to inquire earlier which days they had off each week.

"If I'd been thinking clearly I would have realized sooner that you must be desperate for a few hours away from here," she said.

James smiled. "Not at all, miss. This is our home."

"Of course." She returned his smile. "Still, I suspect a free afternoon would be welcome, wouldn't it?"

An hour later she slid behind the wheel of her rental car and followed Aunt Tilly's vintage Cadillac down the twisting road to Breckenridge. James drove the pristine old car like the treasure it was and Hilda sat beside him wearing her Sunday hat. At the base of the road Hilda turned to wave at Meg through the rear windshield, then they turned left on the road leading to the highway.

As it wasn't two o'clock yet, Meg continued past the Poles and turned onto Main Street, driving slowly past the shops, boutiques and restaurants.

Years ago, Breckenridge had begun as a gold-mining town, but now it mined its gold from the tourist trade. Charm, stunning scenery and fabulous ski runs were the primary attractions. Glittering snowcapped peaks soared above Victorian restorations. Skaters flashed across Maggie Pond. Smiling, bright-cheeked shoppers waited for the light to change at the town's only stoplight. Meg half expected to see a Victorian lady emerge from one of the stained-glass shop fronts on the arm of a turn-of-the-century cowboy.

She could understand why Aunt Tilly had fallen in love with the Kingdom of Breckenridge, as the locals referred to the town. Everything from the ice sculptures lining the streets to the old-fashioned street lamps had a way of seducing visitors and leading them toward daydreams of owning a nearby cabin in the pines.

A person could build a satisfying life here, Meg thought. Even Morgan's Manor was beginning to grow on her. It no longer seemed the oppressive pile of stones she had initially thought, but was in actuality rather quaint and possessed a unique fascination. How could one resist a place where rabbits scampered across the veranda and deer offered a passing nod as they meandered through the backyard? Where mountaintops appeared in every window, and the air was crisp and clean and tasted like cold honey?

When she realized what she was thinking, Meg laughed out loud and shook her head as she turned onto the road to the Poles. She had never felt entirely comfortable living in Manhattan—who did?—but until now she hadn't thought about retreating to a mountainside, either.

She parked the rental car in the Poles lot, then paused beside the car door to look at the hotel and wonder which room was Steven's. And which was Suzanne's. She didn't see the car Suzanne had rented. Could she hope Suzanne had returned to New York? Surely Sheriff Conner didn't seriously consider Suzanne a suspect in Dennis's death. Suzanne had hardly known Dennis. That is, as far as anyone knew.

Sighing, Meg fluffed her hair around her face, then entered the Pole's lobby. Steven and Candida were waiting for her beside a massive moss-rock fireplace that soared toward a two-story pine ceiling.

"I just realized," Steven said when he saw her. "You aren't using the cane anymore."

"Some friend you are," she said lightly, making a joke of it. "I haven't used the cane for two days now and you haven't noticed."

"You're right." A flush of discomfort darkened his face. "I'm sorry."

Meg didn't know what to say. There was nothing worse than an attempted joke that fell flat. She bit her lip and looked around the lobby. "Where are Howard and Suzanne?" She hoped either Steven or Candida would tell her that Suzanne was on a plane back to New York City.

"Suzanne is skiing Keystone today," Steven said. He didn't explain how he knew. "I haven't seen Howard since lunch."

"Never mind them, we're here to have a meeting." Candida led Meg and Steven into a room off the lobby and seated herself at the head of the table. She rapped a gavel on the tabletop and Meg made a face. Where on earth had Candida located a gavel on such short notice, and why did she think she needed one?

In less than five minutes, they agreed to a new slate proposing Candida Ripley as the new MAIMS president. Meg noticed her own name among those listed on the page Candida passed to her.

"I'm not interested in serving another term," Meg said.

"Of course you will." Dangling magenta earrings swung against Candida's cheek when she lifted her head to scowl at Meg. "I want people on my board who aren't afraid to speak up and state an opinion. And I want you where I can keep an eye on you."

"Believe me, I have no political ambitions. I'm not sure being on your board is a good idea, Candida. For a time I thought we might become friends, but I don't think so anymore."

"Friends?" Candida's eyebrows shot toward her hairline. "My dear child, I'm not looking for another friend. I neglect the friends I have. What I need is a worthy enemy to replace that hack, Tillis. You could grow into the job. If you win the Macabre Series, you'll be halfway there."

Aunt Tilly had been correct. Candida was unique.

"I don't think I have the energy to be your pet enemy," Meg said. "But I certainly wouldn't rubber stamp all your opinions."

"Weren't you listening? I don't want a parrot. Your silly arguments will keep the meetings interesting and challenging."

Meg rolled her eyes toward the ceiling. "After such a gracious invitation, how can I refuse?"

"Excellent. Then it's settled." The gavel banged on the table with a nerve-rattling noise. "We are adjourned."

Howard poked his head in the door. "All finished? That didn't take long." Stepping inside, he gave Meg a hug and inquired about her ankle, then told Candida he had made dinner reservations for six o'clock.

"What have you been doing?" Candida scooped her papers into her arms and peered at Howard's wet pant legs. "Were you out wading in the snow?"

He laughed. "I walked down to the Bell Tower Mall to buy the New York newspapers. Took a shortcut through an unshoveled area." He said to Meg and Steven, "I think most of the excitement has died down. There was only one back-page column about the case."

"Good. Maybe we can leave this Podunk town and go home," Candida said as they reentered the lobby. "I'm sick and tired of that good-old-boy sheriff. We've been over the details in this case so many times I'm reeling them off in my sleep."

"You've talked to the sheriff again?" Meg asked in surprise.

"Again?" Candida made a face. "Hardly a day goes by that Sheriff Conner doesn't turn up for 'one more question.' He's worse than Columbo!" She lifted an eyebrow. "Are you saying the sheriff isn't bugging you?"

"No, he isn't."

"That's interesting." Candida looked at Howard. "I don't think he's pestering Suzanne, either. "Good God. Do you think he suspects us?"

"I can't imagine he would." Howard ran a hand over his bald head. "I'm not sorry to have Dennis out of our lives." He winked at Candida. "But I am sorry he was murdered."

The statement reminded them why they were still in Breckenridge. Candida broke the silence by lifting her arm and casting a hurried glance at her watch.

"I have to be running along. The election committee is waiting to hear from me." She patted Meg's sleeve. "Thank you for inviting Howard and me to breakfast tomorrow. Unless something comes up, we'll be there."

Meg released an exasperated breath. All she had said was she thought they should get together sometime before everyone left Breckenridge. Candida had translated a polite comment into an invitation for breakfast.

"I hope you'll come, too," she said to Steven. She didn't mention Suzanne Halverson.

Steven was facing the elevator. "Candida and Howard seem to be getting along better. That's a pleasant surprise."

"Let's hope it lasts." Meg remembered Candida saying she needed drama and lightning in a relationship. As far as Meg could tell, Howard was as nice now as he had ever been. No lightning flashed around his bald head.

"Meg, let's have dinner out tonight."

She looked up at him. "Is that a good idea?" she asked in a quiet voice.

"I don't know." The intensity in his gaze made her feel shaky inside. "I do know there's a strain between us. You and I are going to be business associates for a long time and I'd like that relationship to be comfortable for both of us. Maybe we need to practice being friends. Does that make any sense?"

Practice being friends. The phrase broke her heart. "We are friends, Steven. We were friends before we were anything else."

"I've discovered an Italian restaurant I think you'll love. They have the best veal marsala you ever tasted."

What would they talk about? Against everything sensible Meg heard herself agreeing. And immediately regretting it.

"Good. I'll pick you up about seven."

They gave each other polite smiles, then Meg left the lobby and walked back to her car. After she slid into the driver's seat, she sat for a moment, drumming her gloved fingers against the steering wheel and cursing herself for agreeing to dinner with Steven. Then she drove to Main Street, parked and entered Myrna's Boutique.

When she emerged, her arms were overflowing with parcels. She was the new owner of a long leather skirt, a silver-and-turquoise belt and a silk turquoise blouse and coordinating suede jacket. She had even found a pair of stylish calf-high boots to complete the outfit.

The ensemble didn't carry a designer label, but it was more stylish than what she usually purchased. And it suited her. She drove back to Morgan's Manor and used her key to open the door. "James?" But James and Hilda hadn't returned yet. She really hadn't expected them. In fact, she had suggested they have dinner out and take in a movie if something was playing that they wanted to see.

Humming under her breath, Meg stopped in the kitchen to plug in the coffeepot, then she carried her packages upstairs to her room and arranged her purchases across the bed. When she stepped back to inspect her new outfit, she noticed something out of the corner of her eye.

One of the drawers on the bureau dresser was not pushed all the way shut. Meg disliked open drawers and always closed them firmly. Frowning, she studied the drawer a minute, remembering that she had pushed it shut this morning. Slowly she scanned the room.

There was nothing obviously out of place, nothing she could put her finger on. But something didn't feel right. She distinctly remembered, at least she thought she did, that she had left the new P. D. James novel on the bedside table facing her pillow. Now the cover jacket faced into the room. One corner of the dust ruffle was disturbed as if someone had tipped it up by running a hand between the mattresses. The closet door stood slightly ajar.

Heart hammering, Meg bit her lip, then tiptoed forward and yanked the closet door open. To her vast relief, there was no one hiding inside.

But someone had been in her room, she thought, feeling goose bumps rise on the back of her neck. Someone had been in the house this afternoon and had searched her bedroom. There was no doubt in her mind.

Chapter Eleven

Steven and Meg were shown to a linen-draped table in front of a leaded-glass window overlooking Maggie Pond. Bright lights rimmed the frozen pond illuminating pink-cheeked skaters flashing and whirling across the ice.

Raising his drink, Steven offered a toast above the candlelight flickering within a red hurricane lamp. "To solutions and new beginnings," he said, smiling at her.

New beginnings. Friends instead of lovers? Meg touched her glass to his. "You were right. I love this place." The savory fragrance of garlic and Italian sauces perfumed the air. Opera music drifted from strategically placed speakers. A romantic halo of candlelight glowed over the silver and the rose-colored linen.

"Did I mention that you look sensational tonight?" Steven cast a slow, appreciative gaze over her new turquoise blouse and suede jacket. Meg felt a blush of pleasure appear on her cheeks.

Steven looked wonderful himself. Tonight he wore a herringbone jacket and a navy-and-maroon tie against a dazzlingly white shirt. Meg recognized the familiar scent of an expensive English after-shave.

"Well, what shall we talk about, friend?" Her voice sounded artificial and overly bright. But suddenly she couldn't think of a thing to say. She looked at him and her mouth went dry.

"Your choice," he said, smiling. And she wondered if he couldn't think of anything to say, either.

The one thing Meg did not want to talk about was their changed status. She wanted no references to their past relationship, that was too painful. And she didn't want to think about their altered future. That was also painful.

"What do we do if we can't find the Halverson file?" she asked. "Maybe we should discuss the possibility that Suzanne already has it. That she found the file first."

"I've thought about that, and I really don't think Suzanne found the Halverson file." Steven examined her expression. "I do think it was probably Suzanne who trashed the supply room, but I don't think she found what she was looking for. If she had, I think she'd be asking Sheriff Conner's permission to return to New York."

"How do you know she hasn't?" Meg asked.

Steven met her eyes. "I had dinner with Suzanne last night. She talked about how bored she is. She complained that none of us can leave yet. But she didn't express any urgency."

Meg waited for the familiar stomach roll, the grip of jealous pain that accompanied any mention of Steven and another woman. She felt sorrow and regret, but not the deep, racking emotion she expected. Not trusting the delay, she let herself picture Steven and Suzanne sitting together over a candlelit table like this one, speaking intimately, easily. And still the hideous debilitating jealousy did not bite into her system.

She didn't understand. And then she did. Somehow, without realizing when it had happened, she had accepted that her relationship with Steven was truly ended. Her mind was letting him go, accepting there would be other women in his life. Meg no longer had a claim on him.

"Are you all right?" Steven asked, still watching her.

"Yes," she said, waving a hand and blinking at the moisture in her eyes. She trusted Steven with Suzanne because he was lost to her. Why couldn't she have trusted him when it would have made a difference? "I just realized—we will be able to be friends." There was sadness in that statement, and an aching sense of loss. And the realization that she loved Steven enough to want him to be happy, even if he couldn't find that happiness with her.

"I hope so. Meg, are you sure you're all right? You have a peculiar expression on your face."

There was no way to explain that she was letting go, that right now she was loving him as much as she ever had and at the same time she was setting him free. And feeling a new freedom herself. Maybe the loose ties Aunt Tilly had talked about were the ties of friendship. That was a concept she would ponder later.

Leaning forward into the candlelight, she looked into Steven's puzzled frown and managed a sad smile. "I'm sorry, I was thinking about that old adage, we're too soon foolish and too late smart." If she thought about too late, she would weep. "What were we talking about?"

"The Halverson file."

"Have you considered the possibility that Aunt Tilly did indeed destroy the file as she claimed she did?"

"Meg, what were you thinking about a minute ago?"

She tried to keep her voice light. "I was thinking how often people focus on their own selfish fears instead of focusing on happiness, their own and that of the people they love."

"Do you want to explain that a little more?"

"Steven, please don't ask me to go into this. I'd embarrass us both by breaking into tears. It's simply too late."

"I wish to hell I knew what you were talking about." His frown deepened.

"I know. But it's better this way." She didn't trust her feelings enough to share them. What if these insights were transitory? What if tomorrow she couldn't love him enough to let him go? "Tell me what will happen if we don't find the Halverson file."

For a long moment Steven didn't speak. He studied her with those wonderful brown eyes. Finally he leaned forward, speaking in a low voice.

"All right, let's assume the worst. Let's assume Suzanne was indeed involved in Whitney's murder. Let's further assume she was feeling safe, believing she had gotten away with it. Then Tillis reopened the investigation."

"Go on," Meg said, gazing into his eyes above the hurricane lamp.

"We don't know that Tillis's new evidence implicated Suzanne. That was the suggestion, but Tillis did not confirm it. We could be wrong on that point. It's entirely possible I let my imagination run away with me. It's possible Tillis's new evidence focused on someone else or something else, that it had nothing to do with Suzanne."

The wine steward appeared beside the table to inquire which wine they preferred with dinner. Steven ordered a Chianti, then returned to the subject.

"I'm beginning to think I may have overdramatized Suzanne as a danger."

"Have you decided Suzanne had nothing to do with Whitney's murder?" Meg asked.

Steven didn't answer immediately. "There's no evidence tying her to Whitney's death. Until there is..." He shrugged. "As to Suzanne's interest in Tillis's file, frankly that strikes me as understandable. Of course she would be interested in how Tillis portrayed her. She would be curious about any new evidence. And it seems reasonable that she wouldn't want the case dredged up again."

Briefly Meg considered revealing her uneasy certainty that someone had been in Morgan's Manor while she was at the MAIMS board meeting and shopping. But there was no evidence to support her suspicion. She thought Steven might place the incident in the same category as the icicle incident, merely a case of an overactive imagination.

"On the other hand," she said slowly, "if Suzanne was involved in Whitney's murder and Aunt Tilly found something that proved it . . . it would be a miscarriage of justice if we didn't locate that file."

"Where else can we search?"

Meg turned her gaze to the window, absently watching the ice skaters glide in and out of the lighted areas of the pond.

"I don't know," she said finally. "We've almost reached the end of the line."

The last sentence stayed between them, carrying a personal charge more potent than any speculation about the Halverson file.

Meg was glad when the veal marsala arrived. The fragrance was a delight and so was the first heavenly bite. "This is wonderful," she enthused.

"Remember the marsala at Il Cantorini?" Steven looked as if he immediately regretted the reference.

"I don't think it was better than this. Honestly."

The next time Steven went to Il Cantorini he would take someone else. No, the jealousy was not dead. Meg felt it stir in her breast. But the green-eyed monster had lost its talons. She felt sorrow, but not the claws of jealousy. Jealousy was the fear of losing something one loved. Meg had already lost.

When she looked up, she caught Steven in an unguarded moment and his expression caused her to catch a quick involuntary breath. Candlelight shadowed his eyes, making them appear almost black and darkly intent. He was looking at Meg, but his gaze had turned inward. He, too, was remembering Il Cantorini. The wonderful food, the teasing touches beneath the table, laughing as afterward they ran hand in hand to Meg's apartment breathless with the anticipation of each other.

"Steven?"

"Sorry," he said, giving his head a shake. "I was daydreaming." After pushing at his veal, he gave it up and put his fork down. "Have you given any thought as to what you'll do with Morgan's Manor? Will you put it on the market?"

The food was wonderful, but Meg, too, was having difficulty swallowing. "I haven't decided yet. But I've made up my mind that I won't do anything until I've discovered all the secrets of Morgan's Manor."

"There are more?"

Speaking slowly, expressionlessly, she told him the story her mother had told her. "It seems jealousy runs in the family," she finished, trying to make a joke of it. To her relief, Steven didn't comment on that part of the tale.

Intrigued, Steven asked several questions, most of which Meg couldn't answer. "What do you think your mother and Tillis's secret is?"

"I'm not even sure if the secret is theirs or grandfather's. I don't know what I'm looking for." She smiled and spread her hands. "I hope I'll recognize it if and when I find it."

"If it's a hiding place, maybe that's where Tillis hid the Halverson file." Fresh enthusiasm lit his expression.

"That's what I was hoping. But I'm beginning to think this secret is something I'll stumble across by accident. Apparently James hasn't discovered it in twenty years."

Steven smiled, too. "So you may have to keep Morgan's Manor for a long time."

"This might sound odd, but Tillis hinted that the place might grow on me, and it's beginning to." She met his eyes. "I've been thinking about keeping it and living here."

For a moment he didn't say anything. "You're considering moving to Colorado?"

She turned to look at the skaters spinning on the ice. "There's really no reason to stay in Manhattan," she said quietly. "I've been thinking it might be—easier—to live here." She drew a breath. "Like Aunt Tilly said, what better place for a mystery writer than Morgan's Manor?" She continued to gaze out the windows rather than look at Steven. "Of course, I'd want to do some extensive remodeling..."

"It's odd to think of you living so far away," Steven said after another silence.

Meg ran a glance over the spectators standing in the snow beside the pond rink. As she watched, one of the men stepped back onto the sidewalk and stamped the snow from his wet cuffs. Suddenly she saw Howard in her mind, standing in front of her, his cuffs wet from melting snow.

She sat up straight and blinked.

"Oh my God! That's it."

"What?" Tilting his head, Steven looked out the window, trying to see what Meg was seeing. "Meg? What's wrong?"

"Wait a minute." Staring into space, she ran the memory through her mind, testing it. "Wet pant cuffs. Yes, that's what must have happened. Wait. We were playing bridge, then we heard a noise. You were going to investigate, then..."

"Meg? Talk to me. What are you thinking?"

"Oh, Steven." She raised her head and stared at him, speaking in a voice that was barely audible. Tears filled her eyes and glistened in the candlelight. "I know who flattened the tires and hid the skis. And I know who murdered Dennis."

"You do?" Steven studied her pale expression, then he put his napkin on the table and started to rise. "Stay put. I'll telephone the sheriff."

Meg placed her hand on his sleeve. "No, wait." She pressed her fingertips to her eyes. "There are a couple of things I'm not sure if I'm remembering correctly." She spoke in a soft voice filled with regret. "One more night won't hurt anything. Our murderer isn't going anywhere."

Concern filled Steven's eyes and he took her hand. "Does knowing the killer's identity place you in any danger?"

The warmth of his fingers enclosing her hand shot through her body. For a moment she closed her eyes. "No."

"Do you want to talk about this? With a friend?"

The story didn't take long to relate. Before their after-dinner coffee arrived, Meg had explained her theory to Steven.

He still held her hand, absently rubbing his thumb across her palm. "I think you're right," he said finally.

Without making a point of it, Meg withdrew her hand. She knew he didn't realize how erotic his stroking was. To focus her thoughts, she said, "We still have to check with James and Suzanne before we'll know if we're right."

"Everyone's coming for breakfast, correct?"

"They will be if you'll invite Suzanne and I invite Sheriff Conner."

Steven studied her expression. "You want me to invite Suzanne?"

"Yes, please."

He smiled at her. "This sounds like the old gather all the suspects, then announce the killer's name."

Sadness tightened Meg's throat. "I guess it is, isn't it?" She tried to smile. "Writers always go for the dramatic ending."

After Steven drove her back to Morgan's Manor, he walked her up the veranda steps and faced her under the old-fashioned porch light.

"I'd invite you in for a nightcap," Meg said, starting to shiver in the cold, "but I'm afraid I wouldn't be good company. My mind is racing a mile a minute."

"I understand. I'm as upset as you are."

This was the moment for a good-night kiss. Without it, the moment was awkward and uncomfortable.

Steven placed his large hands on her shoulders and looked down into her eyes. "Is a friend permitted to kiss another friend on the cheek?"

She managed a pale smile. "I think cheek kissing is in the rules, friend."

His warm lips brushed her cold cheek and a shiver rippled through her body.

"You're cold. You'd better go inside." Leaning, he opened the door for her. Then, although he didn't look much like smiling, the corners of his lips turned up. "You might think about this arctic cold before you decide to abandon balmy Manhattan."

"Sometimes," Meg said, trying to keep her voice level, "distant friends are the best friends." Briefly she touched her fingertips to his cheek, then she quickly fled inside.

AS PLANNED, Sheriff Conner was first to arrive. He appeared at Meg's door at eight-thirty. After hanging his hat and coat on the foyer rack, he entered the dining room and glanced at the breakfast buffet laid out on the sideboard. "Do you think anyone's going to be hungry once they discover why they were invited?"

"I don't know." Meg smoothed her hands over her red sweater and dark ski pants. "I might be wasting your time," she admitted. "I could be wrong."

"We have a few minutes before anyone arrives. Why don't we go through this, and you tell me what you've discovered." When Meg finished explaining, Sheriff Conner gazed at her with a thoughtful expression. "That's where I was headed, too. Only I couldn't prove it. I figured that's the only way Parnham could have been murdered."

"Steven and I didn't remember the wet cuffs until last night. I mean, I guess I did remember, I just wasn't seeing the forest for the trees."

"How and when he got back inside was a problem. I wish you'd told me this before."

"I didn't realize what I was seeing before." They turned toward the door as everyone arrived at once.

Candida swept into the dining room, then stopped so abruptly that her jersey skirt flared around her legs. Her eyes widened, then narrowed in irritation. "What are *you* doing here?" she said to Sheriff Conner. "Don't tell me you want to go over Dennis's murder *again!*"

Sheriff Conner did not smile. "One more time, ma'am."

"We can't even have our breakfast in peace." Candida sank into a chair and her bosom lifted in an exaggerated sigh. "You might as well buy that condo you were looking at, Howard. We're never going to get out of this place. Six months from now, Sheriff Conner will still be telling us he'd prefer we didn't leave quite yet. He'll still be popping up wherever we go, asking the same repetitious questions."

"Good morning, friend," Steven murmured, stepping up beside Meg at the coffee service. "Are you all right? You look tired."

"I didn't sleep very well." She glanced at Suzanne and nodded a greeting. "I thought I'd go skiing when this is over. I have a feeling I'll need something that requires concentrating on nothing more than staying upright. I need a break from mysteries." A touch of pink lit her cheeks. "I was wondering if you'd like to join me..."

"I'd love to."

Howard appeared at the sideboard. He dropped his arm around Meg's shoulder and gave her a hug before he placed a muffin on a plate. "You're prettier every time I see you. This climate agrees with you."

Before Meg could reply, Sheriff Conner carried his coffee to the end of the table and rapped a spoon against a glass to get everyone's attention.

"As some of you may have guessed, this isn't entirely a social gathering. Miss Sandler and Mr. Caldwell believe they know who murdered Dennis Parnham. As it happens, I agree with them." A moment of surprised silence followed, then James started for the door. "No, James, we'd like you to stay."

Candida narrowed a cool glance on Meg, watching the color rise in Meg's cheeks. "I find it somewhat incredible that you believe you've solved this when no one else could. But if you're determined to make a fool of yourself, let's get on with it. Who are you accusing of having killed that slug, Dennis?"

"There are a few points I need to confirm." Meg remained standing while the others found seats at the table. "Suzanne, the first question is for you."

Meg looked at Suzanne directly, anticipating a twinge of jealousy. But nothing happened. Suzanne was as beautiful as always, as coolly superior, but her beauty and patrician attitude did not diminish Meg as before. Meg had her strong points, too. Her strengths were different from Suzanne's, but no less worthy.

"Ask away," Suzanne said indifferently.

"When you saw Dennis pass through the foyer that night, then out the front door, did you get a good look at him?"

Suzanne frowned. "I'm not sure I understand what you're asking."

"Would you describe exactly what you saw?"

Suzanne shrugged. "I saw Dennis pass the living room archway. By the time I looked up from my cards, he was reaching for the doorknob. He was dressed to go outside and he was smoking. That's about all I can tell you."

"He was wearing a ski cap and parka?" Meg asked. When Suzanne nodded, she continued. "Where did Dennis get the ski cap and parka? The coatrack is beside the door. Yet you say he was dressed for outdoors when he passed the living room archway. He didn't stop to put on his cap or parka. You're certain that's what he was wearing?"

"Yes. He had the cap pulled down over his ears, the collar of the parka was turned up. It was a blizzard out there. It didn't seem strange at the time."

"Would it be accurate to say that all you really saw was one quick glimpse of Dennis from the side and behind?"

"I suppose so." Suzanne frowned. "But I know it was Dennis. He was smoking. The rest of you also saw the smoke in the foyer."

She drew a breath and turned to James. "When you went outside to fetch the ladder to climb up to Aunt Tilly's bedroom, Howard accompanied you, didn't he?"

James lifted both eyebrows. "I was upset. I'm not sure—yes, I remember now. I believe you're right. I think Mr. Clancy followed behind me."

Meg didn't look at Howard. "But Howard didn't leave the garage when you did, did he?"

James darted an uneasy frown toward Howard who slowly peeled back the paper cup from his muffin and reached for the butter.

"I don't remember, miss. I pulled the ladder down from the hooks and rushed outside. I forgot about Mr. Clancy. I don't recall seeing him again until he came into Madam's room with everyone else."

Now Meg made herself look at Howard and her eyes were sad and filled with regret. "I think you stayed behind in the garage long enough to flatten the tires, Howard, then you noticed the skis and hid them in a snowdrift." When Howard raised his head, Meg said in a low voice, "I'm sorry, Howard. I'm so sorry. But I believe you killed Dennis Parnham. You're the only person who could have done it."

"*What?*" Candida half rose out of her chair. "Are you crazy? Howard didn't murder Dennis! Howard wouldn't hurt a fly!"

"I'm sorry, Candida," Steven said with genuine regret. "But Meg's right."

Meg held Howard's gaze. In the morning sunlight, he looked ruddy faced and as innocent as a baby. He looked like the nice man that he was. Anyone meeting Howard Clancy today would have seen a good-natured, balding middle-aged man dressed in a green sweater and dark slacks, who might have been on a second honeymoon with a wife whom he adored.

"Oh, Howard," Meg whispered.

"It's all right," he answered softly, then he looked away and reached for the raspberry jam to spread over his muffin.

"What?" Candida said again, swiveling toward her husband. "Howard! Aren't you going to deny this outrageous accusation? We'll sue, we'll—" When he said nothing, she fell backward in her chair and stared. A gasp strangled her voice. "Oh my God. No, it can't be! I don't believe this!"

Meg couldn't bear to watch. She turned to Suzanne. "You didn't see Dennis. You assumed it was Dennis because of the cigarette. But the person you actually saw leaving the house was Howard. Dennis was already dead." The room was absolutely silent. Meg's voice sounded overloud in her ears. She shook her head, unable to continue and gave Steven an imploring glance. He took up the explanation.

"Howard suggested bridge," Steven said. "When Dennis declined, Howard declined also. Both men went upstairs. I'm guessing Howard had been waiting for an opportunity. He had already disabled the cars and hidden the skis to give himself time to find that opportunity. He must have taken Dennis's cap and parka to his room earlier in case he found a use for them."

Howard didn't speak. He applied himself to buttering another muffin.

"Howard probably went directly to Dennis's room. Dennis's contempt was so great, he didn't feel himself to be in any danger. Very likely he opened the door, then returned to his chair. Howard moved behind him..."

There was no reason to describe the actual murder. They could all imagine it.

"Then Howard took a cigarette from Dennis's pack," Steven continued, "lit it, pulled Dennis's cap over his head, walked down the steps and out the front door. Because of the cigarette smoke, we all believed we had seen Dennis."

Suzanne stared at Howard. "How did Howard get back inside?"

Meg answered. "I think he walked around the house and climbed in Aunt Tilly's office window." She told them about the tracks in the snow that widened beneath the office windows. "He could have opened the window latch earlier in the evening."

"The noise we heard at the bridge table was Howard climbing in the office window," Steven added.

"When Howard appeared in the living room a minute or two later, we assumed he had come from upstairs. Except...his pant cuffs were wet. If Howard had really been upstairs as he said he was, his cuffs would have been dry."

"Oh my God," Candida said in a choked voice. Her rings flashed as her hands flew to her mouth. "I remember, too. But I didn't make the connection... oh, Howard!"

Meg sat in her chair, unable to say anything more. Deep sorrow constricted her chest. She hadn't wanted the murderer to be Howard. In truth, she hadn't wanted it to be any of them.

Sheriff Conner tied up the loose ends, watching Howard. "The ski cap and parka were a problem. Clancy had to get the cap and parka back on the coatrack to establish that Parnham had returned inside. Most likely Clancy left the cap and parka in Miss Morgan's office until he could retrieve them. He did this near midnight by telling Mrs. Clancy he was going downstairs to get another drink. He asked her to accompany him as far as the landing so she could swear he did not enter Parnham's room at that time."

"He also instructed Candida to stand directly under the sconce," Steven added.

The sheriff nodded. "From that position Mrs. Clancy could not observe the bottom of the staircase. She couldn't see Clancy dash toward Miss Morgan's office, then hang the cap and parka on the coatrack."

"Oh, Howard, tell me this isn't true." Candida's voice was thick with shock. Her hands trembled.

Howard leaned back in his chair and closed his eyes. When he opened them again, he looked at his wife. "I hated the way Dennis talked to you," he said softly. "He didn't treat you with the respect you deserve. He wouldn't release you from his agency agreement, and he wasn't helping your career. Dennis Parnham was a nasty-mouthed, unpleasant man. I never understood what you saw in him, sweetheart." Howard lifted apologetic eyes to the others who watched with sympathy. "I'm sorry for. . . for everything. I'm honestly not sure how this happened. I guess I went a little crazy. I was jealous and—and Dennis just pushed too far."

Suzanne broke the silence. "Well, if you ask me, you deserve a prize. Parnham was a crashing bore."

Sheriff Conner reached for his handcuffs. "Mr. Clancy, I'll have to ask you to come with me."

"Cuffs?" Meg whispered. "Sheriff, is that really necessary?"

"Standard procedure, Miss Sandler."

Candida stumbled to her feet. "You killed Dennis for me." She stared at Howard, her eyes huge and filled with awe. "Howard, do you realize—this is a crime of passion!" Her mouth fell open. "Imagine. I just can't believe it!"

Meg followed them to the door and watched as Sheriff Conner led Howard and Candida to his car. In a moment the car turned down the driveway. Suzanne departed, too, following the sheriff down the twisting road.

When Steven placed his arm around her shoulders, Meg turned blindly and pressed her face against the folds of his warm wool sweater. "Oh, I wish it wasn't Howard," she murmured, feeling the scald of tears against her eyes.

"I know." Steven stroked her hair, watching the cars disappear down the driveway. "Come on. You and I are going to get out of here. We'll ski until you're too exhausted to think about all this."

MEG CONFINED HERSELF to the intermediate slopes as she promised Steven she would to protect her ankle.

At the top of a gently sloped incline, she pushed back her sunglasses and paused to catch her breath. The day was perfect for skiing. A single cottony cloud enhanced the beauty of a frosty blue sky. The snow was deep and sparkling white. Gaily colored parkas flew past Meg, sunlight flashing from poles and bindings. Laughter and cheerful shouts surrounded her. But every time she thought about Howard Clancy, tears glistened in her eyes.

When she reached the bottom of the run, cutting to a halt beside Steven, she looked up at him with an expression that blended confusion and bewilderment.

"I thought we were supposed to hate the bad guys, the murderers. I didn't know it could feel this awful."

Steven removed his glove and cupped her cold face in his hand. "I like Howard, too," he said gently. "But it's over now, Meg. Don't dwell on it."

"No," she disagreed softly, looking at the snow capping the far peaks. "It's not over. Not yet."

There was one more mystery to solve. The ordeal that had begun with Aunt Tilly's dinner party would not truly be over until Meg found the Halverson file and uncovered the final secret of Morgan's Manor.

Chapter Twelve

Meg and Steven had dinner together at Morgan's Manor and carried their brandy into the living room afterward. They sat on the sofa before the fireplace, pleasantly tired from the day on the slopes. Outside, snowflakes floated out of the night sky.

"Now that we're discharged as suspects and free to leave Breckenridge, will you be returning to Manhattan soon?" Meg asked.

She felt comfortably relaxed for the first time since the ordeal had begun. And she had begun to think about the future. Despite the terrible events that had occurred since her arrival at Morgan's Manor, a few good things had also resulted.

Now she was free to engage an agent with whom she would feel more compatible than she ever had with Dennis, and this time she was seasoned enough to make an informed choice. She had inherited Aunt Tilly's sizable estate and presumably would not have to worry about money for a very long time.

And she and Steven had put the bitterness of a failed relationship behind them. She no longer had to dread a chance encounter with him or wonder what they would say to each other in that event. But she had replaced an old pain with a new pain. She still loved him. There was no bitterness now, but there was loss.

Leaning forward, Steven refilled their brandy snifters. "I do need to be getting back. Dick Hines is doing an excellent job of taking care of business—so good, in fact, that I need to return before anyone notices they don't really need me. How about you? Are you still thinking about staying here?"

Meg turned her gaze to the flames dancing in the grate. "I've never really thought of my apartment in Manhattan as home. Adell, Iowa, was always home. Lately I've begun to realize Adell is my parents' home. I haven't made a home of my own yet. Maybe it's time."

Steven stretched his arm along the back of the sofa, his fingertips almost touching her hair. He, too, watched the fire flickering in the fireplace. Occasionally he glanced toward the fat snowflakes melting down the windowpanes.

"I'm beginning to suspect you're falling under the spell of Morgan's Manor." He made a face and smiled. "What's worse—I think I understand it. On a night like tonight the real world seems very far away. It's hard to remember the frantic pace New Yorkers set." Meg felt his gaze shift to her profile. "Do you really think you could live here, Meg? Aren't there things about New York that you would miss?"

She wanted to tell him, yes. She would miss him like she'd miss her own right arm if it was removed from her body. But the pain of saying goodbye to Steven couldn't be any deeper, any worse than the pain of losing him the first time. And she had survived. She was stronger than she had believed. Plus, life would be easier without worrying that she might run into Steven unexpectedly and be reminded of all she had lost.

"Writers can write anywhere," she said slowly. "I'm not tied to a particular place, like a cramped one bedroom in Manhattan. Depending on the size of my inheritance, I may decide to keep the place in New York, though. For those times when I crave the big city, the restaurants, the theaters and all the rest. There are several options."

"I understand the appeal of two residences. In the past day or so I've been pricing condominiums in this area." When Meg shifted on the sofa to look at him, he smiled. "The skiing is terrific, I like the town." His eyes held hers. "And I have a friend here."

"It isn't necessary to buy a condo. You could stay with your—friend—when you came to ski."

In the firelight his eyes looked like warm chocolate. "That's what I was hoping you would say." His voice dropped. "But suppose I wanted to stay longer than two weeks..."

Meg's gaze moved to his lips. "Well, there are some business opportunities in Breckenridge that might interest you."

One of his fingers curled in her hair. "Is that right?" Somehow they had moved closer together. What Meg had mistaken as heat from the fireplace was Steven's thigh pressed against hers.

"Yes," she said, trying to remember what they were talking about. All she could think about was Steven's nearness and the feeling that something important was happening. "I haven't seen any Greek restaurants here."

His dark eyes seemed to caress her face, traveled to the pulse beat in the hollow of her throat, then back up to the tremble at the corner of her lips. He smiled. "Are you saying there is no place in this town where a starving tourist of discriminating taste can enjoy a decent lamb stew?"

His breath flowed over her lips, and Meg felt the resistance drain from her body. She tilted her head to look into his eyes and her mouth moved within an inch of his. "No Greek restaurants," she whispered.

"Beautiful Meg."

Then he kissed her, a slow deliberate kiss that explored her mouth with tender care, building, lingering, until they were both breathless when they eased apart to stare into each other's eyes.

"I don't think you and I can be friends," Steven murmured, his fingertips on her cheek.

His kiss had left her shaken, and she wet her trembling mouth with the tip of her tongue, then heard Steven's groan. Leaning forward, Meg rested her forehead on his chin. Tears sparkled in her eyes.

"What are you saying?" She didn't understand. "You kiss me, then announce we can't be friends?"

His arms enfolded her and he held her close. "I can't be near you without wanting to touch you and hold you. That's more than friendship." His fingers tangled in her hair and he gently pulled her head back until he could look into her eyes. "I love you, Meg. You drive me crazy, I get furious with you. You're stubborn and unreasonable sometimes, and I don't always understand you."

"I think I would like that speech better if you had stopped right after 'I love you.'"

Meg's heart pounded crazily, but she was afraid to let herself hope. Steven had said the words she longed to hear, but he didn't look happy. Confusion flickered in her eyes. Whenever she believed she understood their relationship, it changed. She had arrived at Morgan's Manor believing Steven had betrayed her with Suzanne. Then she learned the truth and realized he had not. But they had not returned to the relationship they'd had before. They had decided they would be only friends and business associates. Now, if she understood correctly, Steven was saying they couldn't be friends because he loved her.

"Do you mean previous lovers can't be friends?" she asked, staring into his eyes. With his face an inch from hers, she could see the green flecks in his warm brown eyes.

"To be honest, I don't know what I mean." Confusion troubled his gaze, too, and frustration. He framed her face between his hands and frowned. "I feel like we're trapped in some kind of emotional limbo. I love you, and I hope you still love me."

"Oh, Steven," Meg whispered. "You know I do."

"The question is what do we do about it? We can't go back and we can't go forward."

Meg drew a deep breath. "I know you've heard this before, but I believe we can be together without me driving both of us crazy with my insecurities." Was that true? Could she trust that the green-eyed monster wouldn't rage back to life, talons extended? "I've witnessed firsthand the destruction jealousy can cause. I know what I've done to us, Steven. I know that jealousy drove Howard to kill Dennis." She touched his lips with her fingers. "I can't blame you if you don't believe this time is any different from the other times I've promised to control the ugly feelings. But it is different. I hope you'll give me a chance to prove that to you."

He stared into her eyes. "I want to believe you. But you weren't the only person who was hurt when you and I couldn't work it out before. I don't want to go through that again."

"Oh, Steven, neither do I."

James cleared his throat behind them and smiled when they hastily broke apart. "You asked me to remind you when it was time for the news, miss."

Before he withdrew, James looked back over his shoulder and smiled again. Meg suspected it had been a long time since lovers exchanged kisses in front of the fireplace at Morgan's Manor. She had an idea James and Hilda were pleased by the thought.

Steven switched on the television and they settled back to watch the ten o'clock news. Actually Meg welcomed the interruption. It gave them both a few minutes to think about what had been said.

Howard's arrest made all the Denver channels. They watched as Howard and Candida stepped out of Sheriff Conner's car and were escorted up the steps into a brick building.

A moment afterward an interview filmed later in the day rolled across the screen. Candida wore what Meg referred to as an "author suit," except Candida's author suit was a violent lemon shade trimmed in black mink with a cape and mink hat to match. Diamonds flashed at her ears and wrist, and only her thumbs were bare of jewels.

"My husband is an extremely passionate man," Candida gushed into the camera in response to the reporters' questions.

"Howard?" Meg repeated. "Passionate?" She and Steven smiled at each other, then turned back to the television.

Candida listed Howard's virtues in such a way that no one who followed the eventual trial could look at Howard's benevolent expression and bald head without wondering and recalling the old platitude about still waters running deep.

"Listen to her," Meg marveled. "Candida believes every word she's saying about Howard being a passionate and possessive lover. Suddenly she's seeing Howard in a wholly different light, and she's enchanted!"

Shaking his head, Steven smiled. "Human nature is filled with surprises."

Candida flirted with the cameras. She batted her false eyelashes and gave the viewers a misty-eyed promise that she would stand by her man. Then she briskly reminded everyone that her next book would appear on the shelves in two months, and she hinted she was already discussing a blockbuster exposé of the hoax and Dennis's murder with her publisher. She gazed squarely into the camera and lifted an auburn eyebrow that seemed to say, *Steven, are you listening?*

There was a message for Meg, too. Before Candida concluded the interview, she announced she had withdrawn from the Macabre Series competition. She gave Meg an arch look from the television screen. "I have more pressing and more important matters to attend to than writing a series. Miss Sandler is welcome to it." Candida left the distinct impression that the Macabre Series, which had been so important to her a few days ago, was actually a trivial project of little consequence.

After Steven turned off the set, he returned to the sofa and gave Meg a thoughtful look. "She's right, you know. The hoax and the murder will make a hell of a book."

"Candida's the perfect choice to write it. I imagine you'll be hearing from her the instant she obtains a new agent." Meg rolled her eyes and smiled. "Meanwhile, I'll be occupied wasting my time writing the insignificant Macabre Series."

Steven returned her smile. "You won't think the series is so insignificant after you see the size of the advance." He paused. "You know we haven't really talked about what will happen to the Halverson book. It's my impression that Tillis expected you would finish the project. Have you thought about it?"

"Some," Meg admitted. "But right now there is no project to complete. No manuscript, no notes, no nothing. I'd say discussing the book is a moot point until and if we find the file. And frankly, that possibility is looking dimmer every day. We're running out of places to search."

Standing, Meg followed him to the door, watching as he pulled on his parka and red ski cap.

"Thank you for dinner and a pleasant evening." Lifting his hand, he stroked his thumb across her lips.

Tilting her head, Meg gazed up at him. "Steven, what are we going to do about us?" she asked in a soft voice.

His arms closed around her waist and he pulled her tight against his body. "I don't know." A sigh stirred the hair on her temple. "I feel like an idiot saying something so trite, but I can't live with you and I can't live without you." He grinned at her. "You'd think a publisher could come up with something more original, but there you are."

Stretching to meet his lips, Meg kissed him. She meant the kiss to be light, a good-night kiss, and that's how it began. But the chemistry she had cursed a few short days ago ignited and their kiss turned passionate and demanding. She felt Steven's urgent need and responded to her own need.

When they pulled apart Meg's heart was hammering and her body was hot and shaking. Feeling the heat pulsing in her cheeks, she cast a meaningful glance toward the staircase and the bedrooms above. "You could stay..." she whispered.

Indecision deepened his intent expression. Then he stroked her throat, his hand coming to rest just above her breast. "I'd love to," he said in a thick voice. "But each of us should think about the next step, Meg, and decide if we want to take it. This time is for keeps. This time we know what to expect. If you and I make a commitment to each other we have to do so knowing you are going to drive me crazy with your jealousy and knowing that I'm going to drive you crazy by refusing to justify every moment I spend away from you. Are you ready to accept that kind of relationship?"

"Are you?"

"That's what I want both of us to think about." He kissed her nose and held her tightly. "I'll see you in the morning."

MEG ROSE EARLY the next morning and watched the sun rise over the mountain peaks as she sipped her first cup of coffee.

Even if she had known where to begin today's search for the Halverson file, she wasn't sure she was in the mood to continue the search. She was thinking, as she had been most of the night, about Steven and everything he had said.

He was right, of course. And he had put his finger on the basic problem between them. In their previous relationship, Steven had wanted Meg to change, and she had wanted him to change. He wanted her to stop driving them both crazy with her jealousy and she wanted him to stop making her jealous. She smiled at how dumb it sounded. In the end neither of them had changed. She had driven him away.

Now they had a second chance. And Steven was suggesting that instead of trying to change each other, they try to accept each other, problem areas and all.

But that wasn't good enough, Meg thought. Steven shouldn't have to accept a destructive element in their relationship. Both of them deserved better. Sighing, she tilted her head back and gazed out the dining room windows at the peaks in the distance.

Jealousy had played such a large role in everything that had happened since she arrived at Morgan's Manor. If losing Steven the first time hadn't been enough of a lesson, she had been surrounded by additional proof since her arrival here. Candida and Aunt Tilly's jealousy of each other had crackled between them. As had the jealousy between Dennis and Howard. And her own jealousy of Suzanne Halverson. Jealousy had almost destroyed her relationship with Steven. It had wrecked Aunt Tilly's marriage. Jealousy had led to Dennis's death. And there was the tragic story her mother had related about Meg's grandparents.

Oh, yes, Aunt Tilly had been so right: jealousy was poison.

If Meg hadn't learned that by now, she never would. But she had learned. Never again was she going to let jealousy get a grip on her emotions. Never again was she going to allow that kind of poison into her life. If her old enemy began to stir, she would remind herself of what her mother had said, and of all that had happened here. And she would remember how strong she had become. Strong enough to withstand the pain of loss if it came to that. Strong enough to believe in herself and in Steven no matter how hard that sometimes seemed.

Feeling better, she tied a bandanna over her short dark curls and turned her attention to today's search for the elusive Halverson file. For a while, at least, she needed to take her mind off personal considerations.

At this point they had searched every room in the house. Steven had torn apart the suit of armor beside the living room door; Meg had pushed a broom handle up the chimney flues. They had pulled the books out of Aunt Tilly's library and searched through them and behind them. Meg was ready to swear she had explored every inch of Morgan's Manor, and the Halverson file was not here.

Except it was. Logic insisted and so did instinct. When all the rhetoric was brushed aside, Candida was right. Writers did not destroy their research notes. If the Halverson file had existed in the first place, then it existed now.

Before she left the dining room, Meg rang for James. "Are you absolutely sure there are no more hidden rooms in this house, like the liquor room, or the fur and silver storage rooms?"

"I've been pondering that question since Miss Ripley raised it." When Meg lifted an eyebrow, he hesitated. "And, well, this is going to sound silly, but . . ."

"We've already eliminated logical and reasonable," Meg said with a smile. "I'm ready to consider silly, so go ahead.

No matter how wild, your suggestions can't be any crazier than some of the things I've been thinking."

"Hilda and I talked about it, and there's something—well, the thing is, sometimes Madam would just—well, it seems that sometimes she would just disappear."

"I beg your pardon?" Meg lowered her coffee cup.

James tugged his collar and looked distinctly uncomfortable. "I would arrive to announce lunch or dinner or a telephone call and Madam would not be in the room where I felt certain she had been just a moment before. Then later she would walk out of the same room. It was enough to make a man think his eyesight or his wits were failing."

Meg stared at him. "How did Aunt Tilly explain this disappearing act?"

"Madam would laugh and say, 'James, you need glasses.' Or she'd say, 'Of course I was there, where do you think I was?' Once—" he looked embarrassed "—she explained quite seriously that she had climbed out the window and gone for a walk. And I can't claim that she didn't, miss. Madam had some unique ways about her."

"How often did this vanishing routine occur?"

"Not often, miss, not often at all. It happened maybe ten or twelve times in twenty years. The last time was about a year ago."

"That you're aware of," Meg said, frowning. "How odd."

"The thing is, neither Hilda nor I ever thought about the possibility of additional secret rooms. But if more secret rooms exist they would explain where Madam disappeared to. So you see, I can't say there are other secret rooms, but I can't say for certain there are not. I can say this. The idea isn't as farfetched as I first thought when Miss Ripley inquired."

Meg poured more coffee, then paced in front of the windows. "Which rooms did Aunt Tilly vanish from?"

James smiled. "Madam could vanish from just about any room in the house, miss."

"Oh." Disappointment diminished the excitement in Meg's eyes. For a moment she had thought they were on to something. But she couldn't accept that every room in Morgan's Manor had a secret room attached into which Aunt Tilly could have vanished.

"It's peculiar that Aunt Tilly vanished on occasion, but I can't believe she disappeared into a dozen secret rooms." She thought James must have erred as Aunt Tilly suggested. Perhaps he did need glasses. She sighed. "It seems likely you would have discovered any additional secret rooms during twenty years."

"That's what Hilda and I concluded, miss. I found the rooms we know about almost immediately after beginning my employment here. If others existed I feel certain I would have stumbled across them, too."

Meg agreed. For a moment her hopes had soared, but it was just another dead end.

"Will you be needing Hilda or me this afternoon, miss?"

"I don't think so," Meg said absently, her mind jumping ahead to Steven's arrival.

"Hilda needs to go grocery shopping for the company we're expecting." This referred to Meg's parents who would arrive late this evening. "And we'd like to stop by the funeral home and pay our last respects to Madam."

"Take the whole day," Meg urged. "Mr. Caldwell will be here soon. We'll manage fine. Take Hilda to lunch and relax a little."

"Thank you, miss. We'll return in time to prepare dinner for you and Mr. Caldwell." He smiled when he mentioned Steven's name and Meg blushed.

Steven arrived an hour later, passing James and Hilda in Aunt Tilly's old Cadillac. Meg offered him a cup of coffee before they resumed the search.

"I have a plan for today," she said, not mentioning any of the conversation from last night. "It's flimsy, but at least I have a plan. Today we concentrate on Aunt Tilly's bedroom. We tear the room apart, and we don't stop until—"

"Meg, we need to talk."

The morning sunshine revealed circles under his eyes, suggesting he was as tired as Meg was. She suspected Steven had spent most of the night, as she had, thinking about their relationship and where it was heading. She looked at his handsome face, at his intense dark eyes, at the mouth she loved, and the Halverson file fell away from her mind.

"I wasn't out of your driveway before I was regretting that I didn't chase you upstairs the minute you suggested it." His lopsided grin made Meg smile in return. "And once I got back to the Poles I could hardly think of anything else."

"But you did," she said softly.

Steven took her hand in his. "I sat up last night and listed all the pros and cons of our relationship. Finally I realized how stupid that was. How do you weigh 'her possessiveness drives me crazy' against 'I love the way she looks in the morning'? How do you balance 'she's the most stubborn woman alive' against 'I want so spend my life with this woman'?"

Meg laughed. "I don't know. How do you?" Happiness lit her eyes.

"You can't." Leaning forward, he kissed her smile. "The bottom line is I love you and I want to be with you. And that outweighs everything else."

Meg put down her coffee cup and sat in his lap, winding her arms around his neck. "Now this is a speech I like." She covered his face with small damp kisses until, laughing, he caught her hands and made her stop.

"So. What are we going to do about this?"

"I don't know," she said, leaning forward to kiss the top of his ear. "For starters, why don't you move in here?" A rush of color fired her cheeks.

"That's exactly the sort of brazen suggestion I was hoping you would make." Catching her chin, he gave her a long kiss filled with promise. "Look, Meg, you and I aren't going to have an easy relationship."

"You might be surprised."

"But that's okay." He looked deeply into her eyes. "I accept that we're going to experience some difficult moments. But I also believe we'll find a way to work things out if we don't lose sight of loving each other."

"I do love you, Steven," Meg whispered against his throat. "I love you so much. I know I have some proving to do to show you that things are different now. Something will happen and you and I will both recognize the moment. We'll understand the jealousy is under control and it isn't going to be a problem for us. Never again."

He tried to look as if he believed her, but Meg knew he didn't. But he loved her and accepted her anyway. Knowing it made her heart soar. They stood and he held her in a loose embrace as if he didn't trust himself to hold her tighter.

"I'm going to drive back to town, check in with my office, fax a copy of the Kowalski agreement to the contracts department, then I'll check out of the Poles and bring my luggage back here. I saw James and Hilda leaving—shall I pick up some lunch?"

"You bring lunch." Meg grinned and kissed his jaw. "And I'll provide dessert."

Steven laughed and patted her on the bottom. "Great. I'll see you in a couple of hours."

In a daze of happiness, Meg stood on the veranda and watched until Steven's rental car curved out of sight. After the car disappeared, she gave herself a shake, then returned inside.

Because she needed something to do to fill up the next two hours, she prepared a coffee tray and carried it upstairs to Aunt Tilly's bedroom. She threw open the curtains to the bright morning sunshine, then turned Aunt Tilly's clock radio to a station that played classical music.

Her plan had been to search every inch of this room, but the truth was she had already searched every place she could think to search. Standing at the window, listening to Mozart, she tasted her coffee and let her mind drift, occasionally glancing at the sepia-toned photographs of her grandparents that hung beside Aunt Tilly's closet door.

Meg's grandmother had been a pretty woman with large sad eyes and a mouth that looked as if it had been trembling seconds before the shutter snapped. Her grandfather didn't look happy, either. He peered out of the portrait frame as if he suspected the viewer of something suspicious. Meg sighed, feeling pity for them both.

She started to turn from the old photographs when a thought struck her and she turned a reflective stare back to her grandfather's wary expression.

"Mother said you were so jealous you resorted to spying on your wife and family," she murmured aloud. She turned in a slow circle, studying the bedroom where her grandmother had retreated in tears. "Now how did you do it?" she asked when she faced her grandfather's stare.

He couldn't have spied through the windows. They were two and a half stories off the ground. The time period precluded listening devices. There was no peephole into the corridor. And the walls were too thick to hear through.

Puzzled, Meg tried to figure it out. For spying to be effective, the person being spied upon couldn't know they were being observed. Her grandfather had to have hidden himself. But where?

A leap of excitement stirred in her breast and Meg sensed she was close to the secret.

All right. The secret was tied to her grandfather's jealous spying. That's why exposing the secret would have embarrassed the family and that's why Tilly and her mother had promised never to reveal whatever it was they discovered. And the secret had to be the method their father used to spy on their mother. How it was done.

Once again Meg turned in a slow thoughtful circle, inspecting the room, dismissing the windows, the door to the corridor, the wall that backed the outside stones. Her gaze came to rest on the closet door.

The closet was the best choice. Her grandfather could have spied from that location. Plus the closet fit her mother's story about two children hiding from the housekeeper.

Meg walked to the large walk-in closet and opened the door. The small room smelled faintly of cedar paneling and of Aunt Tilly's perfume. Meg had searched the closet previously, but she had been looking for a missing file. This time she saw it differently. This time she was trying to solve the family mystery. How had her grandfather spied on her grandmother?

On a hunch, she pulled the closet door shut, then stood in the dark closet feeling a thrill of discovery. A pinpoint of light shone through a tiny hole that she had not noticed previously in the closet door. By lifting on tiptoe, she could peek through the hole and view the bedroom on the other side of the door.

Meg dropped down on her feet and pressed her forehead against the cool wood. It was so sad.

But discovering her grandfather's peephole didn't solve the mystery of how he concealed himself in the closet without her grandmother's knowledge. For his spying to be effective, he had to be able to enter and leave the closet without his wife knowing.

Meg opened the closet door and flipped on the light switch, frowning at the racks of clothing. Then she lowered her gaze to the floor. Maybe a trapdoor? On her hands and knees, she explored every board. And found nothing. But she was convinced she was on the right track.

Next, she pushed Aunt Tilly's clothing this way and that, looking behind the rows of sparkling gowns, looking for a door.

She didn't find a door, but she did find a row of old-fashioned clothing hooks placed about waist high from the floor. A summer belt hung from one of the black hooks. A scarf was tied loosely around another.

Meg pushed down on the first hook, then pushed harder. Nothing happened. She pushed down all four of the hooks and nothing happened. Next she tried pulling up on them. And nothing happened except she almost pulled the last hook out of the wall.

"Okay," she said aloud, squinting at the row of hooks. "We'll try sideways."

The effort felt foolish, and she began to think the whole idea was nonsensical. She didn't even know what she expected to find. Maybe she was wrong entirely. Maybe her grandfather had sat on the side of the mountain with a pair of binoculars or a spyglass or whatever they had in those days.

She pushed the last hook sideways and started to turn away. Then she heard a tiny click. Holding her breath, Meg turned back, then gasped. The wall behind the row of hooks had opened a crack along one of the cedar boards. A steady stream of cool air flowed from the opening.

"Good God," she breathed, feeling a burst of excited astonishment. "There *is* another secret room."

Because Meg possessed the kind of mind that insisted on knowing how things worked, she grasped the old-fashioned clothing hook and pulled the secret door shut. Then she moved the hook sideways again, pushing hard.

The hook did not move easily and she understood why James had never discovered the mechanism. First the hooks were concealed behind Aunt Tilly's clothing. Second, the last hook was the important one and it had to be pressed hard.

Eagerly, heart pounding with excitement and curiosity, Meg pushed the door open wide enough to step through, noticing the hinges didn't make a sound. Either the false wall was built exceptionally well or, and this struck her as more likely, Aunt Tilly had found it useful to keep the hinges oiled.

Meg couldn't believe what she found on the other side of the door. Not in her wildest dreams had she expected anything like this. It was not a room behind the secret door, but a passage. Far ahead shafts of light fell between the boards nailed over an outside window, dimly revealing a passageway.

Heart beating wildly, Meg dashed back into Aunt Tilly's bedroom and jerked open the drawer of the bedside table. Yes. The flashlight was where she remembered.

For a moment she paused and looked at the bedroom door, then she glanced at the clock on the radio. She should wait for Steven. He would be disappointed if she didn't.

She looked back at the door to the closet, biting her lip in indecision. The secret within drew her like a magnet. And Steven wouldn't return for at least another hour.

Curiosity and impatience won out. Steven would understand why she hadn't been able to wait for him. She snatched up the flashlight and ran back into the closet, then stepped through the cedar door and switched on the light.

The first thing she saw was a thick accordion-shaped file on the floor just inside the door. Smiling, Meg bent and directed a beam of light over the file cover. Halverson was written in large block letters across the side. A quick glance confirmed the file was stuffed with manuscript pages, notes, official papers and two video tapes.

She was relieved and happy to find the file, but at the moment the file didn't interest Meg nearly as much as the astonishment of discovering a hidden passageway. She simply could not believe her eyes.

After tucking the file beneath her arm, she trained the flashlight on the dusty floor and followed Aunt Tilly's footprints. Almost immediately Meg lost her bearings as the passageway curved away from the stone outer walls and she realized another passage veered off from the one she followed.

"Amazing," she murmured out loud, shaking her head. "This is simply unbelievable."

Returning to the passage that followed the outside wall, she continued until she reached a short flight of steps that led up, then along a narrow corridor banked on the outside wall by a row of boarded windows. The passage ended at what looked like an ordinary door from Meg's side.

Feeling like a junior sleuth in a Nancy Drew novel, utterly astonished by the stunning maze of passageways she had discovered, Meg pressed the latch on her side of the wall. When she eased the door open, she was looking into a closet at a row of winter coats.

Knowing she was intruding, but unable to resist confirming her guess as to where she was, Meg pushed aside the coats and stepped into the closet, then opened the closet door and peeked out. This was a part of the house she had not seen before, but she could guess that she was standing in the hallway of James and Hilda's third-floor apartment.

A few steps to the left and she peeked into a tidy small bedroom. A few steps to the right and she was standing in a comfortable living room. She spotted the telephone at once. Aunt Tilly could have reached this telephone easily, pulled the wire from the wall and ducked back into the passageway in less than a minute.

Flushed with the pleasure and victory of unraveling secrets, Meg returned to the passageway, pulling the closet door shut behind her. Then she followed the footprints back down the interior staircase and down another flight of stairs. This set of steps took her to the first floor. She discovered a peephole that overlooked the living room and another that looked into one of the oversmall rooms. The only door she located opened into Aunt Tilly's supply room.

Meg leaned her head into the supply room and grinned at the old-fashioned clothing hook on which Aunt Tilly's sweater hung before she went back into the passageway and returned to the second floor.

She felt a little like a voyeur, but Meg couldn't deny that she was having a grand time exploring. It was like being a kid again and living out a childhood fantasy, discovering a labyrinth of secret passages that twisted through an entire house. The concept staggered her. No wonder there were so many odd-shaped rooms. Accommodating hidden staircases and concealed corridors had practically required rebuilding the house.

It was no longer a surprise to discover the passageways provided access to each of the closets in each of the second-floor bedrooms. It would have been ridiculously simple for Aunt Tilly to slip into Candida's room and take the ruby-and-amethyst ring from the bureau top. Candida had been right when she said a thief would have to possess the ability to walk through walls. But Aunt Tilly had that ability.

Maybe Aunt Tilly had planted the phony evidence for a second reason, to pique Meg's curiosity and lead her to discover the passageways and, with them, the Halverson file. But Aunt Tilly, being Aunt Tilly, hadn't revealed the existence of the passageways directly. She had left the excitement and fun of discovery for Meg to unearth on her own.

Reminded of the Halverson file and the final mystery, Meg moved down the dusty corridor toward a pair of boarded windows, hoping a peek through the slats would restore her sense of direction. It was time to examine the file under her arm.

Halting before the rotting boards, Meg wiped away a lacy design of cobwebs and felt her initial excitement begin to fade. The hidden passageways were fantastic and amazing, but there was something sad and depressing about them, too.

The elaborate infrastructure was a hidden monument to one man's sick jealousy. Jealousy had driven her grandfather to enormous expense and extraordinary lengths to satisfy his suspicions. No area of Morgan's Manor was truly private. No one in her grandfather's family had been able to evade surveillance.

Suddenly and with some regret, Meg made a decision she knew she would follow through. The first thing she would do once the paperwork was complete and Morgan's Manor was truly hers would be to tear out the secret passageways. She would obliterate this sad evidence of so much misery and heartache.

Placing her eye to one of the cracks between the boards over the dusty window, Meg discovered she was again on the third floor. Behind her was a staircase that would, if she calculated correctly, carry her over the ceiling of the second-floor bedroom corridor to the bedrooms on the far side of the house.

The boarded windows she peered through faced the front of the house. As it didn't matter anymore, Meg tugged at one of the rotting boards and it came away easily. Midmorning sunshine streamed into the passageway for the first time in nearly half a century.

Now she could see the back of a car parked in front of the veranda. By leaning to one side she glimpsed the trunk and taillights. A smile curved her lips. Steven was going to be astonished. Then she remembered the door was locked and turned to go downstairs and let him inside.

"Stay right where you are. Don't move."

Meg jumped. Her hand flew to her throat and she whirled around from the window, her heart thudding against her rib cage as she peered into the shadows.

Suzanne stood at the top of the stairs leading down to Aunt Tilly's closet. She held a purse-sized .25 caliber automatic in her left hand. And she was pointing the gun squarely at Meg's chest.

Chapter Thirteen

"How did you get in here?" Meg gasped.

Suzanne's smile held a superior edge. "With a key. When I was in the kitchen giving my statement to the deputy, I noticed an extra set of keys on a hook by the back door. I just helped myself."

That explained the afternoon Meg had sensed someone had been in her bedroom. But she wasn't thinking about that experience now.

During the course of her mystery-writing career Meg had written a dozen scenes in which one character aimed a gun at another. What she had failed to comprehend until now was how huge the barrel of even a small gun looked when one was standing on the wrong side of it. The gun Suzanne pointed at her was small, it would easily fit into a purse or a pocket. But Meg stared down the barrel and the opening looked as enormous as the mouth of a cannon. Her throat tightened and she felt her pulse hammering in her temples.

"I let myself in and followed the music upstairs and—" Suzanne shrugged "—discovered the secret door in Tillis's closet. You left it open." She glanced at the narrow passageway, nodded at the staircase visible from where she stood. "I wouldn't have believed this if I hadn't seen it myself. If Tillis built these hidden hallways, she was crazier than I imagined."

Meg wet her lips. A chill tightened her spine. "Put the gun down, Suzanne."

Suzanne moved forward a step and Meg could see her face in the shaft of light falling from the window. Suzanne's gaze was cool and expressionless. Her lack of emotion was almost as terrifying as the gun.

"I want the file. Give it to me, Meg."

"Aunt Tilly's notes? Is that what this is about?" Meg feigned surprise. She glanced down at the heavy file tucked under her arm, then back at Suzanne.

"Don't play stupid. We both know what's in that file."

"You're wrong. I haven't examined the file. And I don't think you know for certain what's in here, either." Meg stared at the gun, then wrenched her gaze up to meet Suzanne's eyes. "It's possible there's nothing in this file to warrant this kind of melodrama. Please, Suzanne. I think we can talk without threats. Put down the gun."

"I know Tillis discovered something important enough that she insisted Steven fly out here and review it with her. I'd have to be an idiot to imagine it didn't have something to do with me." A cold smile curved Suzanne's mouth. "Tillis couldn't resist insinuating that she'd been clever enough to find evidence the police hadn't discovered. But when she realized I was snowed in along with the rest of you, she tried to backpedal by claiming there was no new evidence, after all, that she'd abandoned the book and destroyed her notes. I didn't believe that nonsense any more than the rest of you did." She glanced at the file and moved forward another step.

Meg pressed back against the boards covering the window, dimly hearing the boards creak and crack beneath the strain of her weight. Frantically she darted a quick glance to either side, measuring her chances of escaping and outrunning Suzanne. Such an attempt meant she had to dodge past Suzanne in the narrow passageway, race down the staircase to Aunt Tilly's bedroom and then...and then what?

Every time she looked at the gun it seemed to have grown in size. Perspiration dampened her palms and her jaw clenched. She might outrun Suzanne, but she couldn't outrun a bullet.

"You sent the death threats to Aunt Tilly, didn't you? And you pushed me down the staircase." The accusations blurted out of nowhere. But instinct ordered her to stall, to try to gain a minute or two to think. Fighting panic, Meg tried to imagine what one of her own heroines would do in this situation. Nothing leaped to mind. It was one thing to leisurely plot a heroic escape while safely seated in front of her word processor. It was another thing altogether to instantly create a workable plan when she was staring down the barrel of a loaded gun.

"Give me the file, Meg."

"If I give you the file, what happens to me?"

Even as she asked the question, Meg understood it was rhetorical. They both knew Suzanne intended to kill her. Suzanne would not risk that Meg had examined the Halverson file and knew what it contained. Once Suzanne chose to reveal the gun and aim it, Meg's fate had been decided.

And it could not have happened in a worse place. Biting her lips, Meg darted a glance at the dim passageway and her heart plummeted toward her toes. If Suzanne murdered her inside the passageways, it was unlikely anyone would discover her body. As far as the world was concerned Meg would become an interesting footnote to the hoax and Dennis's murder. She would go down as a missing person. And Suzanne would get away with another murder.

"I think you know what happens to you," Suzanne said softly, confirming Meg's fears. In the shaft of sunlight falling through the dust motes, Suzanne's hair resembled a golden halo. If one didn't notice her emotionless cold eyes, she looked like a lovely young woman enjoying a winter holiday dressed in expensive wool slacks and a cashmere sweater. The gun in her hand was chillingly irreconcilable with the rest of her image.

"Disposing of you will eliminate several small problems." Suzanne's satisfied scan of the passageway suggested she, too, recognized this was an ideal site for a murder.

"You did kill Whitney, didn't you?" Meg forced her gaze up from the barrel of the gun. Her heart was pounding so loudly she had to strain to hear Suzanne's reply.

"With you out of the way and the file destroyed, that damned book will die a natural death and there will be no more talk of reopening the investigation." Suzanne's slate-colored eyes swept Meg's slim figure. "And Steven will be free. You don't know how tired I am of hearing how wonderful you are, how talented, how beautiful, how intelligent, how everything ad nauseam."

Steven. Where was he? What was taking him so long? But she couldn't depend on Steven to arrive on the scene like the mythical hero and rescue her. It wasn't going to happen.

What on earth was she going to do? Just stand here and let Suzanne murder her? But what were her options? Meg's mind whirled in a dozen directions at once.

"Put the file on the floor and slide it over here." Suzanne gestured with the barrel of the gun.

"And if I don't?" It was a stupid question, but Meg felt partially protected, holding the thick file in front of her chest. As if a few inches of paper would stop a bullet.

"No more conversation." Suzanne had advanced until they stood about three feet apart. Her eyes narrowed to slits. "Give me the file, Meg. Let's get this over with."

Meg had read that a person's life passed before his eyes when he was drowning. She discovered the phenomenon also occurred when one was staring down the barrel of a gun held by someone who had pulled the trigger before.

Except what passed through Meg's mind were not the things she had done, but all the things she wanted to do. She wanted to marry Steven and make a home and have children. She wanted to write a bestseller that swept all the lists. She wanted to own a red sports car at least once in her life. She wanted to wake up every morning with Steven's head on the pillow next to her and know he would be there for the rest of her life.

And that might have happened except Suzanne was taking her dreams away from her.

No.

Meg drew a deep breath. She had to believe she deserved her dreams. She had to believe she deserved Steven and a second chance at happiness. She had to find enough confidence in herself to believe she could get through this and that she could win.

Before she could talk herself out of believing, before she could think of all the reasons why she would fail, Meg hurled the Halverson file at Suzanne's face, then leaped forward, her eyes fixed on the gun, her hands extended.

She caught Suzanne's left wrist at the same moment Suzanne clawed at her hair, jerking her head back. The gun fired in the passageway, the sound deafening, blotting the noise they made as they struggled for the weapon.

Suzanne was taller, but Meg was more athletic and her body was charged with adrenaline. The struggle was evenly matched, conducted in desperate jabs and blows. Suzanne slammed her fist against Meg's jaw; Meg flailed with elbows and knees, trying to grab the gun and falling frustratingly short. The gun waved in the air and fired again. Her ears rang as she and Suzanne twisted and fell against the rotting boards covering the windows. Meg saw the sudden cracks running up and across the boards, but she didn't hear the wood splinter because the gunshots had deafened her.

Slowly, teeth bared, Suzanne brought the gun down between them. Meg battled to prevent the terrifying descent, but Suzanne held the advantage as she was braced against the boarded windows. Panicked, Meg felt the gun dig into her ribs before she mustered a burst of strength and shoved hard to turn the barrel away from her body.

The noise of splintering wood and breaking glass tore through the sound of panting breath. Then, so close together that Meg could not separate them, she heard the blast of another gunshot and a scream. Then she felt a searing, burning pain so intense that it dropped her to her knees.

FOR SEVERAL HOURS Meg remembered nothing but fuzzy gray shapes. Only vaguely did she recall dragging herself to the telephone in Aunt Tilly's bedroom where she managed to phone 911 and mumble, "Morgan's Manor. Send ambulance," before she fainted.

The next memory was that of being carried down the staircase on a stretcher and then outside. She saw flashing red bubbles spinning on top of police cars, saw another ambulance pulling out of the driveway and, as her stretcher was tilted up for an instant, she saw a jagged broken window on the third floor. Then the doors of the ambulance closed and she was driven to Vail for emergency surgery. She had a dim recollection of Steven's worried face hovering over her in the ambulance.

Steven was there again when she emerged from surgery, and Sheriff Conner. She thought they might have talked for a few minutes before she drifted into a drug-induced sleep, but she wasn't sure.

By the time Meg struggled awake again and was conscious enough to grasp where she was and to recall part of what had happened, she became aware that her right thigh was heavily bandaged and it hurt like hell.

Steven was sitting beside her bed, holding her hand. When he realized she was awake, he murmured something, then pressed her fingers to his lips. "If you ever again even hint that you lack confidence in yourself, I'm going to shake you until your teeth rattle!"

She gave him a drowsy smile. "Whatever happened to 'Hi, there, I'm glad you're alive'?"

"Hi, there. I'm glad you're alive." He stared at her as if he wasn't sure she was real. "When I saw you—covered with blood..." He covered his eyes and didn't speak again for a moment.

Meg squeezed his hand and looked away. Sunshine glowed on a half-dozen baskets of flowers.

"It's morning?" she asked when Steven raised his head. "How long have I been asleep?"

"Since yesterday afternoon." He stroked her hand between both of his, carefully, as if she might break. Now she noticed his beard and guessed Steven had been at her bedside since yesterday. "You lost a lot of blood."

Despite the growth of beard, and the exhaustion in his eyes, he was the handsomest man Meg had ever seen. It didn't surprise her when a nurse looked in her room and smiled. Every nurse in Vail would be dropping in for a second look at Steven Caldwell.

"I was shot," she said suddenly, trying to sit up. The memory fell on her like a stone. "Steven! Suzanne shot me!" Throwing aside the sheet and blanket covering her, Meg stared down at the bandages wrapping her thigh. A tremble swept her body and she started shaking. She lifted wide dark eyes and spoke in a whisper. "Am I going to be all right?"

"Shh, darling. It's over now," Steven said in a soothing voice. Gently he eased her onto the mound of pillows and pulled up the blankets. "The doctors removed the bullet yesterday. You were lucky. Another fraction of an inch and your thigh bone would have been shattered. The most serious problem was the loss of blood. You're going to be weak for a while, but you'll be good as new in no time."

Twisting, Meg stared up at the IV bottles on the rack over her bed. It was starting to come back to her. "We...we struggled for the gun, and..."

"I know. I was present when you gave your statement to Sheriff Conner."

Meg frowned at him. "I gave a statement to Sheriff Conner?"

"You don't remember? Yes, darling, you did."

She stared at him, but she was reliving that scene in the dim hidden passageway. She saw Suzanne's bared teeth. Heard again the blast of the gun in that confined space, inhaled the stinging odor of cordite, felt a sudden searing pain. And she remembered the blood on her hands, on her leg. The amount of blood had surprised and frightened her. She was light-headed and reeling long before she managed to drag herself into Aunt Tilly's bedroom.

"The passageways, did you...?"

"I saw them." Steven shook his head and smiled gently. "Your parents arrived last night." Before Meg could say anything, he leaned to place a light kiss on her lips. "They were here, but left a few minutes ago to get something to eat. They'll be back soon."

Another thought caused Meg's muscles to tense painfully. Disconnected scenes flashed through her memory. "The file! Steven, I found the Halverson file."

"Shh, try to relax and don't worry about anything, just rest. Sheriff Conner has the file. I'm meeting him in about an hour to review the material."

"Aunt Tilly said something about photos," Meg whispered, her eyes closing.

"Just rest, darling, and get well."

Before she drifted off to sleep, Meg's eyes blinked open and she scowled at him. "I distinctly remember you telling me in the restaurant that you didn't think Suzanne was dangerous, after all."

Steven's fingers caressed her cheek and he smiled. "I remember, too. I'll spend the rest of my life making that up to you."

Meg smiled, leaned her cheek against his hand, then floated away.

WHEN SHE AWOKE again Meg felt rested and alert, relieved to notice the pain in her thigh had diminished to mere discomfort. The shadows lengthening across the room suggested it was late afternoon. A nurse brought her fresh ice water and mentioned that Meg's parents had left five minutes ago without waking her. "They didn't want to disturb you. They said to tell you they'll be back this evening."

To Meg's surprise, Candida had sent a bouquet of roses. Her parents had left magazines and a box of her favorite chocolate creams. James and Hilda had brought a small suitcase of toiletries, one of her own nightgowns and a change of clothing.

After dinner Sheriff Conner arrived with Steven a step behind him. Steven had shaved, showered and changed clothes, but he still looked tired. He bent over her bed and kissed her forehead.

"How are you feeling?" the sheriff inquired.

"Well enough to wonder why Jessica Fletcher never gets shot on *Murder She Wrote,*" Meg said with a rueful smile.

Steven laughed and took the chair beside her bed. "If you can joke about getting shot, I'd say you're on the road to recovery."

The sheriff pulled up a chair on her other side. "Caldwell said you didn't remember giving a statement, so I thought we'd better go over it again in case you've remembered anything you didn't mention before."

Meg pressed Steven's hand, then frowned at Sheriff Conner. "There's something I have to know. What happened to Suzanne?" She touched her temple with her fingertips. "I remember fighting for the gun. I remember hearing the gun fire. Then crawling to Aunt Tilly's bedroom to the telephone. But there's a gap where Suzanne is..." Meg spread her hands. "She's just not there."

"Mrs. Halverson went out the window," the sheriff said in a matter-of-fact tone. "The wood over the windows was rotten, so was the window frame." He watched Meg shudder. "According to your statement, during the struggle Mrs. Halverson was pressed up against the boards." He shrugged. "They gave way and she fell out."

Meg stared at him, then wet her lips. "Did I...did I push her?" she whispered.

"Maybe." A sympathetic smile touched the sheriff's lips. "It wouldn't surprise me. You were fighting for your life."

"We were on the third floor." Meg lifted her face. "Is she...did the fall kill her?"

"She's still on the critical list. By tomorrow the doctors hope to have a better idea if she'll make it or not. She sustained massive injuries from the fall."

"Oh my God." Horror widened Meg's pupils.

Steven took her hand again and held it tightly. "Don't blame yourself. Suzanne was trying to kill you."

The sheriff nodded. "After reviewing your aunt's file, there's enough new evidence to assume Mrs. Halverson was involved in her husband's murder. There's no doubt in my mind that she would have murdered you, too, Miss Sandler."

"I have to know," Meg whispered. "What's in the file?"

As Aunt Tilly had hinted, the new evidence was in the photographs and videos. When Whitney Halverson's body was found, he was clutching a silver earring of an unusual design. A transcript of the inquest revealed Suzanne had sworn she had never seen the earring before. But Aunt Tilly had unearthed a society photo published in a 1987 issue of *Town and Country* that showed Suzanne in profile wearing the same earring.

Steven stroked her hand. "Tillis made another discovery that neither Suzanne nor the police were aware of. The Beverly Hills Hotel, which Suzanne swore she checked into, the Royal Palms, maintains a video file of all registrations. Tillis uncovered that piece of information and obtained a copy of the video showing Suzanne at the registration desk. The video is in the file."

Sheriff Conner took up the story. "There's a full face shot of Mrs. Halverson checking into the hotel, picking up the pen to attempt to sign the register—which she didn't do—and paying for the room. What's interesting about the video, aside from the fact that the woman only marginally resembles Suzanne Halverson, is that the woman checking in is clearly right-handed. As you know—" he nodded to Meg's bandaged leg "—Mrs. Halverson is left-handed. I think a voice print taken from the video will be equally damaging. It should prove Suzanne Halverson did not check into the hotel. I think we'll discover it was her maid."

"The earring places Suzanne at the scene of the murder. The video breaks her alibi," Steven said.

"My office faxed the material to NYPD," the sheriff added. "They're checking it out now, but an early off-the-record opinion says there's enough new evidence to reopen the Halverson case."

"If Suzanne lives," Meg said slowly, "she'll be facing a murder trial."

"You can count on it," the sheriff agreed. "Plus we've got attempted murder right here."

After opening his notebook, he took Meg through her statement again. While she talked, Meg watched a nurse enter her room for no other reason, it appeared, then to flirt with Steven. Steven seemed oblivious to the nurse's attempts to attract his attention.

"Three shots were fired?" Sheriff Conner asked.

Meg nodded, watching the nurse rearrange Meg's flowers and try to catch Steven's eye.

Finally Meg leaned to whisper in his ear. "Oh, for heaven's sake, will you at least smile at her, so she can go check on someone else?"

Steven blinked and became aware of the pretty young nurse for the first time. "What?"

"She's pining away for you. She isn't going to leave until you notice her. So give her a smile." Meg turned back to the sheriff. "What's the next question?"

"Wait a minute." Steven sat up straight and stared at her. "Meg Sandler. Are you urging me to flirt with another woman?" His dark eyebrows lifted. "Maybe you're in worse shape than the doctor said. Are you sure you didn't get hit on the head, too?"

When Meg understood what had just happened, she stared at Steven and her mouth dropped open. A look of recognition dawned on her expression. "The moment," she whispered. "This is the moment. I'm free."

"Uh-oh," Sheriff Conner said. "I think this is my cue to leave." Standing, he closed his notebook and reached for his hat. "If you're feeling well enough to be jealous, I'd say you're going to be up and around very soon now."

"You don't understand," Meg said, looking at him with surprise and joy. "I *don't* feel jealous! I asked him to smile at her!" She turned to Steven with a radiant smile. "I *asked* you to flirt with her." She shook her head and laughed out loud. "I can't quite believe this myself. But it's wonderful!"

The sheriff rolled his eyes, then followed the nurse to the door. "I am never going to understand women. Crime, yes. Women, no. Women do not make sense." He winked and closed the door behind him.

Steven sat on the edge of her bed and smiled down into her happy eyes. His own eyes were warm with love and amusement. "Does this mean you want me to carry on a flirtation with all the nurses in the Vail Medical Center?"

Meg wound her arms around his neck and smiled. "Easy, fella. I'm new at this. I don't think we have to carry it quite that far." She didn't remember ever feeling this happy, this free or this certain of herself, Steven and the future.

She wasn't so naive as to believe there would not be relapses. There would be moments ahead when the caged monster would waken and test her. The difference was Meg now knew she was in control. Trusting Steven had never been a problem. The problem had been believing in herself.

But if she didn't believe in herself after solving one murder and thwarting another, she never would. If she couldn't believe in herself after winning Steven back and caging the green-eyed monster, she was hopeless. But she did believe in herself. And in Steven. And she believed in the future that stretched in front of her like a dream come true.

"I love you, Meg."

She framed his face between her hands and gazed up at him with tears of happiness glistening in her eyes.

"I love you so much."

Tomorrow she would find an architect to redesign Morgan's Manor. By spring the labyrinthine monument to destructive passions would be gone. She would open Morgan's Manor—and her new life with Steven—to sunshine and love.

She felt certain Aunt Tilly would have approved.

OFFICIAL RULES • MILLION DOLLAR WISHBOOK SWEEPSTAKES
NO PURCHASE OR OBLIGATION NECESSARY TO ENTER

To enter, follow the directions published. If the Wishbook Game Card is missing, hand-print your name and address on a 3″ × 5″ card and mail to either: Harlequin Wishbook, 3010 Walden Ave., P.O. Box 1867, Buffalo, NY 14269-1867, or Harlequin Wishbook, P.O. Box 609, Fort Erie, Ontario L2A 5X3, and upon receipt of your entry we will assign you Sweepstakes numbers (Limit: one entry per envelope). For eligibility, entries must be received no later than March 31, 1994 and be sent via 1st-class mail. No liability is assumed for printing errors or lost, late or misdirected entries.

To determine winners, the Sweepstakes numbers on submitted entries will be compared against a list of randomly, pre-selected prizewinning numbers. In the event all prizes are not claimed via the return of prizewinning numbers, random drawings will be held from among all other entries received to award unclaimed prizes.

Prizewinners will be determined no later than May 30, 1994. Selection of winning numbers and random drawings are under the supervision of D.L. Blair, Inc., an independent judging organization whose decisions are final. One prize to a family or organization. No substitution will be made for any prize, except as offered. Taxes and duties on all prizes are the sole responsibility of winners. Winners will be notified by mail. Chances of winning are determined by the number of entries distributed and received.

Sweepstakes open to persons 18 years of age or older, except employees and immediate family members of Torstar Corporation, D.L. Blair, Inc., their affiliates, subsidiaries and all other agencies, entities and persons connected with the use, marketing or conduct of this Sweepstakes. All applicable laws and regulations apply. Sweepstakes offer void wherever prohibited by law. Any litigation within the province of Quebec respecting the conduct and awarding of a prize in this Sweepstakes must be submitted to the Régies des Loteries et Courses du Quebec. In order to win a prize, residents of Canada will be required to correctly answer a time-limited arithmetical skill-testing question. Values of all prizes are in U.S. currency.

Winners of major prizes will be obligated to sign and return an affidavit of eligibility and release of liability within 30 days of notification. In the event of non-compliance within this time period, prize may be awarded to an alternate winner. Any prize or prize notification returned as undeliverable will result in the awarding of the prize to an alternate winner. By acceptance of their prize, winners consent to use of their names, photographs or other likenesses for purposes of advertising, trade and promotion on behalf of Torstar Corporation without further compensation, unless prohibited by law.

This Sweepstakes is presented by Torstar Corporation, its subsidiaries and affiliates in conjunction with book, merchandise and/or product offerings. Prizes are as follows: Grand Prize—$1,000,000 (payable at $33,333.33 a year for 30 years). First through Sixth Prizes may be presented in different creative executions, each with the following approximate values: First Prize—$35,000; Second Prize—$10,000; 2 Third Prizes—$5,000 each; 5 Fourth Prizes—$1,000 each; 10 Fifth Prizes—$250 each; 1,000 Sixth Prizes—$100 each. Prizewinners will have the opportunity of selecting any prize offered for that level. A travel-prize option if offered and selected by winner, must be completed within 12 months of selection and is subject to hotel and flight accommodations availability. Torstar Corporation may present this Sweepstakes utilizing names other than Million Dollar Sweepstakes. For a current list of all prize options offered within prize levels and all names the Sweepstakes may utilize, send a self-addressed stamped envelope (WA residents need not affix return postage) to: Million Dollar Sweepstakes Prize Options/Names, P.O. Box 4710, Blair, NE 68009.

For a list of prizewinners (available after July 31, 1994) send a separate, stamped self-addressed envelope to: Million Dollar Sweepstakes Winners, P.O. Box 4728, Blair NE 68009.

The Extra Bonus Prize will be awarded in a random drawing to be conducted no later than 5/30/94 from among all entries received. To qualify, entries must be received by 3/31/94 and comply with published directions. No purchase necessary. For complete rules, send a self-addressed, stamped envelope (WA residents need not affix return postage) to: Extra Bonus Prize Rules, P.O. Box 4600, Blair, NE 68009.

SW9-92

HARLEQUIN®

INTRIGUE®

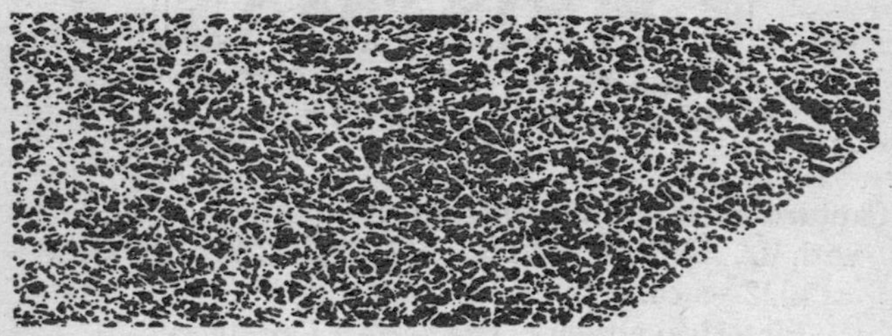

INTRIGUE IS CELEBRATING ITS 200TH BOOK!

Remember all those great adventures you had....

The SHADOW OF THE MOON spills across the stained carpet and the NIGHTWIND howls. You're stuck in a HAUNTED HOUSE in which HIDDEN SERPENTS slither. There's a CALL AFTER MIDNIGHT. It's THE LATE GENTLEMAN ringing to see if that FACE IN THE MIRROR is SUITABLE FOR FRAMING. "What do you mean?" you scream wildly into the phone. But the only reply is WHISPERS IN THE NIGHT.

And the suspense continues! Don't miss Intrigue #200

BREACH OF FAITH
by Aimée Thurlo

Two hundred escapes into suspense and danger with mysterious men brave enough to stop your heart.

IF TRUTH BE KNOWN, a trip through a Harlequin Intrigue can be STRANGER THAN FICTION! HI200